CIRCLES OF DEATH

T0282835

CIRCLES OF DEATH

Marcia Talley

SEVERN HOUSE

First world edition published in Great Britain and the USA in 2024
by Severn House, an imprint of Canongate Books Ltd,
14 High Street, Edinburgh EH1 1TE.

severnhouse.com

British Library Cataloguing-in-Publication Data
A CIP catalogue record for this title is available from the British Library.

ISBN-13: 978-1-4483-0797-5 (cased)
ISBN-13: 978-1-4483-0798-2 (e-book)

All Severn House titles are printed on acid-free paper.

Typeset by Palimpsest Book Production Ltd., Falkirk,
Stirlingshire, Scotland.
Printed and bound in Great Britain by TJ International,
Padstow, Cornwall.

Praise for the Hannah Ives mysteries

"This intelligent mystery series deserves a long run"
Publishers Weekly on *Disco Dead*

"Talley's determined sleuth is more than a match for a ruthless adversary"
Kirkus Reviews on *Done Gone*

"Energetic . . . Hannah's gently amusing observations provide counterpoint to the mayhem. Readers will wish her a long career"
Publishers Weekly on *Done Gone*

"Fast paced and character focused . . . sure to please"
Booklist on *Tangled Roots*

"Entertaining . . . its solution is both surprising and memorable"
Booklist on *Mile High Murder*

"Witty, well-constructed . . . Takes the reader on a timely and illuminating trip"
Publishers Weekly on *Mile High Murder*

About the author

Marcia Talley is the Agatha and Anthony award-winning author of nineteen previous crime novels featuring sleuth Hannah Ives. Her short stories appear in more than a dozen collections and have been reprinted in many best-of-the-year crime story anthologies. She is a past president of Sisters in Crime, Inc. and serves on the Board of the Mystery Writers of America. Marcia lives in Annapolis, Maryland, but spends the winter months in a quaint Loyalist cottage in the Bahamas.

www.marciatalley.com

For Betty, who began subscribing to *Ellery Queen Mystery Magazine* in 1946, the year it went monthly, loyal fan of *Alfred Hitchcock Presents* on television in the fifties and sixties, faithful library patron everywhere her role as a military wife took her, and a passionate reader who never had fewer than seven mystery novels stacked on the end table next to her spot on the sofa. I wish she had lived long enough to see my mystery novels among them. Mom, you were my inspiration.
This one's for you.

Lois Elizabeth Tuckerman Dutton
1917–1980

ACKNOWLEDGMENTS

It was Hilary Clinton who famously said, 'It takes a village to bring a book into the world, as everyone who has written one knows. Many people have helped me to complete this one, sometimes without even knowing it.' Here's a shout-out to my village.

A million thanks to my husband, Barry, who ferociously protects my writing time and now – thank you, Blue Apron – cooks dinner at least three times a week.

To my crack team of advisors:

Donna L. Cole, the multi-award-winning investigative reporter whose dogged reporting on the death of thirteen bald eagles on Maryland's Eastern shore in 2018 brought global attention to this 'dirty little secret.' While taking time out to rescue and transport birds of prey, Donna continues to focus her investigative journalism on the people, places and natural resources of the Chesapeake Bay area, and works tirelessly in support of legislation to ban the possession of carbofuran and rid Maryland of its stockpiles of the toxic pesticide. Donna is the US Navy veteran, bird of prey rescuer, wildlife photographer, breast cancer survivor, neighbor and friend who inspired and informed this book. Keep up with Donna (but you'll need track shoes!) at www.annapoliscreative.com

Suzanne Shoemaker and Malia Hale, Master Wildlife Rehabilitators, Executive Director and Director, respectively, of the Owl Moon Raptor Center in Boyds, Maryland. Thank you for making an exception to your important 'no tours' policy and allowing me to shadow you for half a day while you cared for sick and injured raptors. Owl Moon rescues, rehabilitates, and reconditions raptors with the goal of returning them to the wild. It is totally staffed by volunteers and supported by private donations. Follow Owl Moon and/or donate here: www.owlmoon.org

Kathleen 'Kathy' Woods, a licensed wildlife rehabilitator and bald eagle specialist who explained in detail how she treats raptors for carbofuran poisoning at the Phoenix Wildlife Center in the countryside north of Baltimore, Maryland. See what Kathy and her team of dedicated volunteers are up to here: www.phoenixwildlife.org

If I got anything wrong, it's entirely my fault, not theirs.

I'm grateful to John L. Semcken for his generous donation to Friends of Naval Academy Music in honor of his wife, Mee Hae. I hope Mee enjoys her role as the smart, caring and compassionate director of my fictional Hoots Raptor Rescue Center. I thought Bear should have a supporting role. No extra charge.

To Roger Erickson, highest bidder at a fundraiser for the Junior Sailing program in Hope Town, Abaco, Bahamas, who looked so much like my vision of a Maryland Department of Natural Resources police officer that I made him one, mirrored aviator-style sunglasses and all.

To my Facebook friends on DNA Detectives, you are all search angels.

To my colleagues in the Hope Town Writers' Circle who, like our beloved island, have survived and are back on track following the catastrophic devastation of Hurricane Dorian on September 1, 2019. Hope Town strong!

To my partners in crime in Annapolis, Maryland who have read every word, sometimes more than once, for tough love: Mary Ellen Hughes, Becky Hutchison, Debbi Mack, Lauren Silberman, Rosalie Spielman and Cathy Wiley, and especially to Sherriel Mattingly, beta reader and Hannah's Number One Fan.

And, as always, to Vicky Bijur.

Science doesn't justify [carbofuran's] sale at all. From Africa and Asia to Europe and North and South America, a global collective of biologists documenting animals killed by carbofuran say the sole condition under which it can be safely used – in accordance with label directions – is 'if an area is completely devoid of wildlife.' As each successive poisoning illustrates, carbofuran may instead help create this circumstance. Even decades after environmental officials found the pesticide imperils people and birds, carbofuran's toxic legacy, and its circle of death, still grows.

'Death Spiral,' Rene Ebersole, *Audubon,* Spring, 2020

Skirting the river road, (my forenoon walk, my rest)
Skyward in air a sudden muffled sound, the dalliance of the eagles,
The rushing amorous contact high in space together,
The clinching interlocking claws, a living, fierce, gyrating wheel,
Four beating wings, two beaks, a swirling mass tight grappling,
In tumbling turning clustering loops, straight downward falling,
Till o'er the river pois'd, the twain yet one, a moment's lull,
A motionless still balance in the air, then parting, talons loosing,
Upward again on slow-firm pinions slanting, their separate diverse flight,
She hers, he his, pursuing.

'The Dalliance of the Eagles,' Walt Whitman, *Leaves of*
Grass, 1855

ONE

Twenty-seven years ago

The girl was huddled in a booth at Mama J's Luncheonette, nursing a cup of coffee, her second in as many hours. At her right elbow, a half-eaten bowl of noodle soup sat cooling in a nest of crumpled saltine packets, chicken fat congealing into golden globulettes.

'More coffee, hon?'

'Huh?' The girl stared into the nearly empty cup before looking up.

'More coffee. Looks like you could use some.'

From some dimly remembered place, the girl dredged up a smile to put on for the waitress. 'Yes, please.' As the waitress topped off her cup, the girl watched, smile precariously in position. 'More cream?' she asked.

'Coming right up.'

From a clear glass dispenser, the girl poured a steady stream of sugar into her cup and when the waitress returned with cream in a miniature pitcher, she dumped half of it into her coffee. She stirred it appreciatively. At home she drank her coffee instant and black. Bubs would freak out if she wasted money on luxuries like cream.

Outside Mama J's the rain had turned to snow. Plump, wet flakes hurled themselves against the plate glass window where they melted at once and slid down the pane. With a long, thin finger she traced the path of a drop as it meandered along the glass.

Beyond her moving finger, Christmas garlands sagged across Market Street – snowflakes and bells and rosy-cheeked Santas – intersection after intersection of them. The pavement glistened like wet coal. On the corner, a traffic light blinked amber. She'd been watching it blink for hours, reflected in the stained-glass windows of First Christian Church where, according to a sign on the corner, the Reverend Robert Sinclair would be preaching tomorrow morning at nine thirty. *Who's counted? Who counts? – Luke 2:1–3*, the big black letters declared. The girl leaned her head against the cushion of the booth and closed her eyes for a moment, wondering what accounting had to do with Christmas. Then she remembered. *Ah, yes. It came to pass in those days, that there went out a decree from Caesar Augustus, that all the world should be taxed. And all went to be taxed, every one into his own city.*

Mary and Joseph were already there, in fact, part of a life-size nativity scene the congregation (she imagined) had assembled on the church lawn. The Holy Couple was joined by a cow, a lamb, two kneeling shepherds and a king – only one, for some reason – who carried a jewel-encrusted chest as an offering to the Christ Child. The manger, bathed in a spotlight, was full of straw. And empty. Baby Jesus wouldn't arrive for four more days.

An empty manger. How ironic. The girl's eyes stung and she forced herself to look away.

It wasn't the church she was interested in anyway. It was the parsonage, a pleasant, pale yellow Victorian structure with classical cornices at the eaves, a round fairy-tale tower and one of the tallest and most elaborate chimneys she had ever seen. She sighed and wrapped her fingers more tightly around her cup. The spotlight illuminating the crèche had come on at twilight, but the windows of the parsonage were still dark. The woman had to come home *sometime*, the girl thought. Ministers never went anywhere around the holidays; she knew that for a fact.

The girl turned to a duffle bag sitting half open on the seat beside her. She peeked inside to make sure everything was all right – *good, so good* – took another sip of coffee and waited.

Later she knew they'd say she must have been 'desperate.' She studied her reflection on the inside of the glass – tired eyes set in a moon-round face, hair parted cleanly down the middle, curls cascading loosely to her shoulders. Funny, she thought, you don't look desperate. Weary maybe. Older than your years.

She shrugged. Living with Bubs could do that to you.

The girl drained her cup and was weighing whether to ask for a refill when she saw the white car. It paused at the traffic light at Market and Church Streets, left-turn signal flashing, then swung in her direction, its headlights sweeping across Mama J's window. Instinctively, she ducked. When she looked up again, the car had turned into the driveway of the parsonage. The girl waited, her heart hammering, as the driver switched off the engine, climbed out, bent to retrieve her purse and a paper bag of groceries from the floor of the back seat, and hustled into the house.

The girl was puzzled when lights didn't come on right away until she reasoned that the kitchen must be at the back of the house. She imagined the woman opening cupboards, the refrigerator, putting groceries away – hamburger, tomato sauce, bread, a bunch of celery perhaps – groceries she would turn into Reverend Sinclair's dinner. Maybe she was planning to go out again, the girl thought almost hopefully. After all, she hadn't bothered to put her car in the garage.

But then the entrance hall began to glow honey gold with light from an ornate chandelier framed in the fanlight over the door, and seconds later a Christmas tree sprang cheerfully to life in the living room window. The girl knew there was no turning back. 'It's time,' she whispered.

The girl fumbled in her purse, gathering up her loose change. She carefully arranged a tip – two dimes and a nickel – on the table next to her saucer, then picked up the duffle bag and left the restaurant. She hugged the bag to her chest, protecting it from the wind and driving snow, as she dashed across the street.

But once on the other side she stopped, rooted to the sidewalk. She willed her feet to move – *it's a brave thing you're doing, an unselfish thing* – and at last her feet obeyed, carrying her up the walk and under the shelter of the parsonage porch. She crept to the door on legs like cooked spaghetti; her finger hesitated over the doorbell, then dropped to her side.

Please, dear Jesus, just another minute.

The girl sank to her knees beside the duffle. Carefully she peeled aside the layers – a crocheted afghan, a pink flannel blanket, a Yogi Bear pillowcase – and bent to kiss the sweet-smelling head of her sleeping child, to caress its cheek one final time.

Goodbye, sweet darling, goodbye.

She'd written a note to the woman – on lined paper torn from Bubs' notebook – and she checked once again to make sure that the diaper pin holding it to her infant's T-shirt was securely fastened.

She rang the bell.

And ran.

She had intended to be far down the street by the time the woman answered the door, at least as far as the Sunoco station where she'd parked Bubs' motorbike, but instead she found herself hiding in a hedge of evergreens that edged the driveway. Branches caught her

hair and tugged at her clothing. She moved one aside, just enough
to see the porch. She had to be sure.

What's taking you so long? Answer the door!

The girl shivered; she pulled the hood of her jacket over her
damp hair. Bubs would kill her when she got home to the VW bus
they shared, parked – this month anyway – at nearby Tuckahoe
State Park while he waited on a gizmo for the screwed-up transmission. He'd spent the months of her pregnancy making elaborate
arrangements to sell their baby, finally deciding on a loathsome
couple from Baltimore with nothing to recommend them but the
highest bid. The wife smoked, for heaven's sake, and her husband
wore the veined capillary map of the dedicated alcoholic on his
nose. Bubs had dragged her along on a 'home visit' to their town-
house in Towson where clear vinyl slipcovers protected the all-white
upholstery and plastic runners saved the carpet. 'Neat,' Bubs had
said with a grunt of satisfaction.

'Sterile,' she'd replied.

She'd made a fuss about those awful people, of course she had,
but Bubs flipped out whenever she whined. She touched her cheek,
winced, wondering if her jaw would ever work properly again.

Yeah, Bubs would kill her for sure.

She blew on her fingers to warm them. Still, no one had come
to the door. 'Sweet Jesus,' she prayed, 'don't make me ring the bell
again.'

Five more seconds ticked away and the doubts flooded back.
Maybe this was a sign. Maybe God *wanted* her to change her mind!

To test this theory, she took a tentative step out of the shrubbery.
But the instant her foot hit the pavement a porch light came on,
almost as if she had touched a switch. Startled, the girl merged
back into the shadows, her dark clothing invisible amongst the
trees. She watched as the front door yawned wide and warm light
from the hallway spilled into the night. She studied the woman
standing framed in the doorway – solid and sturdy, built straight
up and down, like a tree. And young. That had been important,
too.

The woman squinted into the dark, looking right, then left. She
shrugged and stepped backwards, moved her foot to close the door,
then spotted the duffle.

Tears coursed down the girl's cheeks. A piece of her heart tore
away. From deep within her chest a wail began, like the cry of a

lost kitten, but the girl clamped her lips shut over it, holding her breath against the pain.

Through tears the girl watched the woman stoop, thrust her hands into the bag and carefully remove the baby, so lovingly and gently that the baby didn't even wake. She saw the woman cradle the child in the crook of her arm, caress its cheek as she had just done.

And then the woman called out, as if she knew the girl was there. 'Hello? Hello? Where are you?'

From the bundle in the woman's arms a tiny hand shot up, grasping, and the baby began to cry. From her hiding place deep within the evergreens, the girl's breasts flushed and began to ache. She crouched, sat back on her heels, gulping for air.

'I can help you!' the woman shouted.

The girl squatted in her hiding place, silently rocking, saying nothing, hearing nothing but the pounding inside her own head and the howling of the wind through the bare branches of the trees, a wind that threw off her hood, lifted her hair and blew it wildly across her face.

On the infant's T-shirt, the note fluttered.

The girl, cheeks wet with snow and tears, sobbed silently as the woman bowed her head to read it: *My name is Noel.*

TWO

Present day

I was jolted out of a deep sleep by the sound of gunfire. World War Three seemed to be going on outside my bedroom window. In the gray light of dawn, my husband, Paul, was a thin dark shadow silhouetted against the French doors of our holiday cottage.

I curled my pillow up over both ears, but it didn't help. 'Make it stop!' I moaned.

'They started early,' Paul observed as he opened the door and stepped out onto the deck. 'It must be the Cast and Blast people. I saw Butler setting up his layout boats yesterday. Their RSA permit must have finally gone through.'

RSA. Reserve Shooting Area. When I first heard the term at one of my local book club meetings, I had to look it up. 'I hate them.'

Paul returned to the bedroom, closing the patio doors behind him, both against the noise of the shotguns and the cool November morning air. 'Would coffee help, Hannah?'

Using the pillow, I propped myself up against the headboard. 'I knew there was a reason why I married you.'

'Hah!' he said as he turned and headed for the kitchen. 'You'll get my bill in the morning.'

'Who's Butler?' I asked a few minutes later when Paul reappeared carrying a steaming mug of coffee – French roast from the aroma – perfectly doctored with sugar and half and half.

'Wesley Butler, the caretaker Dave Tuckerman hired to manage his farm.'

Dave was our neighbor. He owned the farm that shared a property line with ours on the south end, all the way from the road down to Chiconnesick Creek. Unlike our modest three-acre plot, however, the Tuckerman spread covered over a thousand acres of tillable land, including several ponds, wooded lots, streams and almost half a mile of Chesapeake Bay shoreline. After Dave and Sandy moved to New Mexico to be closer to their daughter and young grandchildren, he leased his fields to local corn growers, but the corn had been harvested several weeks before.

'Why can't Dave stick to growing corn?' I grumped as I accepted the mug from Paul's outstretched hand. 'Last thing Tilghman County needs is another shooting preserve.'

Paul sat down on the end of the bed and squeezed my foot where it lay under the blanket. 'It was inevitable, Hannah. Dave started talking about applying for an RSA permit with the breakfast crowd down at the High Spot over two years ago. Once other local farmers began leasing out land to sportsmen—'

'Sportsmen!' I harumphed. 'What's sportsman-like about city slickers blowing the smithereens out of ducks that are specially raised for the occasion?' I took a sip of coffee, then added, 'I don't mind the casting part – at least fish have a fighting chance – but if this blasting goes on much longer, I'm going to march out there and do some blasting myself.'

'We don't own a gun,' Paul pointed out.

'Good thing, then,' I said as I took another sip of coffee.

'They'll run out of ammo before long,' Paul said.

'Hope springs eternal,' I said. 'And when do you think that will be?'

Paul shrugged. 'Just a guess. The dogs will have to round up the dead ducks – I know they have retrievers. Then the hunters will have to peel off their cammies and waders and get all suited up for fishing. Cast and Blast folks will feed them some sort of posh, tail-gate lunch, then welcome them aboard *Reel Time* for the casting part of their manly adventure.'

The last words of Paul's sentence were nearly drowned out by a fusillade of shotgun fire. I flung off the duvet and slid out of bed. 'I give up.' I grabbed a pair of jeans and a T-shirt off the pile of clean clothing still sitting in the laundry basket and headed for the shower.

When I emerged, fully dressed and fluffing my damp hair with a towel, Paul had adjourned to the kitchen table where he was finishing off a carton of vanilla yogurt and the last of a box of granola. I made myself a slice of toast, slathered it with cherry jam and wandered out onto the deck. From that vantage point, I could see three grass-camouflaged boats lined up close to the shoreline. It's illegal to shoot sitting ducks in Maryland, so someone – the dogs? – must have been flushing the birds out. As I watched, a dark

cloud of mallards swirled skyward, and the blasting resumed. Half
a dozen birds spiraled out of the sky and dropped into the
marshland.

'Bastards,' I muttered.

I didn't realize Paul had followed me outside until he rested his
hands on my shoulders and said, 'Fortunately, duck season in
November is the twelfth to the twenty-fifth, so Thanksgiving should
be drama-free, at least.'

'Do they eat them, you think?' I asked, leaning comfortably back
against him.

'I suppose. If they don't mind picking out the pellets.'

I turned my head to look up at him. 'Don't ever ask me to cook
duck for you, boyfriend. Not even if it comes from Whole Foods.
Frozen. In a plastic bag.'

Paul's lips brushed my temple. 'Forewarned is forearmed.' After
a moment, he added, 'I'm about to start on my To-Do List for the
weekend. Anything you need added?'

'Not that I can think of,' I said, returning my attention to the
creek where a handful of ducks were paddling about, enjoying a
temporary ceasefire in our DMZ.

While Paul started in on his chores, beginning with repairing the
front gate latch, I slotted the breakfast dishes into the dishwasher,
then, carrying a second mug of coffee, wandered into the office and
powered up my laptop. There wasn't much in the way of email, so
I texted a good morning to our daughter, paid a couple of bills, then
decided to check in with the Silent Sleuths. Our joint forensic
genealogical and investigative efforts had recently reunited an
orphaned four-year-old named Jamal with his biological grandmother, but we had been in hiatus since then while Jack Shelton
was in Arizona working – half-heartedly, I suspected – on a reconciliation with Nancy, his estranged wife. Meanwhile, Mark Wallis
was serving as interim pastor to a small Congregational church in
northern Vermont. But, in the post-Covid era of Zoom, it was easy
for our team to stay in touch.

I was about to log off when a text popped up from the fourth
member of our team, journalist Isabel Randall.

Astonishing news! Izzy texted.

Astonish me! I texted back.

*Elder abuse blog picked up by WaPo, BaltSun and LonTimes.
WSJ tomorrow.*

Bravo Zulu! I texted in time-honored Naval code for a job well-done.

Quigley's making noises like he wants me back at WBNF. Quigley's name was followed immediately by a green face emoji.

Wanna go back?

Dunno, Izzy texted, finished with a shrug emoji.

Five minutes later as I was slipping into my windbreaker, the back pocket of my jeans vibrated. I checked the message. *Even if he comes begging* – Izzy texted – *crawling on his hands and knees, I'd tell him to shove it.*

I was still smiling when I walked into the kitchen. 'I'm going to the grocery. Do you need anything?'

I was speaking to the pair of eleven and a half B running shoes sticking out from under the sink. The denim-clad legs attached to the shoes gradually emerged, then a faded T-shirt, and finally my entire husband slithered forth, a hose clamp dangling from his index finger as if he'd just caught the gold ring on a carousel.

'Two of these,' he replied. 'Same size.'

I relieved him of the broken hose clamp and tucked it into the canvas shopping bag I'd slung over my shoulder. 'I was going to Acme for yogurt and granola, but I can get those at Mighty Mart, too,' I said.

'Don't use the sink,' Paul warned as he stood up, brushing his hands off on his jeans. 'Not unless you want water all over the floor.'

It's always something in a house as old as ours. The plumbing dated to the 1950s, but the house itself had been built when George the Third still reigned over us as king. The former owners, both attorneys, had remodeled – extending the main floor of the original cottage in both directions – and we'd rebuilt the 1740s era stone fireplace shortly after we'd bought the place. We'd fallen hard for it, changed its name from Legal Ease to Our Song, and loved it warts and all.

'Sorry to take you out of your way,' Paul said as he turned toward the sink as if to wash his hands, paused, chuckled and headed instead for the bathroom.

'Not a problem,' I called out after him. 'Mighty Mart is just a few miles further down the road.'

Mighty Mart was, in fact, exactly thirteen miles further south on US 13, not far from Salisbury airport, and served as the anchor

store for a large outlet mall. It was the go-to place for bulk lots,
family-sized portions (if your family comprised two adults and a
dozen children), and to meet authors who had been featured on
afternoon talk shows as they hawked self-help books at tables sandwiched between towers of snow tires. It's just the two of us now,
Paul and I, so I don't need mayonnaise jars the size of Volkswagens
or whole sides of beef cluttering up our basement freezer. That said,
you can never have too many rolls of toilet paper or paper towels
on hand, so I planned to take advantage of this visit and load up
my cart.

Once through the traffic light that held me up at the mall entrance,
I wound my way past Banana Republic, The Gap, Eddie Bauer and
Chicos, heading toward the far corner where Mighty Mart loomed,
its distinctive red and black MM logo towering so high over the
other outlets that it could probably be seen from outer space. I
parked, grabbed my shopping bag and, leaving the perishable foods
on my shopping list for last, headed straight for the hardware section
of the massive, warehouse-style store. I wandered past the television
and computer section, skirted the small appliances, pausing briefly
to consider an air fryer, then hustled past a wall of gadgets that
beckoned oh so temptingly from hooks, ready to snag me as I
passed. Did I need a microwave S'mores maker? Or a silicone cat
egg mold? Doesn't everyone?

The hardware aisle seemed miles long, but the bins were clearly
labeled – who knew there were so many types and sizes of screws?
– and I eventually kneeled in front of a column of plastic bins
containing worm-gear hose clamps in assorted sizes. I had just
reached into my bag to retrieve the broken clamp for comparison
when I sensed someone staring at me and glanced up.

A young Mighty Mart employee eyed me suspiciously from about
ten feet away, her MM badge standing out like a beacon from the
breast pocket of her turquoise smock. 'Can I help you find
something?'

I smiled and struggled to my feet, waving the replacement hose
clamp triumphantly. I opened my mouth to say, 'No, thank you,
I'm all set,' when the young woman's face brightened and she
chirped, 'Mrs Ives!'

I took a few steps closer, squinting at her in the harsh florescent
lighting. 'Oh my gosh, it's Noel, isn't it?'

The woman nodded, her profusion of coppery-blonde, shoulder-length curls bobbing. Noel Sinclair had been a regular babysitter for my grandchildren while she was a student at St John's College in Annapolis. But that had been, golly . . .

'It's been six or seven years, hasn't it?' Noel supplied. 'How are the kids?'

I filled her in quickly. 'Chloe's in her senior year at St Mary's College, Jake's about to graduate from high school, and I'm sorry to tell you that Baby Tim is learning how to drive.'

'No way!'

'Way,' I said with a grin. 'Whenever I have a death wish, I let Timmy drive me to church on Sunday.'

'That sounds like Timmy! Little daredevil.' Her face suddenly clouded. 'But what are you doing here?'

'Shopping for hose clamps,' I said with a grin, although I knew what she meant. 'But you mean, here, as on the Eastern Shore, rather than on Prince George Street in Annapolis.'

She nodded.

'Paul and I bought a vacation cottage outside of Elizabethtown a few years back and spend weekends over here every chance we get. How about you?'

'Working,' Noel said simply.

'And more importantly,' I said as I scrutinized her employee badge, '"Wendy is Happy to Help You." Who is Wendy and what have you done with her?'

With a hint of a smile, Noel took me gently by the arm, lowered her voice and said, 'Shhh. You'll blow my cover.'

'What?'

'Meet me in the ladies' room in about ten minutes and I'll explain. Alice Kannaday is always watching, so . . .'

As she steered me down the aisle, Noel leaned close to my ear. 'Alice is a tattletale, a mean girl.'

'Is this Mighty Mart or high school?' I whispered back.

'A little of both, I think. But Alice is the pharmacist's daughter, so what'cha gonna do?'

'No kidding, but who's Wendy?'

'Wendy Walker, the manager's niece.'

Clearly Mighty Mart management was a family affair. 'OK, I get it, but why are you wearing her badge?'

'Long story,' Noel said, as she released my arm. 'Ladies' room. Ten minutes.'

'Where's the restroom?' I asked.

'Seafood department. Take a right at the live lobster tank.'

As Noel disappeared around an end cap of knock-off designer handbags, I fingered a Kate Spade tote splashed with flowers as if interested, in case Alice was lurking nearby, then killed a few minutes filling my shopping cart with paper towels, toilet paper and a case of club soda.

Ten minutes later, I parked my cart next to the doomed lobsters and entered the ladies' room.

THREE

Noel was waiting for me, fanning her face with a paper towel. 'Phew! Somebody's been smoking in here. Again! Probably Alice. Pharmacist's kid or no pharmacist's kid, there's no excuse for stinking up the restroom when she can smoke outside on the loading dock.' Noel wiped around the rim of the stainless-steel sink, tossed the paper towel into the trash, turned to me and said, 'I suspect she's hiding her nicotine habit from Daddy.'

While I watched, Noel propped the restroom door open with a yellow Caution Wet Floor (*Cuidado Piso Mojado*) tri-cone, then checked each of the four stalls to make sure they were vacant. 'To answer your question,' Noel said simply, keeping her voice low, 'I needed a job.'

'But . . .' I shook my head in disbelief. 'In a big box store?'

Noel shrugged. 'Not much you can do these days with a graduate degree in Philosophy except teach, and I thought, what's the point of turning out batches of other philosophy majors with no marketable skills?' She grinned. 'Until every major US corporation decides they need a resident philosopher on staff, kids would be better off majoring in business administration.

'After job after job failed to pan out,' she continued, 'I thought I'd better do something before I ended up standing in line for food stamps. So, I'm not proud. I went to a placement service. They gave me a form to fill out, natch, but after I wrote down my name, address, telephone number, yada yada yada, I kind of sat there, staring at the wall. I mean, what practical skills do I have, really? There was a question about keyboarding and I thought, well, I can play "Für Elise" and "Minuet in G" pretty well. Honestly, I was hopeless. I finally figured out they meant typing.'

That made me laugh so hard that I had to lean against the sink, cool against my thigh. 'I can't believe you didn't know about keyboarding!'

She raised her hand. 'Home-schooled, that's me. The term never came up.'

'And after that, they found you *this* job? What do you do?'

'Bag groceries, stock shelves, unload delivery trucks, mop up spills.' Noel smiled grimly. 'Kinda like being a housewife. Look,' she whispered after a long pause, 'it's not what it seems. I'm working undercover for a private security firm.'

'What?' If Noel had claimed to be representing a trade delegation from the planet Jupiter, I couldn't have been more surprised.

'I'm employed by an outfit called Warner Protective Services,' she went on to explain. 'It's a private security firm based in Annapolis founded a decade or so ago by a former Navy Seal named Stuart Warner. Nice guy, by the way. Some high-level muckety-muck at Mighty Mart hired WPS to look into problems they're having with inventory shrinkage,' Noel continued. 'Could be pilfering. Could be bookkeeping errors.' She shrugged. 'Who knows.'

'Doesn't the store have security cameras?'

'They do, but whoever's doing it is managing to get around the cameras. So, for this assignment, I work undercover as a clerk, stocking shelves, making sure all the Froot Loops and Lucky Charms are lined up even. No frozen spinach in with the green beans, that kind of thing. Nobody but the store manager, not even the personnel manager, knows I'm working for security.'

'How could the personnel manager *not* know?'

Noel grinned, revealing a row of even white teeth. 'Because I'm the store manager's beloved niece, taking a gap year from college. Wendy's CV is totally fictional, of course, but since I'm the manager's niece, nobody looked at it too closely.'

'So, what has Wendy found out?' I asked.

'Well, Wendy' – she made quote marks in the air with her fingers – 'had been working the day shift for only a week before learning two valuable lessons. Don't stack cream of mushroom soup more than three cans high, and never let yourself get trapped between Kevin Toomey and the walk-in produce cooler.'

I laughed uneasily. 'He sounds creepy.'

She flapped a hand. 'No worries. A well-aimed kick and a switch to the evening shift took care of the Kevin problem,' she continued with a grin, 'but I was beginning to despair of ever having anything even remotely suspicious to report to Stu, my boss. Not that I *wanted* to catch someone on the staff with their hands in the proverbial cookie jar, mind you. Most of my co-workers, with the exception of the aforementioned Alice Kannaday and the odious Kevin, are genuinely friendly, hard-working people. Still, it's disappointing to have so little of interest to report.'

'How long have you been at it?' I asked.

'This assignment? Two days short of a month,' Noel said.

I shrugged. 'Maybe nothing going on, then.'

'Not exactly nothing,' Noel snorted. 'One afternoon I watched Michael – you might have noticed him, that bulky kid with freckles who fetches things off the tall shelves for you – snitch three varieties of luncheon meat and a selection of gourmet pickles from the deli case. Must have thought nothing of it, because he breezed by me, scooping up plastic packets of mustard and mayonnaise on his way to the Kaiser rolls in the bakery. Hardly a hanging offense,' Noel added, 'but I reported it anyway.'

A young woman burst through the open doorway just then, dragging a screaming toddler by the arm. 'You have to *tell* Mommy when you need to make poo-poo, Tina!'

While she wrestled her daughter into a fresh pair of Pull-Ups in the handicapped stall, I stood quietly at the sink fiddling with my hair. Then, presumably because Tina wasn't being cooperative, I had to make a big job out of applying a little bit of lip gloss. In my peripheral vision, I watched Noel slip a ballpoint pen out of her uniform pocket, yank a paper towel out of the dispenser and scribble something down on it.

After two thunderous flushes that I hoped Mighty Mart's plumbing could handle, the woman and her daughter emerged from the stall. Noel stepped aside so they could wash their hands.

'Let's go look for some big girl panties,' the mother announced more cheerfully than I would have done under similar circumstances.

'Tomorrow's Sunday,' Noel reminded me after they had gone. 'I work late tonight, so I've got the morning off. Can we meet somewhere? I'd love to catch up.' She folded the paper towel into quarters and tucked it into my hand. 'We have to leave cell phones in our lockers, but that's got my number on it. Text me, OK?'

I opened my mouth to respond when another figure darkened the doorway. 'And another thing, Wendy,' I said, raising my voice. 'You can tell your manager for me that if he wants to encourage customers to wash their hands after using the bathroom, he should supply them with soap that isn't pink and doesn't smell like a funeral home!'

And with a polite, 'Excuse me' I flounced out the door past the Mighty Mart employee whose name badge read, *Alice Will Be Happy to Help You.*

FOUR

Nobody was casting and blasting on Sunday, thank goodness. Yesterday's city slickers had loaded their dead ducks and gutted fish into the back of their Escalades and driven home in manly triumph to their wives who, they probably fantasized, were standing by armed with recipes for *confit de canard* or grilled rockfish with cilantro-mint relish they'd downloaded from Epicurious. com. Far more likely, the missus would be rustling up a hamburger casserole, point to the basement door and say, 'The freezer's down there.'

After I got home from Mighty Mart and put my purchases away, I texted Noel to suggest we meet at our cottage around nine the following day. I pinpointed the location with a Google Maps link. 'If you plug in our mailing address,' I warned, 'you'll end up in a pond up to your hubcaps.'

Just in time for breakfast the next morning, Paul finished fiddling with the pipes under the sink so I could run water to my heart's content, or at least until our well ran dry. I used the hour before Noel arrived to bake a cinnamon crumb coffee cake, cheating a bit by using a box mix from Trader Joes.

Noel arrived on time, dressed in dark gray jeans and a classic Simpsons 'Unamused Lisa' sweatshirt in neon yellow. With her pale curls tied back with a rainbow scrunchie, she looked more like the girl I remembered.

'Let's talk in the kitchen,' I said, as I accepted her fleece jacket and hung it on a peg by the door. 'I've made coffee cake, and the Keurig cups come in many delicious flavors, thanks to my Mighty Mart expedition yesterday.'

Noel chose a hazelnut blend and before long we were seated at opposite sides of the small kitchen table I'd found at a flea market in Elizabethtown the previous summer.

'Thanks for saving my life yesterday,' Noel began after sampling the coffee and pronouncing it good.

'What?' I asked, genuinely puzzled.

'With Alice.'

'Oh, that,' I chuckled.

'Academy Award-winning performance,' she said. 'But don't expect to see any change in the soap situation at Mighty Mart any time soon. They have vats of the pink stuff in the warehouse.'

'It really reeks of disinfectant,' I remarked, taking a sip of my own coffee, an aggressive caramel-vanilla-cream I decided I'd not buy again. 'As far as soaps go, I'm partial to the Jergens cherry-almond scent of my youth, but I guess that'd be too much to hope for.'

'If you can't buy it in a fifty-five-gallon drum, Mighty Mart's not interested,' Noel said.

'Moving on,' I said, 'I wanted to ask you about something I've been curious about since yesterday. You told me you went to a placement service looking for a job, but how on earth did you end up in private security?'

'Must have wowed 'em with my résumé.' Noel smiled ruefully. 'Under "supervision" I wrote that I managed a play group of six eight-year-olds twice weekly. You get the picture. I think Mr Warner felt sorry for me.'

'A job's a job's a job, sweetie. Besides, Warner Protective Services sounds like a company with potential.'

'That's true,' she admitted. 'I checked him out, natch. His headquarters is in Annapolis, but he's also got offices in San Diego, Chicago and Pensacola. If everything works out, Stu offered to send me for training. At our last meeting he waxed on and on, almost poetically, about anti-stalking, anti-kidnapping, anti-terrorism . . . anti-this and anti-that until my head swam. When I came up for air, I managed to hold on to two important things: I'd learn to shoot and drive fast, and there's a critical shortage of women in the field.'

'Awesome,' I said, picturing a gun-toting Noel clad head-to-toe in sleek black leather à la Agent 99 or Emma Peel.

'I know what you're thinking,' she said with a smile. 'But how can I deal calmly with potential terrorists when I can't even keep my cool with Alice in the frozen fish department?'

I turned to her in surprise. 'What was that all about?'

Noel shrugged. 'A few days after I started work, we tangled over who had or had not, accidentally or on purpose, unplugged the frozen shrimp cart. The twenty-seven-year-old me would have slinked away from the argument, but the nineteen-year-old student who had taken over my body stood her ground. Before long, Alice and I were trading furious *Did toos* and *Did nots* in front of the cocktail sauce display until Di Hunter, our supervisor, called a time out.

'Embarrassing, really,' she continued. 'A miracle that neither one of us lost our job.' She smiled at me over the rim of her coffee mug. 'Well, not exactly a miracle. What was Di supposed to do with the pharmacist's daughter and the store manager's beloved niece?'

'Sorry, but I find that hysterical,' I said as I retrieved the coffee cake from the kitchen counter, sliced it into squares and set the pan, still warm, in front of her. 'You could always tell Stu that you were really sinking your teeth into the role.'

'Not far from the truth,' she said as she selected a square of cake, took a bite, then set it down on her napkin. 'You filled me in yesterday on the kids, but what's happening with Emily and Dante? Weren't they planning to open a spa?'

I brought Noel up to date on what her former employers had been up to since the last time she babysat for them, highlighting the successful launch of Paradiso, my daughter and son-in-law's spa that had gone so upmarket it had recently been featured in a *Spa World* centerfold.

'Wow, I'm so happy for them,' she said. 'And how about you? The last time we talked you had just signed on to the cast of that reality show, *Patriot House 1774*. Seeing you on TV was awesome!'

'Hard to believe it's been so long,' I said. 'But, to answer your question, I've recently become involved with a group we call the Silent Sleuths. Jack's a retired cop, Mark's a former Navy chaplain and Izzy's a freelance investigative reporter. Working with the police, we've been able to solve a couple of cold cases using forensic genetic genealogy in combination with good, old-fashioned gumshoe work. My specialty is building family trees from DNA data that's been uploaded to recreational databases like Ancestry, 23andMe and GenTree.'

Her green eyes flashed with interest. 'I know about that. My sister, Ginny, bought us both GenTree DNA kits when they went on sale for Amazon Prime day. We spit in the tubes and sent them off. Still waiting for results, although, honestly, we're not expecting any surprises. Mom and Dad are so deeply Minnesotan that hot dish runs in their veins.'

'You never know,' I told her. 'Turns out I'm twenty-five percent Native American.'

She set her mug down on the table with a quiet thud. 'You're kidding.'

'Seriously. My mom was the result of a doomed love affair between a young, pioneering nurse and a Lakota rodeo star.' I set my mug down next to hers and stood up. 'Don't go anywhere. I'll be right back.'

When I returned from the bedroom, I was holding the photo my grandmother had treasured and kept hidden in a trunk for decades. Since it came into my possession, I'd framed it in a punched pewter picture frame.

I gazed at that photo so often, I'd memorized every detail. A man sits astride a white horse. While the horse seems transfixed by the camera, the man stares into the distance, affording a clear view of his chiseled, noble profile. He wears dark trousers, a jacket with fringed leather cuffs and a black Stetson hat. The hand resting on his thigh holds a cigarette. He is Joseph White Bear, my grandfather.

I swallowed the lump in my throat to say, 'Grandmother wrote "My Knight" on the back.'

'Golly, he was handsome! No wonder your grandmother fell for him.'

'Indeed, he was, and she certainly did. Joseph died before having any more children,' I said, without going into the heartbreaking details, 'but he had a brother named Henry, so I have first and second Lakota cousins on the Pine Ridge Reservation in South Dakota, as well as a great-aunt who's still going strong at nearly 106 years old. My niece, Julie, is a teacher's aide out there now, in fact.'

'I'm a preacher's kid. I doubt there's anything so tragically romantic in my background,' Noel said as she set my grandfather's photograph carefully down on the table. 'The disciples might get frissons if their hands accidently brush while filling the mini communion cups with grape juice.' She paused for a moment, then added, 'And then they'd have to pray hard about it.'

'No doubt,' I said with a grin. 'Was Mighty Mart your first gig for Mr Warner?'

She shook her head. 'My fourth, all Eastern Shore-based. I still live in Bentonville – I'm not ashamed to say I've moved back into the parsonage with Mom and Dad. Ginny lives at home, too, at least while she's finishing up nursing school at Salisbury University.'

'What kind of gigs?' I asked, genuinely curious.

'Small jobs,' she replied, avoiding the question. 'He assigns me to places like Mighty Mart because I look young and I'm blonde.' She spread her arms wide. '*Voila!* Your official US government issue Dumb Blonde.'

'You are a nut!' I said, laughing.

'Seriously,' she said. 'It's my secret weapon.'

Somewhere, a cell phone dinged. Instinctively, I reached for my back pocket.

'Mine, I think,' Noel said as she eased her own phone out of her hip pocket and checked the display. 'Yup. That's my signal to leave for work. And if I'm late, the odious Alice will report me. Thanks for the coffee, and the cake.' She got to her feet.

I stood up, too. 'But before you go . . .' While she waited, I covered the remaining coffee cake with a sheet of aluminum foil and crimped the edges around the pan. 'Take this with you,' I said. 'If you don't, Paul will end up eating it all in one sitting.'

'But the pan?' she asked.

I flapped a hand. 'You can return it any time. I have others.'

Carrying the cake, she headed into the hallway, then turned and gave me a one-armed hug. 'It's really good to see you again, Mrs Ives.'

'I'm glad I ran into you, too,' I told her. 'I guess I'll have to shop at Mighty Mart more often.'

'No need to go *overboard*,' Noel said as she reached for her fleece.

FIVE

A week passed before I saw Noel again. A week of second summer: clear cool nights and warm, hazy days. With temperatures soaring into the seventies, Paul and I took full advantage of the weather, often dining on the deck, enjoying the last breath of summer before winter set in with a vengeance.

On Thursday, shortly after lunch, Noel showed up, unannounced. When I answered her knock, she thrust the cake pan in my direction. 'I was passing by and thought I'd return this.'

Nobody simply 'passes by' our cottage. After winding through Elizabethtown, you have to execute a confusing number of lefts and rights off the main roads, down side roads and across one-lane bridges before turning down the rutted gravel lane that ends at our house. Even the Waze app isn't sure where to find us.

'Thank you,' I said, accepting the pan, and then, noting the worried expression on her face, 'Won't you come in?'

'Is this a bad time?'

'Of course not. Don't be silly.' As I closed the door behind her, I said, 'It's a gorgeous day. Why don't we sit out on the deck. Can I get you something to drink?'

'Coca Cola, if you have some.'

'Go on out,' I said, pointing her in the direction of the French doors. 'I'll be only a minute.'

Before long, we were settled into adjoining Adirondack chairs, frosty cans of Coke in hand, gazing out over the creek where Paul's little power boat, tied to the dock, rocked gently. 'I'm not an idiot, Noel. You didn't just happen to stop by. Something's bothering you, I can tell.'

Noel reached for the backpack she'd set down on the deck next to her chair, plopped it in her lap and hugged it to her chest. She must have been holding her breath because she let it out then, long and slow.

'Did you lose your job or something?'

'Oh, no, nothing like that,' she said, sounding a bit more perky.

'It's going well. So well, in fact, that Wendy might be telling Alice to eat her shorts and Di to take this job and shove it.'

'Delicious,' I said, turning my head to face her. 'Can I watch?'

'Ha ha,' she said, but there was no amusement in her voice.

'So, you found the source of the inventory shrinkage, I take it?'

She nodded, her face serious. 'In the majority of such cases, according to Stu, it's due to employee theft or shoplifting, that's why he put me on the job. But this time, it turns out that the thefts were occurring between the suppliers and the Mighty Mart warehouse.' She paused for a moment to take a sip of soda. 'Stu had a guy undercover at the supplier, too, although he didn't tell me that. He's recommended to Mighty Mart that they update their inventory management system. Apparently, the company that sold it to them went out of business five years ago and the software's no longer being supported. Stu calls it abandonware.'

'I love that term,' I said. 'But software or no software, you'd think Mighty Mart would have someone checking bills of lading and so on.'

'Oh, they did, Hannah. One person. One. Epic fail. From now on, they'll be using a double-check system so that two people will have to sign off on deliveries.' She took a deep breath, then let it out slowly. 'But I didn't come here today to talk to you about the problems at Mighty Mart.'

'No, of course you didn't.'

'Ginny and I got our DNA test results the other day.'

The croaking of a frog filled the lengthening silence between us. Whatever their results were, it had to have been a surprise.

'We're not sisters,' she said at last. 'In fact, we don't seem to be related at all.'

'Not even *one* parent in common?' I asked, astonished.

'As I said. Not related. At. All.' Noel unzipped the backpack she still cradled on her lap, reached inside and pulled out a sheaf of papers held together with paper clips. From the green and yellow logo, I recognized the pages immediately as printouts from the GenTree website. 'Here's Ginny's report,' she said, handing one set of papers to me. 'It's what I would expect to see. Our mother was an Olson, and there's plenty of those, along with Larsons, Petersons and Carlsons, first and second cousins up the wazoo, some of whose screen names I actually recognize. But mine?' She shook the second set of papers. 'I don't recognize any of these names! Not a single one! Taylor, Allen, Miller, Butler and Harris. Who the hell are these people?

'And another thing,' she babbled on as she handed her own results over to me. 'I realize that the ethnicity maps can be misleading, but Ginny's map is firmly rooted in Scandinavia while my people, whoever they are, seem to have originated primarily in northern Italy.'

I laid the two printouts out, one on each knee, and did a quick comparison. Noel was right: with the exception of an occasional Smith, the two sisters had not a single family name in common.

'Was Ginny adopted?' I had to ask the question, although I could assume from the data that she wasn't.

Noel shook her head. 'Nope. We're four years apart, and I was old enough to remember Mom being pregnant. When I asked, she told me she'd swallowed a watermelon seed.' Noel snorted softly. 'Put me off watermelon completely for a couple of years.'

'Good grief!'

'Yeah, really.'

'So,' I said, 'the obvious question is, were *you* adopted?'

'I don't see how that's possible either. As far as I know, I had a perfectly normal-looking birth certificate. I needed it when I applied for a passport.'

'It's fairly common for birth certificates to be altered to reflect the names of the adopting parents,' I informed her. 'Have you spoken to your mom and dad about these results?'

Noel turned to me, looking horrified. 'Gosh, no! What if the lab made a mistake?'

'I hate to tell you this, my dear, but the GenTree accuracy rate is close to a hundred percent. And DNA doesn't lie.'

'Well, somebody's lying, that's for sure,' she grumped.

'Can you lay your hands on a copy of your birth certificate?' I asked. 'It might tell us something, like the hospital where you were born, the attending physician . . .'

'It's gotta be around the house somewhere,' she said. 'I'll have to look.'

'What does Ginny say about these results?' I asked.

Noel shrugged. 'That she's my sister and always will be. It's the people who raised us who count, not some random egg or sperm donor.'

'Wise woman, your sister.' After a moment, I added, 'Tell you what. Set me up as a collaborator on your account – I'll show you how to do that – and I'll dig into it. See what I can find out about your matches.'

She sighed deeply, in apparent relief. 'Golly! Would you?'

I reached out and laid a hand on her arm. 'It'd be my pleasure. Seriously, I love this stuff, even more than I love working the *New York Times* crossword puzzle.' I stacked the printouts together and laid them aside, next to my chair. 'Now, sit back. Relax. Finish your drink.'

'I'll try,' she said.

I leaned back in my chair and closed my eyes, enjoying the warmth of the midday sun. 'I could put rum in it.'

'Tempting,' she said, sounding more mellow. 'But I don't drink.'

'Sad,' I said.

'Very,' she replied.

SIX

'Oh my gosh! Is that a bald eagle?'

Shading my eyes against the blinding glare reflecting off the windscreen of a passing powerboat, I squinted where Noel was pointing. 'Could be an osprey. Just a sec.'

I rose from my chair and grabbed the binoculars we keep hanging on a hook just inside the French doors. I uncapped the lenses and held the binoculars to my eyes, panning the sky until the bird came into view. 'Definitely an eagle. You can see its white head. Here, take a look,' I said, and handed the binoculars over.

I watched as Noel followed the flight of the magnificent bird in the general direction of our neighbor's cornfield, soaring over the ancient family cemetery where Nancy Hazlett and her baby, Ella, had been buried.

'My gosh! Wait a minute! It's two bald eagles!' She bobbed on her toes, dizzy with excitement. 'I've never seen one so up close before.'

'We've several nesting pairs in this general area,' I told her. 'One nest is in that big dead tree at the head of our creek. There's another pair nesting on Taylors Island not far from the Blackwater Preserve. Lucy and Desi. They produced two viable eggs last spring. We watched them hatch on an eagle cam the preserve set up. They're almost like family.'

'Wow,' Noel said without lowering the binoculars. 'What do you suppose they're doing?'

'Fishing, I imagine.'

'Holy cow, now there's three,' she said. 'Here, your turn.'

I took the binoculars from her outstretched hand and raised them to my eyes. Three bald eagles, one much larger than the others, seemed to be huddled around something partially hidden by the corn stubble remaining in Tuckerman's field. As I watched, another eagle flapped to a landing and joined them. 'Four now,' I said. 'They appear to be scavenging.' I twiddled with the dial to bring the image more clearly into focus. 'Looks like a dead fox.'

'Gross,' Noel said.

I wasn't familiar with the way eagles behave while feeding on carrion, but I'd observed eagles in the wild before and something was definitely out of whack. One of the birds flapped its wings, rose about six feet in the air, tilted, then fell to the ground, its wings still spread. Two of its companions huddled nearby, wings fully extended, tail feathers splayed and necks flung back. I gasped. 'Something's wrong! Those birds look sick.' The eagle who had most recently arrived waddled up to the carcass, pecked at it curiously, then seemed to reconsider.

'Don't touch it!' I screamed instructions to the bird as the horrific truth dawned on me. The fox must have been poisoned, and now, so had the eagles.

There was no time to consult Professor Google for advice. I tossed the binoculars on the cushion of my chair and raced down the outdoor steps, calling for Noel to follow me. The birds were the length of two football fields away. Maybe we could reach them in time to chase them – and any newcomers – away from what could be a deadly carcass. As we raced across the yard and passed the garden shed, I paused long enough to snatch the tarp off the woodpile.

'What are you going to do?' Noel panted as she wriggled between the strands of barbed wire I held open for her.

'I'm not sure,' I panted back as I crawled through the gap after her, trying not to snag my clothing, 'but step one is to cover that damn carcass.'

The sun was still high, hotly illuminating the scene. Flies buzzed industrially around the dead fox, splayed out on its side, a belly wound red and raw where predators had been picking at it. A halo of dead flies surrounded the wound, a black corona that warned of death, if only the eagles had been able to read it.

I needn't have worried about scattering the birds before medical help arrived. Whatever poison they had ingested must have affected their ability to fly. As if they knew the carcass was bad news, the three eagles had staggered away, forming a wide, protective circle around a fallen comrade who continued to flap its wings ineffectually, making quiet gasping noises.

'I think I'm going to be sick,' Noel said, staring fixedly at me rather than the deathly scene. Holding opposite ends of the tarp and keeping it stretched taut between us, we side-stepped our way over the corn stubble until we reached the fox and spread the tarp over its body.

The eagles barely moved.

To keep the tarp in place, I kicked dirt up to anchor the corners to the ground.

Noel and I backed away slowly, then turned and scurried out of the field onto the shoulder of the gravel road that bordered the Tuckerman property and ours. 'We need to call somebody right away, but who?' I said as I pulled my cell phone out of my pocket and stared helplessly at the screensaver.

'I know someone who will know,' Noel said as she eased her phone out of her pocket. 'Guy named Roger Erickson. He's a Maryland National Resources cop. I met him last spring while Stu was tweaking the security system at Eastern Region headquarters down in Queen Anne.' Noel swiped her iPhone to life, then scrolled quickly through her contacts. 'I have his cell,' she said, her face flushed and not entirely, I suspected, from our exertions and the heat of the afternoon sun. She turned the speakerphone on, and while we waited for Roger to pick up, she explained, 'We went out a couple of times. He's a fun guy, but nothing serious.'

After three rings, Roger answered with a cheerful, 'Noel! What's up?'

'Roger,' she said breathlessly, 'my friend and I have got some pretty sick eagles over here.'

The cheerfulness evaporated. 'Where's here?'

'Our Song cottage, adjoining . . .' She paused and turned to me. 'What's the name of this farm, Mrs Ives?'

'It's the old Hazlett place, Roger. Belongs to David Tuckerman, but he leases it out to some outfitter under the RSA program.'

I started to give him turn-by-turn directions, but he interrupted me. 'I know the place, ma'am. How many eagles we talking about?'

'Four.'

'Shit.'

'Yeah,' I said. 'Two females and two males, I'd guess, based on their relative sizes.'

'Are you sure they're sick?'

I explained about the dead fox and the fact that the eagles didn't fly away when we approached.

'Damn,' Roger said. 'Sit tight. I'll be there. Fifteen minutes, max. In the meantime, don't touch anything. With that many eagles down, we could be looking at a crime scene. Eagles are federally protected, so Fish and Wildlife will need to be involved. I'm calling them now.'

Sit tight. Don't do anything. Hard to stand by helplessly while endangered wildlife is sick, possibly dying, all around you. 'I'm going to take some pictures,' I told Noel after Roger ended the call.

'But . . .' she began.

'Don't worry. I won't disturb anything. I think it's important to document the scene just as we found it.'

Noel flapped a hand, shooing me away. 'I just can't. You go. I'll wait here.'

When I got back to the eagles, the scene was much as we had left it. I took a long, panning video from a distance showing the relative locations of the endangered birds, then moved in for closeups, stepping carefully. The eagle I'd watched plummet from the sky was clearly struggling to stand and the others were staggering, flapping ineffectually. Finally, holding my breath against the stench, I lifted a corner of the tarp and drew it back just far enough to take a still photograph of the late fox.

I had just replaced the tarp when a black Ford pickup with a gold stripe on the side came bouncing over the furrows, speeding in my direction. When it was about twenty feet away, the driver slammed on the brakes, stirring up a cloud of dust. Officer Erickson climbed out, accompanied by Noel who had hitched a ride with her friend. About five foot ten, solid and fit as a rugby player, Erickson wore the olive drab uniform of the Department of Natural Resources police. A Smith and Wesson pistol was strapped to his belt, a Nextel communicator to his left shoulder. He had a pleasant, round face and sported a short, neatly trimmed beard prematurely laced with gray. His eyes were hidden behind blue, mirrored aviator sunglasses. When he reached me, he touched the brim of his trouper hat and said, 'Ma'am.'

'Please, call me Hannah,' I insisted.

'What's wrong with the eagles?' Noel asked in a quiet voice, full of concern.

Roger took only seconds to assess the situation. 'I don't need any lab tests to diagnose this, ladies. I've seen it too many times before. It's carbofuran poisoning.' He pointed a finger. 'See how their wing and tail feathers are all fanned out?'

We nodded.

'Now, check out their talons. They're rigid, almost like claws.'

We saw that they were.

'What's carbofuran?' Noel asked.

'It's a super deadly poison that was actually banned by the EPA back in 2009. A pellet the size of a peppercorn can drop an eagle out of the sky, and only a quarter teaspoon of the stuff will kill a four-hundred-pound bear.'

'If it's banned, then why . . .' I began.

'I'll get to that in a moment. Right now, I want to focus on these birds. Someone from Fish and Wildlife will be here soon, and I've already arranged for a transporter.'

'Transporter?' I asked, flashing to an old *Star Trek* episode and thinking I'd misheard.

'Someone specially trained to capture the birds, pack them up and transport them ASAP to the nearest raptor rescue center. We have a list, so I started calling to see who was available. Not everyone's equipped for so many victims.' He rotated his wrist to check his watch. 'Diana Kingsley should be arriving in about ten minutes.'

Up close and personal, bald eagles, especially the females, are enormous, standing white-feathered head to talon-tip the length of a full-grown man's leg. Well-trained or not, I didn't covet Diana Kingsley's job. I imagined it would be like trying to wrestle a reluctant German shepherd into a shipping crate, if German shepherds had heavy-duty beaks and lethal talons.

While we waited impatiently for the cavalry to arrive, Roger filled us in on carbofuran, a generic pesticide that had been sold under several brand names including Furadan, Curaterr, Rampart and the ludicrously named Carbosip. 'It's illegal to buy and sell the stuff, but it's not illegal to own it. Go figure. No telling how many bags of carbofuran are still stashed away on farms around here.'

'What are they trying to get rid of?' Noel asked. 'Surely not eagles?'

'This farm's an RSA, right?' Roger asked.

'Tell me about it,' I said. 'Trying to sleep late during hunting season is mission impossible.'

'What's an RSA?' Noel wanted to know.

'Regulated shooting area,' I explained, stepping up on my soapbox. 'Otherwise known as a shooting preserve. Whoever's got an RSA license is allowed to raise captive ducks and other fowl on the land for city slickers to blow to smithereens.'

'Gross,' Noel said.

'Eagles are predators,' Roger said. 'They prefer fish, but if there's a pond nearby teeming with ducks—'

'Smorgasbord,' I cut in.

Roger frowned at my inappropriate attempt to lighten the mood. 'Coyotes and foxes take their toll on the captive duck population, too,' he scolded. 'And deer can decimate a corn crop. The lab will be able to determine whether this carcass was laced with carbofuran and left out on purpose, or whether these eagles were victims of secondary poisoning.'

'Somebody did this on *purpose*?' Noel said, clearly as horrified as I was.

'We call it the Circle of Death,' Roger continued after a moment. 'A deer is poisoned with carbofuran and dies. A coyote feeds on the carcass of the deer and dies. A fox feeds on the poisoned coyote, walks one hundred yards away, and dies. Because the fox received a lower dose, it might travel five or six hundred yards before succumbing. A bird that feeds on the dead fox might manage to fly half a mile before dropping out of the sky.' He paused, removed his hat and tucked it under his arm, then wiped the sweat off his forehead with the back of his sleeve. 'The circle of death keeps moving outward. Last year we had a case where there was a five-square-mile radius where we kept finding dead animals. The crime scene kept getting bigger and bigger. And I'm quite certain we never found them all.'

'Is it like DDT?' Noel asked.

Roger shook his head. 'Carbofuran's not like DDT at all. DDT works its way slowly up the food chain to higher and higher concentrations until death occurs. It's not like lead poisoning from lead ammo that gradually builds up in a bird's system, either. Carbofuran is totally deadly. It's use, it's *only* use, is to kill.'

'It must be mega toxic to humans, too,' I commented.

'You betcha.' Roger snorted. 'But incredibly, if you get a chance to read one of the manufacturer's warning labels, and I don't recommend ever getting that close to one, ladies, you'll see that they claim it's perfectly safe when used according to directions. That's bullshit, of course.'

While Roger was talking, I'd opened the Google app on my iPhone and typed in 'carbofuran.' According to Professor Google, carbofuran was an odorless white crystalline substance that when ingested could cause weakness, sweating, nausea, vomiting, abdominal pain, and blurred vision. Higher levels could cause muscle twitching, loss of coordination, and could cause breathing to stop.

My stomach clenched. If it could do all that to a human, those eagles had to be in agony.

I glanced up at Roger from the small screen. 'Along with the usual nausea and vomiting, Google says carbofuran can cause breathing to stop. That's safe? Sounds kinda fatal to me.'

Roger settled his Smokey Bear hat firmly on his head and adjusted the brim. 'Yeah.' He paused for a moment to clear his throat. 'Whoever poisoned this fox, whatever his motives, broke the law. It's illegal to use carbofuran in any form.'

Somewhere close by a car horn toot-tooted. 'Ought to spike his Miller Lite with carbofuran and see how *he* likes it,' Roger muttered as he turned to greet the newcomer.

SEVEN

A full-sized, dark gray Chevy Tahoe screeched to a halt on the gravel road. Its driver backed into the cornfield, expertly lining the vehicle parallel to Roger's truck. The woman who hopped out of the driver's seat wore blue jeans tucked into a pair of heavy leather hiking boots and a red plaid jacket that had to be stifling on such an unseasonably hot day. Her straw-colored hair was twisted into a no-nonsense French braid.

Roger extended his hand. 'Thanks for coming so quickly, Diana. Everyone, this is Diana Kingsley, my favorite transporter.'

Diana bobbed her head in the direction of her SUV. 'I'll need help with the carriers, OK?' Without waiting for an answer, she aimed her key fob at the vehicle and popped the lock. We watched as the rear door slowly rose, revealing a generous cargo area filled to capacity. 'I brought four carriers, Rog, but . . .' She glanced over her shoulder, focusing on the spot where the sickest eagle now lay. 'I think we're only gonna need three.'

'I was afraid of that,' Roger said as he reached for one of the vented pet carriers, seized it by the handle, dragged it out of the vehicle and set it onto the ground.

'OK if I go ahead?' she asked.

'Yeah. I think it's pretty clear what happened here, and the sooner we get these birds some help, the better their chances of survival. We'll comb the scene for evidence after you've gone. Just be careful.'

'Fuck carbofuran,' she said.

As I stood to one side feeling about as useful as a bottomless bucket, Diana put Noel to work lining the bottom of each carrier with terrycloth toweling. Meanwhile, she suited up. She slipped a pair of goggles over her head, parked them temporarily on her forehead, then pulled on a pair of long-sleeve Kevlar welding gloves. 'You, too, Rog,' she instructed. She reached into the bin where she kept her equipment, grabbed a second pair of heavy gloves and tossed them in his direction.

Roger made a one-handed catch. 'I've got my own in the truck, but these are cleaner.'

'Goggles, too,' she ordered, bobbing her head at the bin.

While Roger prepared for action, Diana approached the sickest bird who now lay flat and motionless, its wings uselessly spread. Even from where I stood, I could see that the eagle's eyes were closed. She sat on her heels next to it, forearms resting on her thighs, inspected it silently, then reached out and gently smoothed its ruffled head feathers. She swiped at her cheek with the back of her glove, then stood. 'This little guy didn't make it, I'm afraid. Let's see to the others.'

I watched in fascination as Diana snatched a lightweight, sheet-sized blanket from a pile in the cargo hold, shook out the folds and cautiously approached the largest of the ailing eagles from behind. With precision I suspected was borne of long practice, she tossed the blanket over the eagle's head, covering the bird completely. It struggled briefly, then seemed to relax as she gently smoothed the blanket over its wings, running her gloved hands down and down, all the way to its legs. She seized its legs firmly, somehow avoiding the long, thick toenails, lifted the bird easily and rested it momentarily against her chest.

'Birdy burrito,' Diana announced as she straightened her back and approached the carrier Roger held open and ready.

In a move so swift you'd need slow-motion replay to see exactly how it was accomplished, Diana popped the bird into the carrier, snatched the sheet away and secured the door.

'How did you *do* that?' Noel asked in awe. 'Aren't they heavy?'

'Not really,' Diana said, her brown eyes dark and serious behind her goggles. 'Birds' bones are kinda hollow. I doubt that little lady weighed more than twelve or thirteen pounds.'

'Wow,' Noel said. 'I've carried toddlers around who weighed a lot more than that.'

'Me, too,' Diana said.

After all three birds had been loaded into carriers and slotted into the SUV, Diana draped the carriers with blankets. 'Keeping the birds in the dark helps calm them down,' Diana explained. She stripped off her gloves and goggles, then added, 'These birds are banded, so we'll soon know where they came from.'

'Where will you take them?' I asked.

'Hoots is the raptor center best equipped to handle eagles around here,' she said.

'Hoots?'

'It's named after Hoots, the owl puppet on *Sesame Street*.'

'Ah,' I said. 'I remember Hoots. Played the sax. How soon will we know . . .' I left the thought unsaid.

'I'll keep Roger informed,' she said. 'If you arrange in advance, you might even visit the center at some point. Hoots is off one thirteen, not too far from Pokomoke River State Park. Google it.

'Thank goodness this isn't nesting season,' she continued. 'It takes two adult eagles to incubate eggs and feed and protect young eaglets. If this were springtime, we could be looking at even more victims.'

I thought about Lucy and Desi and their fledglings. About Roger's experience with seemingly endless circles of death. I shivered.

Meanwhile, Diana tended to the dead eagle. She took time to wrap it in a soft cloth, folding the material over the bird as tenderly and lovingly as a human mother swaddling her infant.

'What will happen to the poor thing?' I asked as I watched her work.

'We'll send it to the lab,' Diana said as she passed me, cradling the bundle.

'Lab?'

'Fish and Wildlife has a state-of-the-art crime lab in Oregon,' Roger explained as he accepted the bundled bird. 'Think *CSI* for animals. After they finish with it, the carcass will be frozen and shipped to the National Eagle Repository they also run out in Colorado. Technically, it's illegal to keep a bald eagle feather even if you find one lying on the ground, but Native Americans are an exception. The job of the repository is to store and distribute dead golden and bald eagle parts to enrolled members of federally recognized tribes.'

Noel shot me a glance, and I knew she was thinking about my Native American cousins, as was I.

'How about the dead fox?' I asked.

'After the lab is finished with it, he'll be incinerated.'

'Poor fox,' I said.

'Is your job always so depressing, Roger?' Noel wanted to know.

Before Roger had a chance to answer, Diana interrupted. 'Gotta be going. Thanks for the help, Rog.'

'Any time, Diana.'

'Find out who did this, OK?'

'You can count on it,' he said.

Diana clicked her fob and we watched as the door eased to a close over her suffering cargo. I trailed behind her to the front of the SUV and held the door open while she climbed in. 'What do you do, Diana? When you're not out rescuing raptors, I mean.'

Diana collapsed into the driver's seat and reached around for her seatbelt. 'I'm an independent marine surveyor, inspecting yachts for local marinas and insurance companies.' She clicked her seatbelt closed. 'In my spare time, I fill in for my sister at the High Spot Cafe in Elizabethtown. She and her husband own the place.' Diana leaned forward and pushed a button. The SUV's engine roared, then settled down to a quiet purr. 'Flexibility, that's key, Hannah. Why? Are you interested?'

I shrugged and nodded toward the cargo hold. 'I think I'm going to have nightmares. How can anyone . . .?'

With her right hand resting on the gear shift, Diana turned to me, her face grave. 'Some people are so evil that they forfeit their right to live. You know what I mean?'

EIGHT

With all the drama over the eagles, I'd almost forgotten about Noel's unexpected DNA results until we were back at the cottage and she was preparing to leave for home. She must have had the same thought.

'No rush on the GenTree business, Mrs Ives. Seems selfish to be thinking about that now.'

'I'm still shaking,' I said, holding out my quivering hand for inspection.

'I'm praying that we got to the birds before they had time to, uh, you know . . .'

'I hope so, too,' I said. 'And give yourself credit. If you hadn't been looking at the sky at precisely the right moment, there might have been four dead eagles in that cornfield instead of just one.'

'Do you think they'll make it?' she asked as I accompanied her into the entrance hall.

'Maybe you can check in with Roger tomorrow afternoon for a status report,' I said. 'Since you've got his number handy.'

She flushed. 'OK. You talked me into it.'

I opened the door. 'I don't think it took much arm-twisting on my part.'

'He is kinda cute,' she admitted. 'For an older guy.'

'How old *is* he?' I asked.

She shrugged. 'Honestly? It never came up. Thirty-five, maybe. Forty. Before he joined DNR, he was an avionics technician in the Air Force. Stationed at Andrews.' She hoisted her backpack and settled it onto one shoulder. 'Believe it or not, Roger's read extensively in philosophy, so along with our love of nature, we have that in common.' Halfway down the front steps she paused and turned around to look at me. 'And the fact that he's from Minnesota, just like my, my . . . oh, golly.'

'Don't worry, Noel,' I said, following her thought. 'We'll figure it out.'

'Pretending to be Wendy for a month or so was just a job, Mrs Ives. I never dreamed I'd end up not knowing who I *really* am.'

I stepped through the doorway, but before I could reach Noel to deliver a comforting hug, she turned and fled down the walk to her car, an old but well-maintained dark blue VW Touareg.

It took until nearly three o'clock for the adrenaline rush to wear off. By then, I'd run out of mindless chores and had collapsed in a deck chair, clasping a glass of Petit Sirah, full to the brim.

As I tried to relax, I recalled Diana's words from earlier. 'These birds are banded, so we'll soon know where they came from.' I sipped on the wine, feeling morose, stewing over the sick eagles and worrying about exactly where they had come from.

Were two of them 'our' eagles, the pair that had built their nest in the dead tree at the mouth of Chiconnesick Creek? The pair my grandson, Timmy – a spirited lad blithely untroubled by gender politics – had named Calvin and Hobbes? I set the wine glass down and reached for the binoculars, focusing on the bare, stark-white branches of the old tree. I panned up and up. The nest was still there – giant, hairy with twigs and messy as a college dorm room – but nobody was home.

My gut twisted. I took a generous sip of wine, semi-comforted by its dark, mellow flavor – chocolatey, plummy, a hint of pepper – and tried to relax.

My long, deep funk was interrupted by the crunch of Paul's tires on the driveway. A few minutes later I heard the front door slam and his cheery, 'Hi honey, I'm home. How was your day?'

'I'm out on the deck,' I shouted, then burst into tears.

'What? What did I say?' Paul asked when he found me sitting in the Adirondack chair, clutching my empty wine glass and quietly weeping.

I told him all about my Terrible, Horrible, No Good, Very Bad Day. 'I'm super sad that any birds got poisoned,' I sniffed as I wrapped up my account and tried to reign in my emotions. 'But, but . . . what if it's Calvin and Hobbes?'

Paul leaned over and relieved me of the wine glass, then set it down on the deck. 'I think you've had a little too much wine, Hannah.'

I glanced at him sideways, through damp lashes. 'I needed to relax.'

'Alcohol doesn't help you relax,' Paul said. 'It's a depressant.'

'Not the alcohol,' I insisted. 'Red wine contains resveratrol. Preliminary studies have shown it can help treat anxiety.'

'In rats,' Paul said. 'I read the same article.'

Clearly an argument I was doomed to lose. 'Their nest is empty,' I said, pointing down the creek.

'It's an old nest,' Paul said reasonably. 'And they didn't produce any eggs this season, so perhaps they've moved house. Eagles have been known to do that.' He hauled the second chair around until it was facing mine, then sat down in it. 'When was the last time you saw Calvin and Hobbes?'

Although I racked my brain, I couldn't remember. 'I confess I haven't been paying that much attention. I feel bad about that.'

'I read somewhere that Maryland has more eagles than any state other than Alaska. The guys down at the High Spot tell me there's more than fifty nesting pairs in Tilghman county alone. The victims might not have been our eagles.'

'That's supposed to make me feel better?'

'The transporter told you the birds were tagged, right? So we'll find out soon enough what nest they came from. Jumping to conclusions before we have all the facts is a waste of psychic energy.'

'You're right,' I sniffled. 'As usual. Would you mind fetching me a tissue? My nose seems to be running.'

Paul was back in a minute carrying the whole box. I whipped out a tissue and gave my nose a good blow. 'Thank you,' I said. 'So, how was your day?'

'Same old, same old. I hate grading exams almost as much as the midshipmen hate taking them.' Paul squeezed my knee and stood up. 'Tell you what. Don't worry about fixing dinner. Why don't I grab a pizza out of the freezer?'

I dabbed at my eyes with a fresh tissue. 'Mushroom,' I said. 'Please.'

'Do you feel up to making a salad?'

'Caesar salad OK? If it comes in a bag.'

'Perfect,' Paul said, turning to go. 'I don't suppose you saved any wine for me.'

'I am not a lush, Professor. The bottle's on the sideboard.' I scooted my butt forward, held on to the arms of the chair and began to hoist myself up.

Paul raised a hand, palm out. 'No need to get up, honey. Dinner's under control.'

'Too late,' I said as I staggered to my feet. 'I just thought of something I need to do.'

While Paul busied himself with dinner, bless him, I shuffled to the office – maybe I *had* gone a bit overboard on the wine? – and flopped down on the chair behind the desk. I logged onto the computer and moused over to the icon that would link me to Lucy and Desi's eagle cam. The video came up right away, but my heart froze. Although I stared at the screen for more than five minutes, Lucy and Desi's nest remained empty.

I was beginning to tear up again when one of the pair flapped into view, settled onto a branch and folded its wings. 'Welcome home, Lucy,' I said, sighing with relief. Eagles don't sleep in their nests, I knew that, but the branch where Desi usually preferred to sack out at night remained vacant. 'OK, Desi. Time to knock it off and fly home.'

When Paul announced that dinner was ready, Desi had still not made an appearance. Although the aroma of piping hot pizza wafting in from the kitchen reminded me that I was starving, perhaps because I had missed lunch, I had to drag myself away from the screen.

Thirty minutes later, with garlic heavy on my breath and carrying a chocolate chip cookie, I came back.

And when I refreshed the screen, so had Desi.

NINE

The following morning dawned crisp and cool. I started my day the usual way – carrying a hot mug of coffee out to the deck – but I parked it on the rail almost immediately and zipped back into the house to fetch a hoodie.

The whereabouts of the other pair of eagles, Calvin and Hobbes, still weighed heavily on my mind. On the way back to rejoin my coffee, I snagged the binoculars and used them to check out their tree, but the nest and the branches above and below it all remained empty.

I heard the rumble of the French door sliding open behind me. 'Still no sign of the missing couple?' Paul said.

'Not yet.' My words came out in a puff of mist.

Paul wrapped an arm around my shoulders and drew me close. 'Early days yet, Hannah.'

I laid the binoculars down on the railing next to my mug and leaned into him, appreciating the warmth of his body against my side. 'Who would do such a terrible thing?'

'Well, we know the fox didn't get into the poison here. The most dangerous pesticide in our tool shed is a Black Flag Roach Motel. I know. Last night I double-checked. There's no property closer to the scene of the crime than our good neighbor, Dave's, but he hasn't set foot in Maryland for over a year, as far as I can tell.' Paul squeezed my shoulder. 'My bet? If anyone's responsible, it's the guy who manages Dave's RSA, Wesley Butler.'

'Does Butler run the hunts, too?'

'No, but he manages the stock, so to speak. The Cast and Blasters come from an outfitter in Delaware called Feathers-N-Fins. I've seen their pop-up vans in the driveway. They've got franchises in Virginia and Pennsylvania, too.'

Paul leaned sideways, throwing his weight onto one hip in order to work his cell phone out of his back pocket. He swiped it on, then tapped a few keys. 'Here's their website. Have a look.'

From the date printed underneath the masthead, I could see that the website had been recently updated. *We've added a lot of land to our portfolio!!!* screamed a colorful banner. The announcement included a photograph of dozens of dead ducks laid out in precise rows on the tailgate of a Ford F150. A golden retriever sat nearby looking bored, like, Hey dude, take the picture already and where's my Alpo?

'Ugh,' I said. 'There ought to be a law,' and handed the phone back.

'It's big business, Hannah, and not just for the landowners and outfitters. As part of the package, the punters shell out for two nights at the Sportsmen's Retreat outside of Salisbury.'

'Ah.' I sighed. 'Must be nice.' We'd stayed at the Sportsmen's Retreat a couple of years before, Paul and I, while Our Song's heart pine flooring was being restored. The Retreat, as it was referred to by the locals, was situated on a scenic bluff overlooking the Wicomico River and must have been designed by a decorator who'd been hit over the head by a golf club at birth. How else to explain the relentless golf-themed décor more than ten miles away from the nearest eighteen-hole course? It made my eyes spin. Tartan plaid carpets, heavy overstuffed furniture, brass lamps with green shades. Trophies *I* wouldn't have the time or energy to keep polished decorated the lobby shelves, and vintage covers from sporting magazines, expertly matted and framed, lined the corridors above the wainscotting. The food, especially the Sunday brunch, was three-star Michelin and absolutely to die for, and you'd never hear me complain about the gas log fireplace at the foot of the canopied four-poster in the bedroom suite we'd enjoyed for four days.

'I feel like marching next door right now and . . .' I elbowed Paul gently. 'But don't worry, I won't. I have a better idea.'

'Which is?'

'Talk to Isabel Randall. She's just wrapped up a major story, so I'm hoping she'll have the time and the inclination to investigate this, this . . .' I shook my head. 'I was going to say outrage, Paul, but what happened yesterday is also a flat-out federal crime. Two-hundred-fifty-thousand-dollar fine and two years in prison, if convicted.'

Paul whistled.

'Times four,' I added. 'If I'm reading the law correctly, each bird can be a separate offense. And fines are doubled for organizations.'

'Do the Feds ever successfully nail the bastards?'

'You bet, according to Professor Google, but too often they just get their knuckles rapped with a ruler, fined a couple of thousand dollars and put on probation. You're a bad, bad boy,' I chanted, slapping Paul's hand in time with each word. 'And please don't do it again.'

'Well, if anyone can get to the bottom of it, my money's on Izzy.'

'Have you visited her website recently?' I asked after a moment. 'Totally revamped since she left WBNF-TV and went freelance. Izzy's the queen of multi-media investigative journalism, that's for sure. In addition to the website, she's got a blog, a YouTube channel and just started a series of podcasts called "Tell It Like It Iz." I listened to her most recent podcast on elder abuse, and it was mesmerizing. I'm not surprised the story went viral.'

Like me, Izzy was an early riser, but I decided to wait until the civilized hour of nine before sending her a text. *Got time to chat?*

Give me five, Izzy replied, followed by a coffee cup emoji. *I'll ring you.*

I texted a thumbs-up emoji.

Ten minutes later, my iPhone rang and when I accepted the call, Izzy appeared, head down, fiddling with something on her desk. The image suddenly dove sideways, then a hand loomed large to correct the angle. 'Sorry. Slopped my coffee.'

Izzy was dressed – at least as far down as her waist – in a royal blue, zip-front jacket. Her dark hair was held back from her face by a wide, tie-dye boho bandeau from which blonde-tipped ends escaped, curling softly over her cheeks. 'What's up?'

I told her about Noel, about finding the poisoned eagles, about what we'd learned from the Natural Resources police officer, Roger Erickson, and shared my theory that the origin of the poison was most likely our not-so-friendly, neighborhood reserve shooting area. Izzy gave me her full attention, interrupting only twice to ask for clarification. I noticed she was taking notes.

'Paul forbids me from going full Jessica Fletcher on the caretaker over there,' I said, shading the truth just a tad, 'but I figure if an investigative reporter shows up wanting to interview the guy for a story about eagles . . .'

'I'm interested,' she told me. 'Very. What's the status of the birds taken to Hoots?'

'I don't know yet. Noel will be checking with Roger about their condition later today.'

'Okey dokey. That'll give me time to develop some background.'

'So, you're coming?'

'What? Oh, sure. Didn't I say so?'

'You can stay over with us, if you need to,' I offered. 'We'll give you the yellow room. It's got the best view. No need to call in advance, just show up. If we're not home, the key's under the ceramic turtle.'

'Tempting. I may take you up on it,' Izzy replied. After a moment, she asked, 'Is this kind of mass poisoning unusual?'

'I can't say for sure, but Roger commented that he'd seen enough cases of carbofuran poisoning that he recognized the symptoms, so it can't have been a one-off.'

'Gotcha.'

'I'm sending you a Dropbox link to a video I took at the scene yesterday. I'll let you know as soon as I hear anything more about the birds.'

'Standing by with talons crossed,' she said.

An arm shot forward and Izzy's image vanished. I was left staring at myself. Hair sticking out at odd angles like it had been styled by Edward Scissorhands. Eye bags and wrinkles on terrifying, full-frontal display. LED bulbs might well conserve energy, but the morgue-like illumination emitted by the desk lamp did my complexion no favors. I groaned. It was time for a makeover at my daughter's health spa.

I hoped she had an emergency entrance.

An hour later, my phone rang again. 'Mrs Ives!' Noel chirped. 'Roger just called. The eagles are going to be fine!'

'I'm so relieved,' I said, although the pent-up sigh I puffed into my cell phone probably made that obvious.

'They're still too sick to be released, but Roger says there's no reason to think that they can't be returned to the wild. In due course, he says, whatever that means in real people time.'

'Did Roger learn anything about where the birds came from?'

'There's some sort of database . . . wait a minute, I wrote it down.' I heard paper rustling, and then Noel was back. 'Here it is. Wanted to get it right. According to the US National Bird Banding Database – whew, that's a mouthful, isn't it – anyway, one pair had purple bands, which means Maryland or Virginia. Reading the letter and number code on it, the female fledged from a nest down in St Mary's City and is about eight years old. Her mate came from Yorktown, Virginia. He's seven. The other sick female had a green band, which means she fledged in New Jersey, but there isn't any record of where she went after that. She's nine years old.'

I dreaded to ask but I had to. 'How about the eagle that didn't make it?'

'A local boy, Mrs Ives. He's also nine years old, and the nest he fledged from was not far from here, near Mardela Springs, but he wasn't successfully tracked after that.'

'Shit, shit shit,' I said, feeling sick. 'I'm worried he might be Calvin, one of our nesting pair. If so, the sick female is also one of ours, Hobbes.'

'Hobbes?'

'Timmy named them.'

'Ah, that explains it.'

I snorted. 'Timmy's first choice was Beavis and Butthead, so you can understand why we caved on Calvin and Hobbes. I wanted to name them Sonny and Cher, but I was outvoted.'

'How can you be sure it's Calvin and Hobbes?'

'I can't, of course. Their nest isn't monitored, except in a casual way, and if the birds were banded, I never got close enough to even see, let alone read any bands. I have a really bad feeling about it, is all. Their nest sits at the head of the creek that borders both our property and the Tuckerman place and, well, I haven't seen either of the birds for a couple of days.'

'That sucks.'

'Yeah. But I don't think we'll ever know for sure. Paul did some research. He tells me that eagles start working on their nests in November – either tidying up old ones or building new ones in preparation for mating in January – so it's possible Calvin and Hobbes simply decided to move.'

'Let's pray that they did, Mrs Ives.'

'Amen, Noel,' I said.

TEN

Two mornings later, Isabel Randall arrived at Our Song fully armed, toting a briefcase and carrying an overnight bag. I showed her up to the yellow bedroom, gave her directions to the bathroom and instructions on how to keep the showerhead from dripping, then invited her to join me in the kitchen once she got settled in.

It didn't take her long.

'The room is charming,' she said as she sat down at the kitchen table. 'Very cheerful. And I love the fabric on the Roman shades.'

'My granddaughter Chloe picked it out. It's called Citrus Garden, from Schumacher and Greeff. Don't even ask how much it cost per yard.'

'Girl has champagne tastes, huh?'

'Indeed she does, and we have a beer pocketbook. Thank goodness for remnants.'

While I boiled water for tea, Izzy briefed me on her plans. She'd set up an interview with Roger Erickson for late that afternoon. Roger had put her in touch with Kendrick Fenelus, the US Fish and Wildlife Service officer assigned to the case who she hoped to be meeting at the scene of the crime the following day. 'What's on your schedule for tomorrow afternoon?' she asked as she pawed through the assortment of tea bags I'd set out in a glass canister in front of her.

'A luncheon date with Paul McCartney, but, hey, no problem. I'm sure Sir Paul won't mind rescheduling.'

She grinned. 'You wish.' Izzy selected a lemon-mint tea bag and lowered it into her cup. While I covered the bag with boiling water, she said, 'I've arranged for us to visit Hoots at two tomorrow afternoon. I'm guessing Noel would want to come along, too, but she'll have to wait. The woman who runs Hoots, Mee Semcken, says she can't deal with more than two visitors at a time. Her first priority has to be the birds.'

'Squeee! You rock!' I set the electric kettle back on its base and joined her at the table, eager for details.

Izzy had set up interviews with other locals, too, I soon learned, including liaising with reporters at the *Star Democrat*, one of the last surviving Eastern Shore newspapers. It's first issue appeared on the streets of Easton, Maryland in 1799, when John Adams was president.

'In the meantime,' she continued, 'I thought perhaps you could introduce me to your neighbors.'

'Easier said than done,' I told her. 'I met the guy who actually owns the farm a couple of years ago when we bought our place, but he and his wife moved to New Mexico. Paul tells me there's a caretaker living in the house now, managing Tuckerman's whole farm operation. His name is Wesley Butler, but I've never laid eyes on the guy. Until recently, we've just been spending Paul's summer break and our long weekends here. And we don't get out much.'

'Family? Kids?'

I shrugged. 'I have no idea.'

'Perhaps it's time to introduce yourself, then.' She shot me an impish grin. 'What do you say? We'll just stroll over, all casual. Pay our respects, neighborly-like.'

'You got it. A show of good, old-fashioned southern hospitality.'

'For that, you'll need to bake cookies.'

'Pepperidge Farm won't do?' I hooked a finger under the plate of Dublin shortbread in the center of the table and tipped it in her direction.

She shook a finger. 'Martha Stewart would be appalled.'

I wagged a finger back. 'Martha Stewart doesn't live here.'

In the end, we bundled up in lightweight fleeces against a cool breeze that had clocked around to the north and set out on our visit empty-handed.

Because the Tuckerman estate was so vast, the farmhouse of our nearest neighbor was over a mile away, a straight shot down the gravel road that fronted both our properties and eventually dead-ended at the Chesapeake Bay. On the way, I took Izzy as close as we could get to the spot where Noel and I had discovered the poisoned eagles.

'Thank goodness you recorded that video the other day,' Izzy remarked as we stood side by side on a furrow in the cornfield, reluctant to cross over into an area that was still cordoned off with crime scene tape. Nevertheless, she plucked a cell phone out of her fanny pack and used it to take a few pictures while I waited, trying, but failing miserably, to erase the nauseating images of that gawd-awful day from my mind. I averted my eyes and stared at the horizon instead, following a long line of dry, stalk-littered furrows until they disappeared, merging into a marshland of tall grasses and reeds.

My heart beat a quick *rat-a-tat-tat*. 'What the heck is that?'

Izzy had her head bent over her phone, shading the screen from the glare of the sun while she tapped away at something. Her head shot up, eyes wide with alarm. 'What? Where?'

I pointed to a spot perhaps a hundred yards away where a scrap of yellow tape flapping in the breeze caught my attention. What Roger told us about a circle of death sprang immediately to mind. 'If that's marking another crime scene area, there must have been another victim,' I said.

We stood in respectful silence for a while, then began speculating about the species of the victim and hypothesizing about its place in the deadly circle. Before the fox? After? Fish and Wildlife would be handling the investigation, I knew, but we hoped Roger would be willing to fill her in when Izzy met with him later on.

Next to me, Izzy suddenly stiffened. When she spoke, her voice was low and gravelly. 'And there's another one, Hannah. Damn it. Over by that stand of trees.' Even from a distance, the yellow crime scene tape stood out.

'I feel like this is going to go on forever,' I said, feeling sick to my stomach.

'C'mon.' Izzy's face wore a look of grim determination as she turned away from me and trudged off in the direction of the nearest marked-off area.

I plodded along in her wake.

Once again, Izzy, a consummate professional, documented what we saw. Other than the residual crime scene tape and, at the third location, a yellow crime scene marker tent bearing the numeral five, it was nothing.

'Now, I *really* want to talk to that caretaker.' Izzy stowed her phone, did an about face and set off in the direction of the road. She took long strides and I had to jog to keep up.

'You can't appear casual if you're descending on the man's house like an avenging angel,' I panted, aiming my words at her back.

Izzy slowed her pace, waiting for me to catch up.

'When we get there, let me do the talking, OK, Iz? With Natural

Resources and Fish and Wildlife crawling all over the place, Butler has to know about the poisonings on Tuckerman's property, so I worry he'll clam up if he discovers you're a reporter. Me, I'm just a nosy, pain-in-the-butt neighbor.'

Izzy stopped in her tracks and faced me, grinning. 'You expect me to argue with that?'

'You could put up a *little* resistance,' I said as we set off again, walking side by side.

'I know very well who I'm dealing with, Miss Oh-Please-Kind-Sir-Have-You-Seen-My-Lost-Cat?'

'How was I supposed to know I was talking to a serial killer? Not for sure, anyway,' I added, just to be clear.

'That's why you're fun to hang out with, Hannah Ives.'

'Ditto, ditto, Miz Randall.'

The Tuckerman house, a raised rancher covered with white vinyl siding and sporting cheerful, neon blue shutters, sat in the shade of a stand of mature tulip poplars. Someone was showering the house with love. The boxwood hedges surrounding its solid brick foundation were neatly trimmed. Flower boxes under windows flanking the front door showcased a variety of yellow, orange and white chrysanthemums; purple pansies poked their cheerful heads out from underneath the taller mums. The lawn had been recently mowed and the concrete sidewalk that led to the front door neatly edged.

A late-model Honda Civic was parked in the driveway.

While Izzy waited on the sidewalk, I stepped up onto the stoop and rang the doorbell. Nobody answered. I pushed the button again, mashing it down hard just to be sure, with the same results. 'Somebody has to be here,' I said, bobbing my head in the direction of the Honda. 'Maybe he's out in the barn?'

Izzy and I wandered down the driveway. It wrapped around the house in a semi-circle, then angled off to the left, terminating at an enormous barn. In contrast to the meticulously maintained home, the barn was in need of some serious TLC. The hip roof sagged. One of the doors had come off its overhead track and was propped crookedly against the weathered red wood siding. My mother, bless her, would have said that the structure was 'standing on the promises of God.' Just beyond the barn stood a child's swing and slide set and, next to it, a kid-sized, above-ground swimming pool, fitted with a blue canvas cover. 'Guess that answers the question about family,' Izzy said.

On a wide, circular dirt apron in front of the barn, a man dressed

in jeans and a dark blue windbreaker had his head under the raised
hood of a bright green utility tractor.

'Mr Butler?' I called out. 'Wesley?'

The head that emerged from under the hood sported a blue knit
watch cap pulled down over the ears. Strands of auburn hair escaped
from under the band, curling gently over the ribbing. He held a
torque wrench in a hand covered with grease. 'Not guilty,' he replied.
'I'm just the cheap labor hired to fix the tractor.' He laid the wrench
down on the motor block, pulled a pink rag out of his back pocket
and used it to thoroughly wipe his hands. 'Steve Heberling, at your
service. Tidewater Farm and Supply.'

'Heberling?' I asked as he pumped my hand. 'Any relation to
Dwight Heberling?'

'He's my uncle.'

'Ah, so you must be Rusty's cousin.' I freed my hand from his
grasp and gestured vaguely in the direction of our cottage. 'I live
next door. Dwight rebuilt our chimney a few years back and Rusty
does yard work for us from time to time.'

Heberling's face brightened, apparently impressed by my creden-
tials. 'Pleased to meet you, Mrs, uh . . .'

'Sorry! I'm Hannah Ives and this is my friend visiting from
Annapolis, Isabel Randall.'

Heberling shook Izzy's hand. 'Any way I can help you?'

'As I said, my friend and I are looking for Wesley Butler. We
want to talk to him about the sick eagles I found near my property
the other day.'

Heberling shook his head. 'Heard all about that. Was the talk of
the town over coffee at the High Spot this morning. You found the
eagles, you say?'

I nodded.

'Four of 'em, they say.'

I nodded again.

'Ew, sorry.'

If Heberling was hoping I'd go into detail, I must have disappointed him. 'Thanks,' I said simply.

'Look,' Heberling continued after a pregnant pause. 'I don't know
where Wes is. He took Beau and zipped out in the Whaler a couple
of hours ago. Didn't say where he was going or when he was coming
back, not that it's any of my business. Might be checking his crab
pots?' He shrugged.

'Crabbing? You'd think he'd have enough on his hands catering to Feathers-N-Fins and the other outfitters.'

'Oyster beds, too,' Heberling added.

'Hannah tells me the ducks are, for lack of a better word, planted here?' Izzy cut in.

Heberling's eyes twinkled, the same lively blue as his cousin's. 'That's about the size of it, ma'am.' He waved his arm in a wide arc, indicating an area due west of the barn. 'He's got three ponds out back and they're planted with milo, wheat, millet and sorghum to keep 'em fed. Last year, Tuckerman released five hundred ducks just to get started.'

'I don't get it,' Izzy said. 'How come the ducks don't fly away? Don't they head south for the winter or something?'

'These ducks? Nah. Got everything they need here. Why fly anyplace else?' He chuckled. 'If you're staying at the Ritz, why check out and move to a Holiday Inn? Most of 'em couldn't survive in the wild anyway. They're tamies.' He snatched the cap off his head, combed his hair with his fingers, then tucked the cap into his back pocket along with the rag. 'They run 'em up in boats to keep 'em flying. Blammo! Send the dogs out to fetch. That's killing, in my opinion, not hunting.'

'Doesn't seem fair to the ducks,' Izzy mused. 'Kinda like a cross between a petting zoo and Auschwitz.'

'Yeah, but while we're pointing fingers, how about Frank Perdue? He's got a chicken processing plant not far from here. None of *those* pen-raised birds get away.'

'All the more reason to eat vegetarian,' Izzy muttered.

'Don't get me wrong,' Heberling said. 'I've been hunting since I was six, but there's hunting and then there's . . .' He paused. 'Whatever this is. Begging your pardon, ladies, but finding out your first duck was a tamie would be like finding out your first girlfriend was a hooker hired by your dad.'

I laughed. I couldn't help it.

Turning to Izzy, he said, 'Most of the ducks 'round here are mallards, Ms Randall, but we've got mottled ducks, canvasback, pintails and a handful of other breeds that show up to party.' He aimed a long, grease-stained finger at the sky. 'Eastern Shore's on a flyway. I'm no naturalist, Lord knows, but I worry when these birds take their whacked-out genes, migrate north with their wild cousins and interbreed.'

'And I'm no expert on the sexual proclivities of ducks, but I don't suppose there's much anyone can do about it,' she said.

'Has this ever happened on the Tuckerman farm before?' I asked, trying to steer the conversation back to the sick eagles. 'Mass poisonings, I mean.'

'Not that I know of. Not in this county, anyway. Big one down in Caroline County some years back. Thirteen eagles, that was. A case in Chestertown, too, not so long ago.' He shook his head. 'Accidental, maybe? Never heard that they pinned 'em on anyone specific anyway.'

'Why would anyone do such a thing? Intentionally, I mean.'

'Remember when I told you Dave Tuckerman stocked his ponds with five hundred ducks last year? Well,' he continued, not waiting for a response, 'he complained to Wes a couple'a weeks ago that there's only 'bout three hundred of 'em left.'

'After what you said about this farm being Duck Nirvana, I'm betting you're not going to tell us that two hundred ducks decided to up and fly away,' Izzy said.

'No, ma'am. We've got plenty'a fox and coyote around here. Raccoons. Eagles, ospreys and owls. Even feral cats. They all gotta eat.'

Heberling reached out and retrieved the wrench. 'And I gotta get back to work on this engine, ladies, but I'll tell you one thing. Wes Butler was down at the High Spot one morning complaining that he watched one eagle eat eleven ducks in three hours. Total bullshit, of course.' As he spoke, Heberling emphasized each point by whacking the business end of the wrench rhythmically against the palm of his left hand. 'An eagle can eat about a pound of food at one sitting. He can store food in his crop, sure, but even on a big bird, a crop's only got room for about two pounds of meat. Now, a duck weighs about four pounds. Eleven ducks? Pah! You do the math.'

'Are you suggesting that Wes blamed the eagles for his stock losses?' Izzy asked.

'I'm not suggesting anything, ma'am. Let's just say that I can see a guy who thinks like that getting pissed off and trying to do something about it.'

'Thanks for taking the time to talk to us,' I said. 'Sorry to interrupt your work.'

'Any time. No problemo.' Heberling turned and stuck his head back under the tractor's hood.

'What's the best way to get ahold of Wes Butler?' I asked, addressing his back.

'The wife and kids are away, so he hangs out most mornings at the High Spot,' Heberling said, both hands busy, his voice muffled by the hood.

'OK, thanks,' I said.

We had taken a few steps down the driveway when Heberling called us back with a cheerful, 'Hey!'

When we turned around, he was propped against the tractor on one elbow, a goofy grin spread across his face. 'Do you know what you get when you mix a mallard duck with a mottled duck?'

'I'll bite,' Izzy said. 'What do you get?'

'A muddled duck.' Heberling chuckled. 'Farmer joke, ladies. Have a blessed day.'

ELEVEN

Although I continued to fret over the missing eagles, I knew there was nothing I could do about it. As for the sick birds, I kept telling myself they were in the best of hands at Hoots, so relax, already. Read a book. Work a jigsaw puzzle. Dig out that sweater you've been knitting on since the Winter Olympic Games in Sochi.

It's not that I had forgotten about my promise to dig into Noel's perplexing DNA test results. It's just that genealogy research could be so complex and detail-oriented that in order to do the job properly, I had to clear my desk . . . and my mind.

Noel had made me a collaborator on her GenTree account, so shortly after finishing lunch, while Izzy was out conducting her interviews, I cleared off the dining room table, set up my laptop, gave Paul strict instructions that I was not to be interrupted for anything short of a North Korean nuclear attack, and signed on.

With the exception of a single 'root-person' record for Donna Noel Sinclair consisting of what I recognized as her Facebook photo and a birth date of December 25, 1997, I was staring at an empty family tree. Putting myself into Noel's shoes, it must have been wrenching to see her absence of a biological family so baldly and graphically illustrated.

First, I clicked on Noel's DNA History tab. Not that I doubted what Noel had told me earlier, but when working with genealogy, I've learned that making assumptions can send you so far down a false trail that you practically have to erase everything and start over.

Noel was right about one thing. Fifty percent of her DNA came from Parent A whose ancestors hailed from geographical areas around northern Italy. There was a generous dose of Scots–Irish in that line, too. Parent B's genes came primarily from Sweden, Denmark and Norway *avec un petit peu* from France. However, GenTree doesn't differentiate between the mother's and father's side of the DNA they tested. I remained hopeful that we could sort that out later.

Next, I clicked on the link that would lay a map over the geograph-ical data. I saw that Parent A's ancestors, in general, had been part of the wave of immigrants who migrated to the United States from Ireland in the mid-nineteenth century and had settled primarily in the Midwest. Parent B's antecedents seemed to have arrived much earlier, in the mid-1600s, and were clustered in the area we refer to now as the Delaware River Valley.

That was interesting background material, but it brought me no closer to finding any of Noel's existing relatives who, centuries and generations later, could be living anywhere on the planet.

Much more important information was to be found in her DNA data.

I clicked on the DNA Matches tab and, as usual, held my breath while waiting for the results to populate the screen. If one were incredibly, amazingly, unbelievably lucky, her mother or father would have been tested by GenTree. Their record could pop up at the head of Noel's list of matches at any time, boldly captioned 'Parent/Child.' Alas, not today. Noel had over six thousand matches, however – not that unusual – but nothing closer than a handful of first and second cousins. I'd built trees successfully with fewer matches, but with so many of Noel's matches in the distant fourth- to sixth-cousin range, it might be an uphill slog. I hoped that some of those second cousins had extensive family trees attached to their records.

Noel's best match was an excellent one, a first cousin with 866 centimorgans in common. His account name was SimonSez, but his family tree of several hundred records was set to private, damn him. I sent Simon a message, politely requesting he give me permission to access his tree, but according to GenTree's records, he hadn't shown up online for six months, so I couldn't count on hearing back from the guy. A few of Noel's second- and third-cousin matches did have public family trees, but with fewer centimorgans in common than SimonSez, it was hard to tell at this stage where they might intersect with Noel.

It was time to turn to the Leeds method for help.

Back in 2018, while working with an adoptee to help identify her biological father, a genealogy 'search angel' named Dana Leeds developed a brilliantly simple method of clustering second-, third- and fourth-cousin DNA matches by color, making it easier to identify the ancestors they had in common.

After several hours of work on Noel's data, I ended up with four color sets which represented the eight individuals – four sets of great-grandparents – that Noel shared with each of them. Next came the tedious job of reviewing each of the matches, looking (hoping!) for public family trees from which I could 'borrow' records to identify those individuals and start building Noel's tree.

Around three thirty, I took a break. I grabbed a Coke from the fridge, popped the top and leaned against the sink to drink it while I used my thumb to check my iPhone for messages. Izzy reported that she had been invited to do a ride-along with Roger Erickson and that we shouldn't hold dinner for her. The second message was from Noel. She got off work at four and asked if it was OK to stop by. *Of course*, I texted back. *Wanna see your tree?*

TWELVE

While I waited for Noel, I took some chicken breasts from the freezer and set them out on the kitchen counter to thaw. I'd just finished emptying the dishwasher when she arrived, wreathed in smiles and carrying a Mighty Mart shopping bag. 'This is for you,' she said, lifting the bag by its string handles.

'Thank you! What's the occasion?'

'No occasion.' She draped her jacket casually over a peg on the coat rack. 'Rum cakes were on sale. Just don't look too closely at the sell-by date.'

I had to laugh. 'Sell-by dates are mere suggestions. Besides . . . rum. Doesn't it last forever?'

I left the rum cake – a welcome addition to the dinner menu – on the kitchen counter and invited Noel to follow me into the dining room. I drew a second chair around so we could sit side by side in front of my laptop, but before launching into a demonstration of the GenTree website, I filled her in on that morning's visit to the Tuckerman farm. 'We didn't learn all that much, to tell you the truth, except for Heberling's opinion that a farmer losing stock to predators might be tempted to do something about it.'

I also told her about the appointment Izzy had made for a visit to the Hoots Raptor Rescue Center. Although Noel expressed disappointment at not being able to go along *this time*, it turned out to be, in her words, just as well. 'It's my last week at Mighty Mart, Mrs Ives, and I plan on quitting Friday, going out in grand style.'

'I hope it doesn't involve a loaded gun,' I said.

'Hah! I wish. No, the original plan was to have me arrested.' She drew quote marks in the air. 'I'd be caught shoplifting. As an object lesson for the rest of the sales associates.'

'That seems harsh.'

'Totally agree. And since I was using Wendy Walker's ID . . .' She let the sentence die, leaving me to draw my own conclusion.

'Would have been awkward,' I said. 'Especially for young Wendy, the manager's beloved niece. So what's the plan now?'

Noel grinned. 'Not sure, but a certain song popularized in the
Seventies by Johnny Paycheck comes to mind.'

'"Take This Job and Shove It"?'

'Exactly. And flouncing will be involved, too. Hair-flipping and
flouncing.'

Just picturing the scene made me smile. 'I hope somebody takes
a video.'

Noel chuckled, then bumped my arm lightly with her elbow. 'But
I didn't come over to talk about that. You were going to show me
something.'

'Genealogy one oh one,' I said. 'Are you ready?'

'You bet.'

'Fasten your seatbelt.'

I clicked the touchpad and brought up Noel's list of DNA matches.
'Let's start with this guy, SimonSez. His match is a really good
one,' I told her. 'Eight hundred and sixty-six centimorgans.'

'Centi-what?'

'Centimorgans. Abbreviated cM and named after Thomas Hunt
Morgan who got the Nobel Prize in 1933 for his work on the role
that chromosomes play in heredity.

'Centimorgans are a measure of the total length of your chromosomes,' I continued. 'In a normal person, that's about seven thousand
four hundred centimorgans. Think of it like a math problem.' I
grabbed a blank piece of paper and a pen, scribbled down the number
7,400 and drew a box around it.

'I was never particularly good at math, Mrs Ives.'

'No worries. It's really pretty simple.' I drew two more boxes,
connected them to the first and wrote 3,700 in each of them.
'Logically, if you inherit half your DNA from each parent, that
means you get about three thousand seven hundred centimorgans
from each, and—'

'I get it,' she interrupted. 'And a grandchild of those same people
would inherit one-quarter of their centimorgans from each, and a
great-grandchild, one eighth.'

'Gold star pupil,' I said as I added more boxes to the diagram
and wrote 1,750 or 875 in each, as appropriate.

'Pretty straightforward.'

'Not so fast. It's a bit more complicated than that.' I took a deep
breath and let it out. 'Lesson two. Let's say you match another
person at one thousand seven hundred and fifty-nine centimorgans.

Based on certain formulas . . . wait a minute.' I pawed through the pile of printouts strewn across the tabletop until I found the color-coded chart I was looking for. 'This is called DNA Painter, and it's really helpful in predicting possible relationships from centimorgan counts, but you still need more information before deciding how you may be related to someone. Obviously, if the one thousand seven hundred and fifty-nine centimorgan match is to an eighty-five-year-old, it's not going to be your grandchild.'

Noel giggled. 'I get it.'

'It helps me to think of the relationships as reciprocal,' I said, indicating the chart. 'The relationship between two individuals at one thousand seven hundred and fifty-nine centimorgans, mathematically speaking, could be half-sibling to half-sibling, niece to aunt or uncle, or grandchild to grandparent. All greats are in the eight hundred range and great-greats somewhere in the four hundreds.

'A word of caution, though,' I continued. 'DNA can be a bit messy. You notice on the chart that there's a wide range of centi-morgans in each category. That's because nobody inherits equally from any particular ancestor. I'll give you a personal example. Although we have the same mother and father, my older sister Ruth and I match at two thousand three hundred and fifty centimorgans, while Georgina and I are at two thousand three hundred and two. That's a super close sister-to-sister match, though. My sisters and I have known first cousins who range from the low seven hundreds to the high nine hundreds in centimorgans, so you can see that it's not always easy to sort a relationship out.'

'I think I need an aspirin.'

I squeezed her hand. 'The good news is we have this guy, SimonSez. As I said, he's an excellent eight hundred and sixty-six centimorgan match with you. That means he's probably your first cousin and you have grandparents in common. The bad news is that he's got his family tree set to private. I've emailed him to ask for access, but . . .'

'What about these other matches?' Noel asked, leaning closer and brushing my laptop screen lightly with her finger. She was indicating two individuals, SharynG and RPL at 267 and 244 cM respectively.

'I was just getting to them. They're in range for second cousin, but you can tell by the colored dots I've assigned that they're both on Parent A's side while SimonSez is related to Parent B. SharynG has an extensive family tree, and it's public, so let's start with her.'

'Doesn't everyone on GenTree have a family tree?'

'Sadly, no. Anyone can get their DNA tested and uploaded, but there's no requirement to build a family tree and link that data to it.'

Noel snorted. 'How rude!'

I had to laugh. 'Exactly. But to be fair, a lot of people are not interested in finding genetic matches. They're simply interested in their ethnicity estimates, like you were.'

'Tell me about it,' Noel said. 'My sister and I checked our DNA matches just for kicks. Ginny's totally cool with what we found out, but I'm still in shock.'

'Just out of curiosity, what was Ginny's ethnicity, do you remember?'

'Pretty much a snapshot of Minnesota where our parents came from. More than half German and about a quarter Norwegian. Irish and English figured in at around ten percent each, as I recall, and the rest – which is going to come as a huge surprise to the good Reverend Robert Sinclair if Sis and I ever decide to tell him about it – is Russian Jew.'

'Mom or Dad's side?' I asked.

'I haven't had the time or the expertise to figure it out. Maybe after we . . .' She bobbed her head in the direction of my laptop, one eyebrow raised.

'Right,' I said. 'OK, so the first thing you need to do is start building your family tree. As I said, let's start with SharynG. For work like this, I always set the chart to display vertically so the root person is at the bottom and the ancestors are in rows above, arranged by generation.'

Sharyn C. Green, we soon learned, was two years older than Noel, married with two children. She was one of three sisters. 'From the number of centimorgans you share with Sharyn,' I said, 'we are assuming she's a second cousin, so let's climb up her family tree generation by generation: parents, grandparents, great-grandparents.' I stopped there, my finger lingering on the boxes displayed on the screen. 'Meet your great-grandparents, Noel.'

'Gosh! I've got butterflies in my stomach.' She scooted her chair closer to the table and leaned in. 'Hello there, Howard Leonard Smith 1914 to 1979 and Letitia Mae Smith née Swanson 1915 to 1977.'

'When you get home, you can click on each of their individual GenTree records to find out more about them, but right now, let's drill down a bit. You can see from Sharyn's tree that Howard and Letitia had three children: two boys, Thomas and Andrew, and a girl named Felicity. One of those three children is either your grandmother or your grandfather on Parent A's side. Howard and Letitia had ten grandchildren. One of those grandchildren is either your mother or your father. Going a step further, according to Sharyn's tree, Howard and Letitia had thirty-two known great-grandchildren. You would be great-grandchild number thirty-three.'

Noel flopped back in her chair, an open hand pressed flat against her chest. 'I can hardly breathe.' After a moment, she said, 'But, thirty-two kids is huge! How on earth do I narrow it down?'

'Well, you can eliminate Andrew right away. He's Sharyn's grandfather, so he can't be your grandfather, too, or you'd be first cousins sharing twice as many centimorgans. That leaves you with Thomas or Felicity.

'Next, you need to check out RPL's family tree. If RPL is Sharyn's sister, you won't be much further along, but . . .'

My session with Noel was interrupted by a knock on the front door. I checked the time: four thirty. Way too early for Izzy to be coming back, and besides, I'd given her a key.

I don't know where Paul had been hiding out, but I heard him yell, 'Never mind, Hannah, I'll get it.' Half a minute later, he appeared in the doorway. 'Somebody here to see you, Hannah. Is this a good time?'

'It's OK. I'll be right out.'

I pushed my chair back, stood and laid a hand on Noel's shoulder. 'I think you're ready to fly solo. Why don't you work on RPL while I go see to this.'

Noel grinned and bent over the keyboard. 'I'm on it.'

I followed Paul into the hallway to greet our visitor.

THIRTEEN

An angular beanpole of a man wearing heavy work boots and dressed in chinos and a red polo shirt waited in the hallway just inside our front door, shifting nervously from one foot to the other. His lank, sandy hair was tied back in a low ponytail and he carried a ball cap in a hand gnarled by hard labor or injury, perhaps.

'Wes Butler came over to see us, Hannah. From the farm next door.'

I didn't extend a hand and neither did he. 'Glad to finally meet you, Wes.'

Wes fixed me with blue eyes, so pale they look bleached by the sun. 'Steve tells me you stopped by this morning.'

I drew a blank. 'Steve?'

'Steve Heberling, the guy tinkering with the tractor.'

'Of course! Sorry. I'd forgotten his first name. Yes, I did. I wanted to ask you about the poisoned eagles I found near our property line yesterday.'

'Heard about that,' he said. 'Terrible business, but I'm not surprised. They're our national bird, God bless America and all that, but now that they're off the endangered list, some folks are saying eagles are getting out of hand.'

Was that a confession? For someone who considered it good sport to murder defenseless waterfowl by the dozens, I didn't suppose killing any bird, including an eagle, would cause Wes to lose much sleep.

Luckily, before I could open my mouth to point this out, Paul opened his. 'After Hannah told me about the eagles, I checked our garden shed thoroughly, Wes, just in case there was poison left over from the previous owner. Zip. Nada. Do you have any theories about where the poison might have come from?'

'Fish and Wildlife already sent someone out to talk to me. I'll tell you what I told him. The only pesticide we use is RoundUp, on the corn. Low toxicity and totally legal. Rumor has it those birds were killed by carbofuran. If so, it sure as hell didn't come from us. We haven't used that kind of stuff for years.'

'Any theories?' I asked.

'I hate to state the obvious, but there are other farms hereabouts. Watson's, for example. I wouldn't trust Watson as far as I could throw him, which wouldn't be very far because the old coot weighs at least three hundred pounds.' He grinned, revealing a row of bright, well-maintained teeth, with one incisor slightly overlapping the other. 'No telling what he's got lying around. He never throws anything away.'

I'd never met Mr Watson, but we knew he ran an extensive soybean operation on a six-hundred-acre spread about three miles to the south of us. That he never threw anything away, I believed. His front yard was an eyesore, littered with rusting farm equipment, old tires, electrical cable spools and, taking pride of place near the mailbox, a discarded claw-foot bathtub.

'On my walk over yesterday, I noticed that somebody'd marked off two other areas in the cornfield,' I said.

'Three,' Wes said.

'Damn. Another poisoning, do you think?'

Wes shrugged. 'Fish and Wildlife didn't say, but I was the one who pointed out a dead bobcat behind the barn.'

'Bobcat? We have bobcats in Maryland?' I squeaked.

'Yes ma'am. Mostly out Garrett and Allegheny way, but we see them around here from time to time. Heard muttering about carbofuran taking that one down too, but don't ask me. I'm no scientist.'

I stared at Wes and bit my tongue. In that brief second, I had a flashback to my junior high school days, when my dad, then a commander in the US Navy, had been stationed in Taiwan. Poisonous snakes abound on that sub-tropical island, including pit vipers, known as Hundred Pacers by the locals. Watch out, we kids were warned. Get bitten by one of them and a hundred steps later, you're dead.

No bobcat got into any carbofuran miles away and lived long enough to wander away and die behind the Tuckerman barn. I'd seen how quickly the poison worked on the eagles. After ingesting the poison, that bobcat would probably have dropped in its tracks. I made a note to ask Roger Erickson if they'd thoroughly searched the Tuckerman barn.

'Mrs Ives?'

Noel spoke from behind me. When I turned, I saw she was

hugging a sheaf of printouts to her chest. 'I've got to get going, but I wanted to make sure it was OK to take these with me.'

'Of course you can.'

'And thanks so much! I think I've got the hang of it now.' She headed for the door, passing by Wes with a smile and a casual, 'Hi.'

Paul made a proper introduction. 'Wes, this is Hannah's friend, Noel Sinclair.'

Wes squinted at Noel, looking momentarily puzzled. 'Have we met before?'

Noel considered him blandly. 'I don't think so.'

'You look sorta familiar.'

'Do you shop at Mighty Mart?' she asked brightly. 'I worked there for a while.'

'Nah. Don't think so. Costco's more my speed.'

'At church maybe? My dad's been pastor at First Christian Church in Bentonville for simply ages.'

''Fraid I'm not the church-going type, miss.'

Noel reached for the doorknob. 'Oh, well. They say we all have a doppelgänger somewhere.' After a moment, she added, 'Mrs Ives, I've left something out for you on the table. Forgot all about it until I started to pack up.'

Noel had just opened the front door when Wes blurted, 'Wait a minute. I know! You look just like that girl on, uh, uh . . .'

Noel paused, waiting politely for more information, one pale eyebrow raised.

He snapped his fingers. 'I got it. That girl on *Game of Thrones*, what's her name?'

'Daenerys?' Noel offered helpfully. 'Arya?'

I studied Noel in profile, comparing her face to the cast of female characters I remembered from eight seasons of the popular television series and thinking, Golly, this guessing game could go on all day.

He shook his head. 'Uh uh. The one who's forced to marry the dwarf.'

'Sansa Stark?' she suggested.

Wes snapped his fingers. 'Yeah! That's the one.'

Noel favored him with a smile. 'I'll take that as a compliment, then.'

While Paul yakked with Wes about what it was like working with the Cast and Blasters, I accompanied Noel to her car. 'At least I don't remind him of Yara,' Noel said as she slid into the driver seat. 'Or, God forbid, that evil witch Cersei.'

'He has a point, though. You do look a bit like Sansa Stark, or rather the actress playing the role.'

Noel snorted. 'Sansa's a redhead. I'm a blonde. She's also Queen of the North, while I work at Mighty Mart.'

'The hair color's easily fixed. Only your beautician will know for sure.'

'You are a riot, Mrs Ives.' She slotted the key into the ignition and the engine whirred noisily to life.

'What did you leave for me, Noel?' I yelled after the car as it pulled away.

She waved lazily from the open window. 'You'll see.'

FOURTEEN

What Noel left out for me, in a nine-by-twelve manila envelope, were two documents, a certified copy of her birth certificate and another document I'd never seen the like of before – a certificate of live birth. It contained a wealth of information, including her birth weight (3200 grams) and Apgar score (8). A Post-it note stuck to the top read: *Dug these out of Mom's files. Color me confused.*

A quick search of the Internet explained the difference between the two documents. The Certificate of Live Birth is the first unofficial draft of the fact that your mother gave birth to you. Once this information has been completed, usually by the hospital where you were born, the Certificate of Live Birth is sent to the Office of Vital Statistics which creates the Official Birth Certificate you use for school, insurance, and tax purposes, and to apply for identification cards and passports. If Noel's Certificate of Live Birth had been filed by a hospital, I would take it as rock-solid proof that the mother listed on the document had actually given birth to her, unless she had been switched with another baby in the hospital nursery.

But according to a checked box, Noel's birth had taken place in a 'residence,' at a street address in Bentonville I took to be the parsonage. Hers was a home birth duly attested to by Edward Matthew Stone, MD with Mary Elizabeth Short in attendance. Mary Elizabeth was not a nurse, midwife or doula, as one might expect. 'Friend' was written on the line following the checked box marked 'Other.'

Babies arrive unexpectedly all the time, I reasoned. They're born in cars and on buses, in the back seats of taxis and patrol cars, all without doctors in attendance. The level of detail in Noel's live birth certificate – the date of her mother's last normal menses (March 15) and the number of prenatal visits (9) – was convincing. Unless the mother, the doctor and his witness all lied.

I sat back, stumped. Until now, I never had reason to question a GenTree DNA test, but, as my late mother was fond of saying, there's a first time for everything.

I Googled around for a while, found what I was looking for, picked up my phone and used it to text Noel.

Color me confused x2.

Advise you and Ginny get 2d DNA test.

3 day TAT, results via email.

And I sent her the link to an accredited home DNA testing lab in Maryland with over 1,000 five-star reviews.

Noel responded in less than five minutes with a thumbs-up emoji followed, seconds later, by an emoji picturing two girls – one blonde, one brunette – linked by a heart. My own heart lurched. I had the feeling she'd used that emoji before.

Orange-gold shafts of the setting sun sliced across the braided rug, suggesting it might be time to turn my thoughts to what to do about dinner. I'd heard Paul making goodbye noises and hustling Wesley Butler out the front door some time before and, from the sound of the television playing quietly in the living room, he was now watching Nicole Wallace on MSNBC. I sighed, got up, cleared the dining table of my laptop and piles of printouts and lugged everything back to the office.

Although Izzy had advised me not to count on her for dinner, I was a professional at ignoring such advice. Back in the kitchen, while still puzzling over Noel's DNA test results, I pounded the three chicken breasts into submission with the rim of a saucer, dredged the flattened pieces in seasoned flour and set them aside on a paper towel until the moment I would magically turn them into chicken piccata. While I rummaged in the fridge holding a lemon in one hand and searching for the jar of capers I knew had to be in there somewhere, Paul joined me. 'What can I do to help?'

'A salad would be nice,' I suggested, glancing up from my stooped position over the open vegetable drawer. 'And see if you can find the capers while you're at it.'

While Paul shredded, peeled, sliced and chopped, I scrounged around in the pantry until I came up with a twelve-ounce package of egg noodles. I set it out on the kitchen counter. 'Wine?' I asked my husband.

He paused in mid-chop. 'I thought you'd never ask.'

I poured us each a glass of chilled Viognier, pulled up a chair and brought him up to date on the research I was doing with Noel.

Paul bit the pointy end off a peeled carrot and chewed it

thoughtfully. 'Sounds like everything's on hold till the results from the second DNA test come in.'

'Fingers crossed that the GenTree test was in error. Much less drama under that scenario.'

'Have the girls already confronted their parents?'

I rested my wineglass on the table, turning it idly as I spoke. 'No, thank goodness. I've never met the mother, but I gather she's easily rattled.'

'As a preacher's wife, you'd think she's seen everything.'

I shrugged. 'Maybe, but I got the impression from Noel that her mother's a bit fragile.'

'What about her father?'

'Never met either of her parents, but I know it's a strictly conservative household. Everyone was astonished when they allowed Noel to enroll at St John's, that hotbed of left-wing liberalism, but the college gave her a full ride so it was a no-brainer. Noel says she bites her tongue whenever the conversation turns to politics these days, but she's respectful of her parents' faith-based views.'

I'd filled a pot with water and set it on the stove to boil when I heard the front door slam.

'Hello, honey! I'm home.' Izzy breezed into the kitchen, still wearing a jacket and clutching a fistful of keys. Eyeing the dinner preparations, she said, 'Goody. I'm not too late.'

'No rush,' I said. 'We're just getting started.'

Paul paused in mid-slice to wave a paring knife at the wine bottle. 'May I pour you a glass?'

'Yes, please. It's been a day.' She shrugged her backpack off her shoulder and let it dangle from a strap at her side. 'I'll just freshen up, then come down and give you a hand.'

Fifteen minutes later, she reappeared, her face cleansed of makeup and her wild hair brushed and tamed with a tie-dyed scrunchy. She inhaled deeply. 'God, that smells good.'

When I told her dinner was under control, no help needed, she plopped down in a chair and accepted the wine Paul offered. She tasted it and sighed. 'Ah, that's refreshing. Chardonnay?'

'Viognier,' I corrected. 'Some kind of blend. It was on special at Rudy's.'

With a finger, Izzy drew a smile in the condensation on the glass and dotted it with two eyes.

Using tongs, I turned the chicken filets over in the skillet so they could brown on the other side. 'So, how'd it go?'

'I'm sure Roger has had more exciting days during his time as a Natural Resources police officer, but today wasn't one of them. We got to check the fishing licenses of everyone fishing off the Bill Burton Pier in Cambridge, though.'

'Were they catching anything?' Paul wanted to know.

'Croakers, whatever they are, and catfish.'

'Croakers are light and sweet, but kinda bony,' Paul explained. 'They average around twelve inches, so I like to fry them whole.'

'Only chicken tonight. Sorry,' I said.

'A doomed day from the git-go,' Izzy reported. 'The chicken's a highlight, believe me. In the time between citing a power boater for an oil slick and testing the Choptank River for dissolved oxygen, salinity and E. coli, I tried to pump him for information about your eagles, but he insisted he couldn't comment on any ongoing investigation.' She sighed, tipped the wineglass to her lips and emptied it in several swallows. 'But I did get a body count.'

'I'm afraid to ask.' I tore open the package of egg noodles and dumped them into the boiling water.

'In addition to the dead fox and the eagle you found, one bobcat, two foxes, a badger and a great horned owl.' She held out her empty glass. Paul topped it up. 'They could have died of old age, of course, or some deadly disease. Nothing's official until their bodies have been autopsied.'

Izzy leaned back in her chair, rested her glass on the tabletop and rotated it absent-mindedly. 'Honestly, the man could be infuriating. Clearly, I'm going to have to file a FOIA with Fish and Wildlife in order to get additional information, but from my experience, it'll be a wasted effort. They either slow-walk it or ignore you altogether.

'However, he did share good background on confirmed cases of carbofuran poisoning on Maryland's Eastern Shore.' She raised up on one hip to retrieve her cell phone from the back pocket of her chinos. While I drained the cooked noodles, dumped them in a bowl and topped them with a lump of butter, she consulted her notes.

'Starting in 2009, two bald eagles in Cordova, two in Easton, thirteen in Federalsburg, for God's sake. Here's Easton again for five more, another one in Cordova and most recently in Chestertown, six.' She glanced up from the screen as I brought the noodles over to the table. 'And that's just the birds that died. Many more were poisoned but pulled through thanks to quick intervention by Tri-State, Phoenix, Owl Moon and Hoots.'

'I can't tell you how much I'm looking forward to visiting Hoots tomorrow.' I turned down the gas, added lemon juice and capers to the drippings in the pan and gave them a good swirl with a wooden spoon.

'I'm sure *they* won't be asking us to file a FOIA request,' Izzy said, using the tongs to help herself to a generous serving of noodles.

I poured the sauce over the chicken, carried the platter over to the table and sat down. 'Definitely not,' I said, digging into the noodles myself. 'Just a donation.'

FIFTEEN

For the trip to Hoots the following afternoon, Izzy insisted on driving, allowing me the luxury of enjoying the scenery – cornfields, family-run farm shops, beach-themed eateries – as it scrolled past the window. Just before Ocean Highway passes over the Pokomoke River and all four lanes are swallowed by a huge shopping mall, we were stopped by a traffic light near a big liquor store. When the left turn arrow flashed green, Izzy headed north on Dividing Creek Road. Approximately half a mile past Tindly Chapel, Waze directed her right onto a single-lane road that came to an abrupt dead end at a steel utility gate secured with a chain latch. A sign on the gate read: *Restricted Area*. To the right was a gravel parking area just large enough to accommodate three cars, and a forest-green porta-potty from Gotügo. Izzy pulled in next to the porta-potty and switched off the engine.

'We're supposed to call from here and wait by the gate,' Izzy said as she reached for the cell phone.

We called as instructed, then climbed out of the car. Two minutes later, a wooly, terrifyingly huge brown dog with a black muzzle bounded up to the other side of the gate and promptly sat down.

'Well, hello,' I said, bravely facing what was surely a deadly hound from the Baskervilles.

The dog replied with a throaty, welcoming woof.

A woman I took to be the dog's owner, Mee Semcken, emerged from a ranch-style house about fifty yards away and hustled down the drive in our direction. About my height, Mee was dressed in jeans and a red Polar-tec vest zipped over a pink-and-white striped shirt. She wore sensible, lace-up leather shoes. 'I see you've met Bear,' she said as she unlatched the gate.

'An appropriate name,' I said while we waited for her to pull the gate aside. 'What kind of dog is he?'

She smiled and tucked an unruly strand of dark brown hair behind her ear. 'A Mastiff-Jindo mix. Jindos are native to South Korea, just like me.'

'From his size, it looks like he inherited more from the mastiff side,' Izzy said.

Mee chuckled. 'Bear's an absolute love. Watch out or he'll lick you to death.'

After introductions, Mee turned to me, her eyes dark and sad behind her trifocals. 'Diana told me it was you who found the eagles.'

'I did. I'm still having nightmares about it.'

'You never get used to it.' She ushered us through the gate, dragged it back across the road and latched it behind us. Bear sniffed my pants leg curiously then trotted on ahead, as if leading the expedition.

'How are the birds doing?' I asked as we trailed after Bear along a gravel drive.

She smiled. 'Would you like to see for yourself?'

'Yes, please.'

'Go play now,' Mee ordered, addressing her dog. Guard duty done, Bear wandered off on some canine mission of his own.

Mee continued down the drive as it curved away from the house, then led us through the doors of a surprisingly bright, airy barn. A fully equipped tool shop ranged along the wall to the far right. Between us and the tools, plastic tubs filled with old newspapers, trash bags, paper towels and other supplies were stacked shoulder high. The area to our left seemed to be dedicated to the storage of miscellaneous, lesser-used equipment, fitted together as neatly as pieces of a jigsaw puzzle. Should the need arise, I thought as I took in the jumble, getting that molded plastic wading pool out of the middle might be a challenge.

'Follow me,' Mee said as she steered us through a maze of brooms, stools, ladders, wheelbarrows, heat lamps, empty galvanized trash cans and the occasional pair of mismatched rubber boots to a row of tall cages stretching along the back wall. One wall panel had been rolled aside to allow sunshine in and fresh air to circulate.

Mee stopped at the first cage. 'First, I'd like you to meet Peggy.'

Peggy was a mature bald eagle, we learned and, as her name suggested, a female. Head cocked to one side, she eyed us curiously, but seemingly without fear, from the far corner of a cage that I estimated to be about eight by four feet in dimension and at least eight feet high. The cage was sheathed up to the level of Mee's shoulders with sheets of stainless steel; closely spaced bars extended above that. Peggy's temporary home had been carpeted with artificial grass and she stood in a pile of shredded newspapers. I suspected she had shredded them herself out of boredom as the only other objects in the cage were a gnarly log and a shallow ceramic dish filled with gravel and water. Peggy took a step toward her water bowl, lurched to one side and fixed Mee with unblinking golden eyes.

'She's expecting a fishy treat,' Mee explained. 'That's how we deliver her meds.' Turning to the bird she soothed, 'John'll be along in a minute, precious.

'John's one of our volunteers,' Mee added with a smile. 'He's a retired real estate developer, still very active in community affairs, but he manages to give us a couple of hours every day.

'Peggy's not one of yours,' Mee said, addressing me. To Izzy, she added, 'I need to tell you about her case, though, because it'll be important for the article you told me you're writing. Did you notice how she staggers, how she seems disoriented?'

'That little bobble just then?' Izzy asked.

Mee nodded. 'That's the result of lead poisoning.'

Izzy's eyebrows disappeared beneath her bangs. 'Lead? I thought the use of lead shot was illegal.'

'A popular misconception, I'm afraid. In 1991 lead shot was banned for use in hunting waterfowl, but that didn't come close to addressing the problem because you can still use lead shot to hunt other game. People don't understand that lead ammo kills birds long after it's fired from a gun.' Mee aimed her right index finger at her left palm, like a gun, and stabbed at it. 'When a bullet enters the body of a deer or a pig, it shatters into hundreds of pieces, some of them invisible to the naked eye. These are the lead fragments that can poison eagles, and, I might add, that humans often ingest as well. I read somewhere – I'll see if I can lay my hands on the citation for you, Izzy – that the US Geological Survey estimates that a regularly-used upland hunting field contains approximately four hundred thousand pieces of lead shot. Per acre!'

Izzy whipped out a small, spiral-bound notebook, flipped it open and started rooting around in her handbag for a pen. 'Yikes. I think I better start taking notes.'

'When Peggy came to us,' Mee continued once Izzy clicked her pen, 'she was all hunched over and droopy, like an old man, and her tail feathers were stained green. Classic symptoms of lead poisoning. It's more common than you'd think. About a year ago, *Science* magazine reported on a thirty-eight-state study of over two thousand eagles, and nearly half of them showed signs of chronic lead poisoning. I've got that issue in my office somewhere. Remind me to give it to you before you go.'

'I'm astonished,' Izzy said. 'As a government, we've managed to ban lead-based paint and leaded gasoline. You'd think the Feds could get their act together and ban lead-based shot, too, especially when alternatives like steel work equally well.'

'They almost did,' Mee said. 'At the tail end of the Obama administration, the US Fish and Wildlife Service quietly issued an order to phase out the use of lead ammunition and lead fishing tackle on all federal lands by 2022. We were all quietly high-fiving over it, but it took the new Interior Secretary exactly one day on the job to strike it all down. So, now it's up to each individual state to make its own laws concerning the use of toxic shot and, believe me, the regs are all over the place.'

'So, what do you do to treat birds like Peggy?' I asked.

'Depends on the level of lead in their blood. Peggy tested in at forty-nine point eight which is super high. When she first came to us, she got five days of EDTA injections.'

Mee held up a hand. 'Before you ask, EDTA stands for ethylene diamine tetra acetic acid.'

Izzy's pen flew over the page.

Mee flapped a hand, dismissing the big words. 'Just call it calcium disodium. It binds to the lead and flushes it out of the blood in a process called chelation. Now Peggy's well enough to take her meds orally. We were using a brand name called Chemet, but it costs fifteen dollars a tablet. Fortunately, we found a compounding chemist in Elkton who mixes it up from scratch for one third of that amount.' She patted the door to Peggy's cage. 'Her level is now down to ten, so we're getting there, slowly but surely. Honestly, there are enough hazards for a raptor living in the wild – collisions with cars, crashing into windows, flying into high voltage power lines – without poisoning their food source. We suspect Peggy may have eaten a fish that had swallowed a lead sinker.'

'Where does the money to pay for the meds come from?' I asked.

'Donations.'

'The government doesn't pay for any of it?'

'Not even a nickel.'

'Considering all the cockamamie projects the government wastes money on every day, that seems very wrong,' I said.

Izzy looked up from her notes to ask, 'Are you telling us that the eagles Hannah found were suffering from lead poisoning?'

'Not at all. Somehow your birds got into carbofuran or a pesticide like it. Mass poisonings like this, where the birds practically fall out of the sky, are definitely not lead-related. The clenched feet and poor vision are giveaways.'

'That's what Roger Erickson suspected and told Hannah at the scene,' Izzy chimed in. 'But Kendrick Fenelus, the officer from the US Fish and Wildlife Service who I recently interviewed, seems to be maintaining radio silence. He declines to confirm anything because it's part of an ongoing investigation.'

'Kenny? Yeah, he's one of the good guys. Originally from the Bahamas but joined up with Fish and Wildlife in Florida and transferred to Maryland after cutting his teeth in the Everglades. He can sometimes be maddeningly by the book.' She heaved a sigh. 'Well, Officer Fenelus can wait weeks for the lab report, but we can't afford to. We're treating your birds for carbofuran poisoning and I'm happy to report that they're doing quite well.' She motioned us forward. 'See for yourself.'

Mee led us to a separate row of cages further back, which on close inspection appeared identical to Peggy's. Mee stepped to one side in the narrow passageway to allow us to pass, then waited patiently, arms folded across her chest, while Izzy and I visited each of 'our' ailing birds.

'That's absolutely astonishing!' I exclaimed, recalling the birds as I had last seen them. In a few short days the two females had gone from stooped, paralyzed and convulsed to standing upright on two feet and walking, albeit unsteadily. The male, who I figured had been closest to death, was comfortably nestled in a mound of terrycloth toweling, but seemed alert. He turned his head and blinked – the eye membrane moving sideways in an unexpected and startling way – when I passed between him and the light coming in through the window.

'If it's not lead poisoning, how have you been treating them?' Izzy asked.

'The same way I'd treat you if you were unlucky enough to get into carbofuran – atropine injections. Atropine is the go-to antidote for all kinds of organophosphate-carbarmate poisoning. We adjust the dosage according to weight. The girls improved pretty quickly, as you can see, but the little guy needed a bit of help, so we flushed out his crop with activated charcoal. It's called gavage,' she explained, and spelled the word out for Izzy. 'In humans, it's like having your stomach pumped.'

Thinking about Peggy, I asked, 'Have you named our eagles?'

'No, we haven't, and that's good news. We only name the birds we determine can't survive in the wild. Peggy, for example, will most likely end up being an ambassador bird for our outreach programs. Sometime before she came to us, she injured her wing. The veterinary surgeon repaired the damage as best she could, but the injury may impair her ability to fly. We'll make a final determination once she's well enough to move into the flight cage.

'Speaking of which,' she continued, 'follow me.'

Mee led us out the back door and down a narrow dirt path shaded by trees. When we emerged into the open, we found ourselves standing in a field before an enormous, rectangular cage. Anchored at the four corners and at regular intervals along the sides by telephone poles, it was constructed primarily out of two-by-fours, wooden slats and screening. Canvas sails stretched across the roof provided ample shade for the birds, and two wooden platforms and half a dozen perches installed at various heights throughout the enclosure offered comfortable places for them to roost.

'Volunteers helped build this last year,' Mee reported. 'The materials were donated by a local builder. And before you whip out a tape measure, Izzy, it's one hundred-and-forty feet long, twenty-four feet high and twenty feet wide.'

As Mee described the features of the enclosure and Izzy scribbled away, a bald eagle that had been rooting around in the wood chips covering the floor took flight, landed on one of the perches and neatly folded its wings. 'That's the Colonel,' Mee said by way of introduction. 'When he came to us, he had a deep gash across the top of his beak, probably from being caught in a heavy-duty fishing line. A local dentist repaired it with the same kind of putty he uses to make temporary crowns for humans.' She chuckled. 'He even colored it yellow with a highlighter pen we had lying around the clinic.'

'Do you think the Colonel will be able to return to the wild?' I asked.

Mee shrugged. 'It's wait and see time. We do a lot of that around here. The Colonel will probably be able to eat whole fish soon, but right now we're giving him pinkies until we're sure the repair will hold.'

I thought I'd misheard. 'Pinkies?'

'Newborn mice,' she said. 'We buy them by the bag, frozen.'

'Ugh,' I said.

'You have to feed raptors what they like, Hannah, especially when they're recovering.'

Isn't that the truth, I thought. I remembered my hospital stay following breast cancer surgery. The dietician may have considered chicken broth, strawberry Jello, lemon ice and hot tea 'food,' but I certainly had not. I'd shoved the tray aside and wept in frustration until a sympathetic nurse managed to rustle up a turkey sandwich from the hospital cafeteria.

'What happens to the birds that can't survive in the wild?' I asked. 'Surely, you can't keep them all.'

'Sadly, no. I hate to tell you this, but almost half the raptors brought in to Hoots by the transporters have to be euthanized.'

Thinking about Peggy and the Colonel, I began to tear up.

'It's humanly done,' Mee soothed, her face serious. 'We use isoflourane. It's a general anesthesia that relaxes the muscles, relieves pain and puts them quietly to sleep.'

I was willing to leave it at that, but Izzy pressed on. 'And then what?'

'Incineration, unless it's an eagle. Fish and Wildlife is required to ship dead eagles out to the National Eagle Repository in Colorado. The law is fascinating. I recommend you check out their website for details. So . . .' Mee rubbed her palms briskly together. 'Let's move on, shall we?'

'Great idea,' I said, hoping to change the subject and lighten the mood.

'As you've probably observed, eagles are social beings, so the Colonel will soon be sharing the flight cage with the Three Musketeers in there,' Mee said, bobbing her head in the direction of the barn.

Izzy grinned. 'How long before the Three Musketeers can be released?'

'Depends on how long it takes them to recondition their muscles and regain their strength,' she said. 'I promise to keep you informed.'

Before we left Hoots, Mee Semcken gave us a quick guided tour of the clinic, a space that had formerly been the walk-in basement of her home. Like any proper clinic, it had pale green walls and privacy curtains. The space where packing boxes, rusting bicycles and old furniture might once have been stored was now filled to bursting with medical equipment and supplies. It was hard to imagine where one would set down something even as small as a coffee mug and, if you did, you'd have to send out a search party to find it.

Once she'd secured the clinic door behind us, Mee reached out to her right and drew a colorful shower curtain aside, revealing floor-to-ceiling shelves stocked with medications. The laundry room on our immediate left contained an ordinary household washer and dryer, but the shelves above the machines had been repurposed for the storage of neatly rolled bath towels, stacked end facing out, like a rainbow of sausages. 'It's harder and harder to get newspapers these days,' Mee pointed out as we passed by, 'but people always seem to have worn-out towels they're willing to donate.'

While music played softly in the background, a slow and easy rendition of 'Tougher Than the Rest' by Bruce Springsteen, a woman introduced to us as Mee's assistant, Charlene, hovered busily over a center island. Charlene wore a leather apron and her eyes were protected by a pair of industrial-style goggles. A young woman I took to be a volunteer from the University of Delaware – the Fighting Blue Hens T-shirt she wore was a dead giveaway – cradled a hawk in heavily-gloved hands while Charlene administered eye drops, then fed the bird red meat she'd cut into slivers using heavy-duty scissors.

'With so many patients, we keep track of dosages and feeding schedules on this whiteboard,' Mee said, indicating a chart tacked to the back of a door that led upstairs to the main floor of the house. The board was marked off in rows and columns, each space filled with data written in dry mark in minute capital letters.

Bruce began singing 'Dream Baby Dream' when Mee invited us to stick our heads into a lab area equipped with a sink and several tables, all made of stainless steel, cluttered with plastic tubs overflowing with necessities, and underneath them, buckets and cleaning supplies. Food-cutting guides, safety warnings, picture postcards possibly sent in by vacationing volunteers and a couple of *Far Side* cartoons were taped to the walls using blue tape.

'And this is where we store their food,' Mee said as she moved a package of paper towels aside, raised the lid of the chest freezer and invited us to peek inside. Just like my freezer at home, it contained plastic-wrapped trays and frost-covered bags of items I couldn't begin to identify. But unlike mine, thank goodness, this freezer held a pillow-sized bag of frozen pinkies, each newborn mouse only as big as my thumb, not counting its tail. I shuddered and stepped back.

Mee escorted us out of the clinic through the former two-car garage, now dedicated to bird cages draped in dark gray cloth which housed smaller raptors, like owls, red-shouldered hawks and kestrels. 'You just missed the vulture,' Mee told us, indicating one of the larger cages, now empty and being cleaned with hot soap and water by one of the volunteers. 'Some creep shot him through the back with an arrow, but fortunately, with the veterinary surgeon's help, we were able to save him.'

I had mixed feelings about vultures which I decided to keep to myself. I'd observed them in our Annapolis neighborhood, gorging on roadkill, dozing on rooftops – black and brooding like Dracula mini-mes – notorious for vomiting all over their feet. I'd never smelled a rotting corpse, but . . . like that.

At a nearby table which seemed to be doing double duty as a desk and a catch-all, Mee spent a few minutes rummaging and muttering to herself – *I know it's here somewhere* – before laying her hands on the issue of *Science* she'd promised Izzy.

Back at the gate where we'd left Izzy's car, I thanked Mee profusely for spending so much time with us. 'Before we go, may I give you this?' I reached into my handbag for the check I'd made out to Hoots Raptor Rescue Center earlier that morning. 'It's not a lot, I know. Just a hundred dollars for each bird.'

Mee folded the check precisely in half and slipped it into a pocket of her vest. 'The birds and I thank you, Hannah. Every penny helps.'

SIXTEEN

That Tuesday, just as Paul and I were packing the car for a return to Annapolis, where we planned to spend the long Thanksgiving weekend with our daughter and her family, Noel texted: *Results back. Plz call.*

I had left my cellphone on my bedside table, so it was twenty minutes before I saw the message and returned her call.

Noel picked up right away, sounding breathless. 'Some of this is gobbledegook, Mrs Ives, but the bottom line is GenTree was right. Ginny and I are not sisters.'

I hadn't exactly been cooling my heels waiting for the news, and it didn't surprise me.

'Let me read it to you,' she rushed on before I could get a word in. '"Biological specimens corresponding to Alleged Sibling One and Alleged Sibling Two were submitted for genetic testing to help determine whether they are siblings. Based upon the genetic data, the combined sibling index is zero point zero zero zero six and indicates that these data are one thousand six hundred and sixty-seven times more likely if X and Y are unrelated than if they are siblings. Based on testing results obtained from analyses of the DNA loci listed, the probability of full-siblingship is zero percent."'

'Well, that says it all, Noel. What does Ginny think?'

'Nothing much to think about, is there? Was it Neil deGrasse Tyson who said, "The good thing about science is that it's true, whether or not you believe in it"?' She snorted. 'I'm afraid my parents are in the latter camp.'

'Have you talked to them yet?'

'Ginny and I had a confab down at Starbucks this morning. We know our mother. No matter how many tests we take, she'll simply claim the lab made a mistake. And as long as she has my Certificate of Live Birth to wave around as proof we'll never get the truth out of her.' She paused. 'The doctor who signed the certificate is key. We need to talk to Dr Stone.'

My heart did a quick *rat-a-tat-tat*. 'You know him? The doctor's still alive?'

'Yes and yes. Dr Stone was our GP growing up. He and his wife have been members of Dad's church, like, forever. In his late seventies and retired now, but they still attend church fairly regularly. She sings in the choir.'

'And how about the witness? What was her name? Short?'

'Knew her, too. Mary Elizabeth Short was the church secretary back then. Sadly, she died of pancreatic cancer when I was around fifteen.'

'So, do you and Ginny have a plan?'

'We do. The Stones lived in downtown Bentonville for years, in the same house as his office, but when I looked them up in the church directory this morning, I see they've moved to one of those fifty-five plus condo communities at Kent Narrows.'

'The blue and gray ones?'

'Those are the ones. Not exactly to my taste, but the water views are stunning.'

I chuckled. 'I'm not ready to join the mahjong and pickleball set just yet, but when I do, trust me, it won't be to a condominium at Kent Narrows.'

'Long way off for me, and who knows what the world will be like by then. Maybe they'll be flash freezing all the old people and shipping them off to colonies on Mars.'

'Ouch! That hurt,' I said.

Noel laughed. 'Sorry. Um . . . back to business. Just before you called, I telephoned the doctor and asked if I could come over to discuss a medical issue. He said sure, if I could make it today around three because they're flying to Amsterdam in the morning to catch a Viking riverboat cruise. Thing is Ginny has final exams and can't go with me, and I don't want to do it alone. I really think I need a witness.'

Breaking the pregnant pause that followed, I said, 'I feel a request coming on.'

'Could you, please?'

'We're leaving tomorrow morning ourselves, but, sure, I'll be happy to hold your hand if you think it'll help.'

'Thank you! The way I figure it, Mrs Ives, Dr Stone will be less likely to blow me off if I have somebody with me. To his mind, I'm probably still a pigtailed little girl.'

'But wait until Stuart Warner gets finished with you, Noel. You'll be a lean, mean, kickass machine.'

'Don't tell my mother that. She thinks working security means I'll be trailing around after movie stars while they shop for Oscar gowns on Rodeo Drive.'

'Doesn't it?' I chuckled. 'When does your training start, by the way?'

'January the second. In Miami. For ten weeks. Another reason to get this sorted before I go.'

Several hours later, a woman I took to be Mrs Stone buzzed us in. When we wandered down the elegant hallway, she was waiting at the open door of the condo she shared with her husband. 'Noel, welcome.' An eyebrow quirked when she saw Noel wasn't alone. 'And your friend.'

'This is, um . . .' Noel began, but I saved her the trouble of trying to explain me, a woman clearly old enough to be her grandmother. 'I'm Hannah Ives. A long-time friend of the family.'

'Well, don't just stand there letting all the cold air in,' the doctor's wife scolded cheerfully, stepping aside to let us pass into their foyer. 'Eddie will join us in a minute. In the meantime, would you care for some tea?'

We said we would.

'Your parents are well, I hope?' our hostess said, her voice tinged with worry.

'Perfectly well, thank you,' Noel said as we followed Mrs Stone into a spacious, ultra-modern kitchen reminiscent of the 'After' pictures on a home makeover show. 'I came to talk to the doctor about another matter.'

Because she had been expecting us, the doctor's wife had a large, rectangular tea tray sitting ready on the opalescent granite countertop. 'Lady Grey OK?' she asked, looking at me as if she already knew it would be OK with Noel.

'Perfectly,' I said.

Mrs Stone picked up the electric kettle, poured boiling water into the teapot, set the lid back in place and lifted the tray. 'Follow me.'

Five minutes later, when the doctor breezed into the enclosed balcony where we were sitting, we were already politely oh-ing and ah-ing over the Chesapeake Bay view and using dainty silver spoons to stir sugar into our cups. Proper porcelain cups, too, with gilded rims, a matched set hand-painted with violets, roses and peonies.

'Sorry to keep you waiting,' Dr Stone apologized. 'But I got tied up with an important call.'

I'd been envisioning a tweedy, avuncular, professorial sort, but I was way off base. Edward Stone was tall and buff, dressed in a close-fitting black turtleneck sweater over dove gray pleated slacks. He wore his abundant salt and pepper hair slightly long and combed straight back. On his feet, tassel loafers seemed back in style.

In contrast to her husband, Mrs Stone – please, call me Barbara – was comfortably plump and wore her hair in a salon-fresh silver bubble that prettily framed her face. For the occasion, she had chosen a classic, long-sleeved shirtwaist dress in navy blue, accessorized with a double strand of pearls and matching earrings. 'I was just telling Noel how good it was to see her again, Eddie.' Turning to Noel, she said, 'We've missed you in choir, dear.'

'I've been busy with work lately, Mrs Stone. But I'll be at practice next Thursday, I promise.' She favored the woman with a radiant smile. 'I hear they're doing Vivaldi's *Gloria*. It's one of my faves.'

'Mine, too, dear,' she said, before turning her attention to her husband. 'Sit down, Eddie, why don't you?'

Palms upturned, the doctor shrugged – what's a guy gonna do? – pulled out the chair between Noel and his wife and sat down as instructed.

After Dr Stone had been served tea and a dish of lemon slices had made the rounds, Noel set her cup down on its saucer with a delicate clink, reached for her handbag and balanced it on her knees. 'I need to talk to you about this, Doctor,' she said, as she pulled out the live birth certificate, laid it on the damask tablecloth in front of him and smoothed out the creases.

Dr Stone's eyes ping-ponged from the certificate to his wife and back again. 'That seems a very long time ago.'

'Twenty-seven years,' Noel prompted.

'We'd been having a long, cold, rainy spell the night you were born,' the doctor said in a barely audible voice.

Noel's eyes didn't stray from his face. 'So, I was born at home?'

'You were.' He double-tapped the upper right-hand corner of the certificate with a slim, neatly manicured finger. 'Mary was there, too.'

'Well, that's where I'm having a bit of a problem, Doctor. Ginny and I – you remember my sister, Ginny?'

He nodded.

'Well, we had our DNA tested,' she said bluntly. 'My sister and I are not even remotely related.'

'Oh, honey!' Barbara cut in. 'Those ancestry tests are notoriously unreliable.'

'So, we had our DNA tested again,' Noel barreled on, 'by a certified DNA lab this time.' Her head swiveled from the doctor to his wife and back again. 'And I can tell by the looks on your faces that you know what *those* results were.'

Indeed, Dr Stone's face had drained of color; tiny beads of sweat glistened on his temples. 'I feared this day would come,' he began.

'Eddie, don't . . .!' his wife began.

Dr Stone reached out, took his wife's hand, squeezed and held on tightly. 'No, it's all right, Babs. It's an epidemic. Everybody's getting their DNA tested these days. It was just a matter of time before the truth came out.'

Noel pressed on. 'If Robert and Anna Sinclair aren't my parents, Doctor, then who are?'

'I have absolutely no idea.' The statement fell on the room with a thud.

After a few seconds, Noel squeaked, 'Was I *kidnapped*?'

'Oh my gosh, no!' Barbara cut in. 'Whatever gave you that idea?'

'What else am I supposed to think, Mrs Stone, with so little information to go on?' Noel turned back to the doctor. 'And why did you sign this certificate? Aren't doctors sworn to tell the truth or something?'

'You're thinking of the Hippocratic Oath. First, do no harm.' He paused, his tea – indeed, everyone's tea – forgotten. 'I hope you'll believe me when I tell you that at the time, after considering all the options, signing that certificate seemed best for everyone concerned.'

'You'll need to explain it to me,' Noel softly urged. 'Please. I need convincing.'

Dr Stone frowned, looking years older than the man who had entered the room ten minutes before. 'I can't, Noel. Not without breaching doctor–patient confidentiality.'

'What?' Noel rose from her chair and exploded. 'Whose birth certificate is this anyway? This is *my* medical history we're talking about, Doctor, nobody else's. I deserve to know!'

Barbara turned sideways so she could face her husband. Still holding his hand, she said, 'Eddie, she's right. And if you don't tell her, I will. You may think you have an obligation to keep Anna's secret, but I certainly don't.'

Barbara Stone released her husband's hand, rolled her shoulders, folded her hands in her lap and, staring out the window at the view rather than at Noel, began to speak. 'It was brutally cold that night, spitting snow. Someone rang the doorbell at the parsonage, and when your mother answered it, she discovered you on the doorstep, stuffed into a duffle bag and wrapped up in a blanket. Robert was working on his Christmas sermon at the church but he rushed right home when Anna called, and after an hour or so, they called Eddie.'

'You were only a few days old,' the doctor said, continuing the story. 'Your umbilical cord was still attached and it had been tied off with a shoelace, but you were a perfectly healthy, full-term baby girl.'

'Why didn't anyone call the police?'

'Because there was a note, Noel. Your mother, whoever she was, willingly gave you away. We discussed what to do for several hours, and we prayed about it together. It was our belief, one that I still hold today, that your mother wanted the Sinclairs to have you.'

'So, you lied?'

Edward Stone shifted in his chair, his back rigid.

Noel pounced. 'Date of last menses! Number of prenatal visits!' she cried, stabbing at the certificate to emphasize her point. 'All lies?'

'No, I didn't lie about those, Noel.'

When he didn't elaborate, Barbara stepped in. 'Your mother had been pregnant, Noel, but early in September she suffered a miscarriage. At the time you arrived on her doorstep, Eddie was treating her for post-partum depression.'

Barbara gave that bombshell a moment to sink in before continuing. 'She'd been praying hard, you see. Praying fervently for another pregnancy. And then, a miracle! You appeared on the doorstep and it seemed like God had answered her prayers. And, who knows, maybe he did.'

'I just don't understand,' Noel blurted. 'Again, why didn't they call the police?'

'And turn you over to Social Services?' Barbara Stone asked. 'What kind of life would that be for a child? Do you think you would have been better off in the foster care system, Noel?'

Noel stared at her folded hands, shook her head.

'Have you had a good life, Noel?' Barbara asked, her voice soothing, gentle.

Noel glanced up, seemingly surprised at the question. 'Of course I have.'

'Do you love your parents?'

'Of course I do.'

'You and your sister, Ginny, are close?'

'You know we are.'

Barbara picked up the certificate, refolded it along its well-creased lines and handed it back. 'Put this away then, Noel. File it away. Forget about it.'

All along, I'd been biting my tongue, fighting the urge to jump into the discussion. I couldn't stay quiet one second longer. 'But, how on earth did they pull it off?'

Dr Stone raised a hand, volunteering to explain. 'Anna and Robert hadn't told anyone about the pregnancy, Mrs Ives. Some of my patients start shouting the news even before the home pregnancy test has a chance to dry, but not Noel's mother. She was superstitious, so afraid she'd jinx the pregnancy that she wanted to wait until at least twenty-two weeks. We had just scheduled the first ultrasound when she lost the baby.' He paused; winced as if in pain. 'A little girl.'

'Everything was ready,' Barbara rushed to add. 'In her grief, Anna refused to put anything away. The crib, the bassinette, boxes of disposable diapers, even the yellow outfit she planned to dress you . . .' she paused, swallowed hard. 'Dress the baby in when they brought it home from the hospital.' She pressed a hand to her bosom, took a deep, steadying breath. 'When Eddie arrived that night, he found Anna in the nursery feeding you a bottle and rocking, rocking, rocking.'

'But still—' I began, before the doctor interrupted, as if anticipating my question.

'Do you know Anna, Mrs Ives?'

I had to confess that I'd never met her.

'Well, Anna is sturdily built, one might even say Rubenesque. And it didn't matter what skimpy little fashions were currently in style. As a minister's wife, Anna always dressed conservatively. Nobody questioned the home birth story.'

'Nobody,' his wife added, her eyes narrowing, as if daring us not to upset the applecart, even at this late date.

Noel got the message. 'I'll have to think about it, Mrs Stone, Dr Stone. In the meantime, I have to ask you not to mention this conversation to my parents.'

'Very wise,' said the doctor.

'It's for the best, dear. Then and now, for the best.'

SEVENTEEN

During the hour-long drive back to Bentonville, Maryland from the Stone's condo on Kent Island, Noel and I exchanged few words. After several attempts to draw her out were met with either silence or a terse, 'I need to think, OK?' I gave up and focused on my driving.

Twenty miles south of the Queenstown Outlet Mall, the dam burst. I pulled off the four-lane highway as soon as I could, slotted the car into a parking space at the CVS outside of Easton, released our seatbelts and wrapped Noel in my arms, stroking her back until her sobbing subsided. Then I reached into the glove compartment for the box of tissues I keep handy for snotty noses and sticky fingers, offered her one and waited while she wiped her cheeks, dried her eyes and gave her nose a honking good blow. 'I could be anybody,' she hiccuped, fumbling for a fresh tissue. 'A drug addict's kid. The offspring of a serial killer, or . . .' She turned to me, eyes red-rimmed, lashes glistening. 'Even the product of rape, or, dear God, incest.'

'Or, you could be the love child of a famous rock star,' I suggested, hoping to lighten the mood. 'Or maybe a dotcom gabillionaire.'

'I hadn't thought of that.' She sniffed while dabbing her nose.

'You know what I'm going to suggest now, don't you?'

Noel nodded. 'Get back to work on the GenTree stuff.'

'Exactly. And I'll be happy to help.'

'No, thank you, Mrs Ives. You've already given me a good head start, and I think . . . I hope, I'll be able to do it myself.' She managed a smile. 'Will you be on call?'

'Of course. Any time.'

'Thirty-two possible second cousins are a lot to process.'

'Yes, but you've already eliminated approximately one third of them, the ones that descend from, what was his name, Andrew?'

She nodded.

I buckled my seat belt and waited for Noel to do the same.

We were cruising down Route 50 and well past Easton when Noel spoke again. 'The hardest part is the lies. All these years, they lied. Mom, Dad, the doctor and his wife, even poor, dead Mary Elizabeth Short. Big fat liars, the whole lot of 'em.'

'I gather you're not buying their explanation for why they did what they did.'

'What good Christian wouldn't at least *try* to find the mother of an abandoned child?' She paused. 'Otherwise, how do they know the mother didn't regret her decision, change her mind?'

'To be fair, Noel, unless and until your parents move away, the woman who is your mother will always know where to find you.'

'Why didn't she come back for me?' Noel barely managed to choke out the words.

'That's a good question.' I reached out and squeezed her knee. 'It's impossible to know, but maybe GenTree will sort it out for you.'

Twenty minutes later, I brought my Volvo to a halt in front of the Sinclairs' well-kept, Victorian-style parsonage. A man and a woman, dressed warmly – she in a puffy jacket, he in a windbreaker and both wearing knit caps and gloves – were stringing Christmas lights on the hedges that lined and partially hid the brick foundation. As I pulled on the emergency brake to keep the car from rolling further along Church Street, they paused in mid-task – he from the top step of a ladder – to wave cheerfully at the car.

'Your parents?' I asked, reaching for the ignition key.

'Yup.'

Noel opened the passenger door, stepped out onto the curb and before closing the door, leaned in to say, 'Not a word, please. This is something I need to sort out on my own.'

'Are you planning to introduce me?' I asked.

She shook her head vigorously. 'Not just now, please. I'm barely holding it together.'

To tell the truth, I was worried about Noel. I have Eva Haberman, the priest at St Catherine's Episcopal Church in West Annapolis, to turn to for spiritual guidance and advice. But what do you do when your pastor is part of the problem?

'Do you have someone you can talk to?' I asked.

'My sister.'

'Other than Ginny, I mean.'

'Don't worry, Mrs Ives. I'll be fine. Who knows? As you say, maybe I'll turn out to be the long-lost heir to a vast family fortune.

Or, the granddaughter of a Sicilian crime boss, whisked out of the safety of the Witness Protection Program into a more normal life.' She grinned. 'I'd get a lucrative book deal out of that, I'll bet.'

I had to laugh. 'Yeah. You're gonna be fine, kid.'

EIGHTEEN

On the post-Thanksgiving, Black Friday, college football and pumpkin pie Monday, Paul and I unloaded the car and settled back in at Our Song for a lunch of leftover leftovers – my famous turkey tetrazzini. I'd just cleaned up the kitchen when Izzy breezed in, face flushed and bubbling over with post-holiday cheer.

'Did you have a good Thanksgiving?' I asked, genuinely curious about how my friend had spent the holiday. The last time we'd been together, her plans had been up in the air.

'I did,' she said as she shrugged off her parka and draped it over the back of a kitchen chair. 'Spent it with Jack.'

That news surprised me. 'Seriously? I assumed he'd be spending it with family.'

'The visit with his in-laws in Flagstaff wasn't going well, so he packed up and flew home early,' Izzy explained as she helped herself to a K-cup and popped it into the Keurig.

'Oh, too bad. Jack mentioned he and his wife were working on a reconciliation. Sounds like there's been a setback.'

'One might say so,' she said, reaching for one of the clean mugs I keep next to the coffee machine.

'What I suspect is that you may be one of the reasons it's not working out.' I raised a hand, palm out. 'Not judging, just commenting.'

Izzy pushed the brew button and waited while the machine gurgled and hissed. 'You may be right.'

I decided to change the subject. 'Did you get time to visit your mother?' Izzy's mom was a resident at Symphony Manor, an assisted living facility in Baltimore's Roland Park neighborhood. Vascular dementia had taken a toll. Her mother's loss of memory, erratic mood swings and trips down Fantasy Lane had been a continuing source of worry and frustration for her daughter.

Izzy grinned. 'Yes, I did. Jack was kind enough to go along for moral support. Turned out to be painless. Mother mistook Jack for my ex, so she gushed all over him for two and a half hours.

When we left, Jack was totally confused, but Mother was happy as a clam.'

Izzy's ex was James Terrance Campbell, aka Terry, the WBNF-TV weather guy. Izzy always joked that their eight-year relationship had been stormy.

'Hey, after I finish my coffee, how about going for a walk?'

'Sure,' I agreed. 'Where to?'

Izzy took a sip of coffee, then set the mug down on the counter. 'It's a bit on the down-low.'

'All the better,' I said with a grin. 'How low?'

'I still haven't been able to interview Wesley Butler. I've emailed, texted and telephoned, but he keeps giving me the runaround, which only makes me suspect he has something to hide. I stopped by just now to see him in person, but he put me off again. Said he had to pick his wife and kids up from BWI airport.' Izzy shot her sleeve to check her Apple watch. 'I figure two hours there, two hours back. Gives us plenty of time.'

'Time for what?'

'To search the joint, silly.'

'Including his house?'

'No, I'm not particularly interested in the house. He's got little kids. If he's hoarding any deadly poisons, they won't be kept in the house unless he's certifiably insane. I propose we have a casual look around the outbuildings, starting with the barn.'

I gave the countertop a final wipe and draped the towel over the handle of the oven to dry. 'I don't believe for a minute that Wesley didn't have anything to do with the eagles being poisoned, but what will we be looking for exactly? Has there been any official verdict from the lab?'

'According to Officer Fenelus, those tests take time, and sadly, there's a backlog, but I have a feeling he knows something and simply isn't saying.'

'Noel's got an off-again, on-again relationship with Roger Erickson at Natural Resources. It's been on recently, so maybe she can coax information out of him.'

'It can't hurt to ask.' Izzy finished off her coffee in three swallows, then handed the empty mug to me. 'So, you're game?'

I inverted the mug over a peg in the dishwasher, closed the door and punched a few buttons. 'Lead on, then, Nancy Drew.'

Izzy reached for her parka. 'As I was turning into your driveway,

Wesley's red Kia drove past, so the clock started ticking about ten minutes ago.'

She was out the door and well ahead of me by the time I collected my jacket, hat and gloves and caught up with her by the front gate.

'Just two friends, out for a stroll on a crisp, sunny day,' I muttered as I mashed my hat down over my curls and fell into step beside her.

'Walking off Thanksgiving calories,' Izzy added, her words turning to white mist.

'Let's go the back way,' I suggested, taking the lead. 'Noel and I climbed through the barbed wire the other day, but a bit further on, there's a utility gate where they drive the combines in and out. Kinder to clothing.'

Once the gate had been pulled shut behind us, Izzy and I trudged straight across the field, high-stepping over lumpy furrows strewn with dried corn stalks. I was glad we'd taken that route because it bypassed the scene of the crime. Even though the yellow caution tape had already been removed, I didn't relish any reminders.

'Are you sure the farm's deserted?' I asked as the Tuckerman barn loomed on the far horizon.

'I've been asking around,' Izzy said. 'Down at the High Spot they say that Tuckerman runs it lean and mean. Have you ever met him?'

'Once, at a fancy garden party thrown by a local real estate agent, back in the summer when we first bought the place.' I stumbled and made a grab for Izzy's arm. 'Our hostess ended up dead, strangled by her Hermes scarf,' I continued after regaining my footing. 'Quite the bitch, so the list of suspects was as long as your arm, but they eventually caught up with the guy.'

'So, other than that, Mrs Ives, how did you enjoy the party?'

'Well, everybody got a beach towel, a floating keychain and a free iPad mini, so not a complete loss. Except for the victim, of course.'

'That's harsh, Hannah.'

'You didn't know her,' I said.

The closer we got to the barn, the more my stomach fluttered. Was it nervous excitement or simply fear? 'What's your plan if somebody's here?'

Izzy stopped in her tracks. 'Well, I figure we'll just use the patented Hannah Ives Have-You-Seen-My-Lost-Cat technique. Do you still have a picture of Hobie on your phone?'

'He's my screensaver,' I told her. Hobie was a handsome lynx point Siamese who belonged to Pete and Trish, our across-the-street neighbors in Annapolis. For more than a year now, Hobie had taken to dividing his time between our place and theirs, usually showing up just after dinner. We like to think he enjoys *On the Beat* with Ari Melber just as much as we do, but it might have more to do with the gourmet cat treats we keep in a glass jar on top of the mantle.

'Hobie, check. We're good to go, then,' Izzy said.

We set off at speed, approaching the barn from behind. 'Walk like you own the place,' Izzy called to me over her shoulder as she circled the barn with confident strides. I caught up with her on the drive out in front.

Since our previous visit, the broken door had not been repaired, but Wes – or somebody – had pulled a tall sheet of corrugated sheet metal across the opening. It was a simple matter for the two of us to drag it to one side and walk in.

Once inside, I realized the barn was in worse shape than I'd thought. Patches of blue sky could be glimpsed through ragged holes in the roof. The sun shining through gaps in the siding slashed across the dirt floor like prison bars. The tractor Steve Heberling had been tinkering with had been parked to our immediate left and partially covered with a tarp, presumably because the roof couldn't be trusted to keep it dry. To our right, bales of hay were stacked like children's blocks all the way up to the level of the loft.

From a spot dead center in the barn, Izzy executed a 360-degree turn and said, 'Hmmm. If I were a container of carbofuran, where would I be?'

I volunteered to check the loft and headed for the wooden ladder that led up to it. On the third rung I paused to look down, comforted by the fact that, should I fall, it would be into a bed of hay. When I reached the top, six rungs further up, I took a quick look around. 'Nothing up here except stacks of lumber,' I called down to my co-conspirator. 'Two-by-fours, mostly, but a lot of one-by-sixes, too. Maybe they're planning to repair the place. Sure could use a bit of TLC. Oh, and several coils of rope.'

When I rejoined Izzy on the floor below, she'd discovered a storage area behind the tractor where she was methodically reading the label of every bottle, jar and can on the shelves, as well as those stacked beside and in front of them. 'Paint,' she announced, hoisting one large paint can by the handle. 'Matches the shutters on the house.' She set it down. 'Thinner, piles of rags.'

While Izzy continued her inventory, I wandered over to a shelf nearby where automotive supplies – oil, additives, filters, transmission fluids – were kept, but found nothing labeled with a skull and crossbones or even Mr Ick.

A Craftsman tool cabinet on casters caught my eye, not only because of its color – fire engine red – but because it was the neatest, cleanest thing in the place. It had ten drawers and each contained what one would expect: tools. I rolled it aside and looked behind, revealing two wooden boxes of duck decoys, so roughly carved that even a myopic duck wouldn't be fooled into a hookup.

'What the hell's this?' I heard Izzy say.

I shoved the tool cabinet back into place and turned around. Izzy had discovered a roll of raffia grass, unrolled it and was holding it up to her waist. 'Makes a nice hula skirt,' she said, giving her hips a little wiggle. Half a dozen other rolls were stacked nearby, almost indistinguishable from the bales of hay they were propped up against.

'It's raffia grass. I've seen them use it to camouflage the flat boats.'

'Good for tiki huts, too, I imagine.' Izzy rolled the raffia back up and returned it to the top of the pile.

That's when I noticed that tucked into a nook just beyond the wall of hay was a makeshift office equipped with a battered mahogany dining room table and a vintage swivel-tilt office chair, its plastic upholstery mended with duct tape. Neatly stacked piles of what on closer inspection proved to be Cast and Blast brochures as well as magazines – separate piles for issues on hunting and fishing and another for agriculture – covered the table.

Wes was obviously on top of his job. The In tray of his In-and-Out box was empty, while the Out tray contained a wad of invoices marked *Paid*. A dark blue ceramic mug with a broken handle from the High Spot Café held an odd assortment of pens and pencils, and above it tacked to the wall with push pins was an illustrated calendar from Tidewater Farm and Supply. Wes had already turned it over to the page for December where the pinup girl of the month was a cow and her calf in a snowstorm, gazing mournfully through ice-rimed lashes into the photographer's lens. Calendar squares had been filled out in a precise hand with ink, using black for the Cast and Blast schedule and, paging back through previous months, red for other farm operations such as tilling, planting, pruning, spraying and irrigation, most of which I assumed would be handled by the tenant farmer. Doctor and dental appointments for Wes and his family were noted in blue.

From the number of planned Cast and Blast excursions scheduled, two of them designated specifically for greenhorns, I made a mental note that it might be wise for Paul and me to stay back home in Annapolis from December 15 through to the end of January.

A filing cabinet, rusting through where the gray paint was chipped, stood to the left of the table and to the right a push-button wall phone was mounted adjacent to a closed door. I lifted the receiver, listened for a dial tone. 'Dead,' I reported to Izzy and hung up.

'Not surprised,' Izzy said. 'Do you know anybody with a landline these days?'

I had to admit that I didn't.

'Do you notice anything odd?' I asked my partner in crime a moment later.

Izzy's eyes did a quick survey. 'Not really.'

'Everything else in this place is covered with hay dust, but not the desk or the chair. It's clear Wesley actually uses them.'

'Not this filing cabinet, though,' Izzy noted. The top drawer was torqued and slightly ajar but she tugged at the handle hopefully. With a teeth-clenching screech of metal on metal, it inched open just far enough for us to see it was empty. The two drawers below it were filled with back issues of magazines, their covers faded and brittle with age.

The closed door, however, was another matter. Other than the pristine Craftsman tool chest, its shiny brass knob had to be the newest thing in the barn. Izzy grasped the doorknob and turned. When the door didn't open, she rattled the knob, 'Locked, of course.'

I made a shooing motion. 'Move over and let a professional handle this.'

Izzy smiled at me in puzzled amusement, but let go of the knob and stepped to one side. 'Over to you, then, Houdini.'

As I bent to examine the lock – a simple key entry knob – I muttered, 'I used to be pretty good at picking locks back in college.' I glanced up at her sideways through a fringe of bangs that badly needed a trim. 'I'm not as proud of that as I am of my degree in

French, but I have to admit that it's a skill that's proven to be a lot handier than being able to recite the whole of *"Demain, dès l'aube"*.' I grinned. 'Victor Hugo, in case you're wondering.'

Izzy laughed out loud, then stifled the laugh with the back of her hand as if worrying about eavesdroppers.

'At Oberlin, I'd used bobby pins,' I confessed, 'but I don't think we're going to find any bobby pins lying around in this barn. Maybe, though . . .' My eyes took in the clutter on the tabletop. There were no drawers to rummage through, but if the coffee mug was anything like the one I had on my desk at home . . . I grabbed the October issue of *Progressive Farmer* magazine, opened it to the middle and dumped the contents of the mug out on top of an article on improving irrigation efficiency. My haul was four ballpoint pens, a couple of No. 2 pencils that badly needed sharpening, a dried-out eraser, a pair of drug-store reading glasses, a rubber band, and two brass Chuck-E-Cheese tokens.

While I was putting everything back in the mug, Izzy had been pawing through the piles of papers in Wes's outbox. 'Will this help?' she asked, indicating a paper clip that Wes had apparently been using to keep a canceled check attached to an invoice.

'Yes!' I said. 'Do you think you can find another one?'

Several minutes later, we'd come up with three paper clips – a pair and a spare – one of which I straightened out to its full length, the other I twisted into an L.

Izzy's shadow loomed over me as I worked my magic on the lock. 'You're blocking my light,' I scolded. In the time it took for Izzy to step away, the tumblers fell into place, the knob turned and I opened the door.

For a moment, all Izzy could do was gape. 'Wow,' she said at last. 'That was impressive.'

'A survival skill,' I told her. 'Freshman year I had a party-hearty roommate who kept locking me out while I was in the shower. She finally transferred to the University of Michigan, but by then . . .' I pushed the door wide. '*Et voilà!*'

Izzy stepped through the door ahead of me, then turned round, arms akimbo. 'I can't believe you picked a lock just so we could get into a toilet.'

Along with a large cardboard carton tucked under the sink and a portable Honda generator in the corner, the two of us filled the tiny lavatory almost to capacity.

'Why would you put a lock like that on a lavatory?' Izzy asked.

I shrugged. 'The generator maybe? Paul's sister has one on her farm and it's worth about fifteen hundred dollars.'

I twisted the cold-water knob on the sink, but no water spewed from the faucet. 'No water.'

Izzy peered into the open toilet bowl and wrinkled her nose. 'Ugh! Don't guys ever flush?' She jiggled the handle, but the toilet wouldn't flush. 'No water here, either.'

I peered into the bowl which was stained black with a greenish ring. 'Ugh is right. Do you think we need hazmat suits?'

Izzy lifted the lid to the toilet tank. 'Well, well, well, what have we here?' She stepped to one side and motioned me forward for a closer view. Someone had removed the float ball to make room for two white plastic bottles with red and black lettering. Using my gloved hand, I picked one of the bottles up by its cap and eased it far enough out of the toilet tank so we could determine what was in it. 'Furadan,' I read aloud. 'One liter.'

'And it's not the old stuff, either.' Izzy pointed at the label. '"*Hecho en E.U.A./México.*"' She looked at me, eyes wide. 'This hasn't been lying around the farm for the past ten years. Someone's deliberately smuggled these bottles into the country.'

My second language was French, but I had no trouble translating the label. *Peligro. Mortal en case de ingestión. Mortel si se inhala.* My hand began to tremble. 'We need to leave everything exactly where we found it,' I warned as I carefully slid the deadly bottle of Furadan back into the tank.

'Have they been opened?'

'I don't know, and I don't plan to find out,' I said, peeling off my leather gloves and stuffing them in my pocket. I made a mental note to throw them into the fireplace as soon as I got home. I didn't need to *Lea el instructivo anexo* to know that Furadan could also be absorbed through the skin.

'Now I'm really curious about what's in the box,' I said, indicating the carton Wes – or somebody – had stashed under the sink. 'It must be important enough to keep under lock and key.'

Izzy squatted down in front of it for a closer look. 'Unopened,' she announced while exploring the lid with a gloved finger. 'But it's from Amazon. It's got that smiley swoosh on it.'

'Any other labels?'

'Wait a minute. This bit of tape is loose.' As I watched, Izzy inserted her finger under the packing tape and gently lifted the flap. 'Can't see a damn thing,' she announced, 'but I don't want to mess up the cardboard.' She sat back on her heels, reached for her iPhone and swiped the flashlight on with her nose. 'Here,' she said, handing the phone to me. 'Shine the light on it while I peek through the crack.'

Izzy bent her head close to the box, face screwed up in a squint. 'It's another box. It's bright red, with . . . um, Titus, it says. Can you move the light a bit to the right?' After a second of silence, she jerked her finger away from the flap, almost as if she'd been stung.

'What?'

The light from the iPhone shone full on her astonished face. 'Shit, Hannah. Titus makes sardines. Tins of sardines. Fifty to a box.' Without ceremony, she whipped the iPhone out of my hand. 'I'm taking pictures.'

Izzy stripped off her gloves and began snapping away. Meanwhile, I dashed off in search of the box of blue latex gloves I'd noticed when Izzy was checking out the paint cans. Then, with my assistance as a freshly gloved prop holder, Izzy took close-ups of the contents of the toilet tank and then, being careful not to tear the packing tape any more than necessary, of what was in the cardboard box. 'If the poison that killed that eagle wasn't Furadan and the fox didn't have sardines in his stomach, this'll mean nothing, of course,' she muttered as she backed out the door, rotated her phone ninety degrees and aimed for a long, wide-angle shot.

'But we don't know that,' I said reasonably.

Izzy tapped a few keys. 'I'm emailing the photos to myself for security.' She looked up. 'And when I get back to the house, I'm going to send them to Officer Fenelus.'

'Oh, swell,' I huffed. 'And confess that we trespassed on David Tuckerman's property and broke into a locked bathroom?'

'Locked? I don't see any locked room, do you?' she said as she closed the lavatory door firmly behind us. 'Tsk, tsk. So easy to forget to push that little button in when you come out of the loo.'

I couldn't suppress a grin. 'Yes, it's quite unlike Wes to be so careless.'

'And, sadly, although we looked everywhere, we never found your cat.'

'Seriously, Izzy. Thank God I don't actually have a cat,' I

commented as Izzy and I dragged the makeshift metal door back into place in front of the barn. 'How long would a cat survive in a place where deadly cans of sardines are left lying around? I'm with Diana Kingsley on this one.'

Izzy slapped at her jeans, sending puffs of hay dust into the air. 'Who's Diana Kingsley?'

'She's the trained transporter who took the eagles to Hoots. She believes that some people are so evil they forfeit their right to live.' I stripped off the blue latex gloves and tucked them into my pocket.

'As an investigative reporter who cut her teeth on the mean streets of Baltimore, there's not much I haven't seen, Hannah, and I couldn't agree more.'

NINETEEN

'*Mmmm, ooooh.*'

I spun around. 'Did you say something, Izzy?'

'Me? No. Why?'

'I thought you said something.'

'Not me. I thought it was you.'

'*Ahhhh, ooooh.*'

'There it is again,' I said. 'Listen.'

Izzy and I paused, our ears on full alert.

'*Ahhhh . . .*'

Izzy turned and grabbed the makeshift barn door. 'It's coming from inside the barn. Do you suppose we've shut an animal up in there?'

'We can find out,' I said as I helped her drag the metal door aside and prop it up again against the siding. We stepped back into the shadowy interior, dimly illuminated by the broad shaft of light coming in through the opening we'd just made.

'Help . . . me.' A woman's voice, faint.

'We hear you,' I called out. 'Where are you?'

'Dunno.'

'Over there,' Izzy said, pointing toward the ladder that led up to the loft.

I dashed in the direction of the ladder, weaving around bits of rusting farm equipment and stumbling over cans of paint until I reached the bales of hay that effectively walled that part of the barn off from the area we'd recently searched.

'*Ooooh,*' the woman groaned.

'Coming!' I called out. I leaned over the chest high stack of bales and peered behind them. From beneath a heap of loose straw, a red tennis shoe protruded. The leg attached to the shoe twitched.

Panting and heaving, Izzy and I dismantled the wall a bale at a time until the gap was wide enough to wade through. With the exception of her blue jean-clad leg, the woman was completely buried under the straw. We fell to our knees and began pawing it away.

The woman lay face down on the floor of the barn, her abundant blonde hair tangled and matted. 'Thank . . . you!' She gasped. 'Couldn't breathe. Too much . . .'

'You're OK now, Diana,' I said, recognizing the plaid shirt the raptor transporter had been wearing the first time I'd met her. 'We're here to help.'

Gently, Izzy cleared straw away from Diana's cheek. 'What happened?'

Diana moved her head slightly and groaned. A jagged gash, glistening and bubbly with partially clotted blood, marred her pale, white forehead. 'Dunno.'

'You've had a nasty blow to the head,' I told her.

Diana stirred; her hand twitched. 'Hurts.'

'Best not to touch it,' Izzy said, gently staying Diana's hand. 'We'll need to get you to the hospital. Looks like you'll need stitches.'

'Do you think you can stand up?' I asked.

'Dunno,' Diana rasped again.

'Let's give it a try, shall we?'

Izzy took one of Diana's arms and I took the other. Between us, we eased her to her knees and then to her feet, where she slumped between us like an empty suit.

'Ready?' I asked.

After a moment Diana nodded and we took a baby step forward. Immediately, her left leg buckled and she screamed in pain.

While I continued to support the patient, Izzy knelt and rolled up Diana's left pant leg. No one was reassured when she sucked air in through her teeth. 'Ouch! I'm no doctor, but it sure looks broken to me.'

Even from my vantage point, I could see that Diana's ankle was an angry purple, unnaturally twisted and swollen to twice normal size. Diana wasn't walking anywhere on that.

Together, we dragged her over to a bale of hay and helped her sit down.

Once she was settled, Izzy reached for her cell phone. 'I'm calling nine one one.'

'No!' Diana's hand dug into my arm, so deeply her fingernails left half-moons on my skin. 'No!'

'But you need medical attention, Diana,' I said reasonably.

'I can't be found here,' she said, her voice weak but emphatic. 'You drive?'

Izzy and I exchanged glances. We'd left both our cars at Our Song, more than a mile up the road. We'd hiked to the Tuckerman farm, but presumably Diana had driven there and parked somewhere nearby, but out of sight.

'Where's your SUV, Diana?' I asked.

'Old cemetery,' she said. She released the death grip on my arm and patted the pocket of her shirt. 'Keys.'

'I'll go,' I said as I eased the key ring out of her pocket. 'It's not far.'

Diana was right, of course. She couldn't be found in the Tuckerman barn – none of us could. We were trespassing, big time. A rusted, bullet-pocked sign tacked up on the outside of the barn – possibly as a joke – warned *NO TRESPASSING: Trespassers Will be Shot. Survivors Will Be Shot Again.*

In less than ten minutes I was back, parked as close to the barn as I could get.

'We need to hurry,' I said, feeling the clock tick-tick-ticking as we helped Diana hop to her car. 'Wesley could be coming back any minute.'

'Son of a bitch,' Diana muttered as we eased her into the back seat and fastened the seat belt around her. 'I'll—'

'Shhh,' I said. 'There'll be time for explanations later.'

Izzy and I made quick work of closing up the barn. 'You drive,' she said. 'I'll sit in the back with Diana. Where are we taking her?'

'Emergency room at the hospital in Salisbury,' I said as I figured out how to start the unfamiliar vehicle and put it into drive. I drove south on Route 50 as fast as the speed limit allowed, balancing our need for speed against the moans emerging from the back seat every time the SUV hit a pothole or drove over a hump.

'I shouldn't have been there,' Diana announced to the ceiling from her prone position on a gurney in a curtained-off cubicle of the ER. The shot she'd been given for pain had apparently taken effect.

Not long after I'd commandeered a wheelchair and rolled her into the ER, the doctor on duty in the ER had cleaned Diana's head wound and closed it with five stitches. A nurse had decorated his work with a gauze bandage that wrapped around Diana's head like a Seventies era headband. and announced that, because of the head wound, they would be keeping her overnight for observation. Now we waited for the results of the X-rays they'd taken of her ankle.

'None of us should have been there,' I pointed out.

Diana turned her head on the pillow and looked straight at me. 'I've been warned more than once about getting too emotionally invested in my cases. Every time I step out of line, I risk being struck off the list of approved transporters. But some of these guys are so evil . . .'

I patted her hand. 'Tell me what happened, Diana. Did you fall?'

She smirked. 'In a manner of speaking.'

'I'm back,' Izzy said as she breezed into the cubicle after having successfully parked the car. 'They said only one visitor at a time, but I told them I was your sister.'

I was occupying the only chair in the room, so Izzy made herself comfortable by leaning against the sink.

'What happened, Diana?' I asked again.

Diana laced her fingers together, rested her hands on her stomach and stared at the ceiling tiles, as cool and immutable as a noble-woman on a medieval sarcophagus. 'It's still a bit foggy, Hannah. I remember parking under a tree by that little cemetery not far from your place, then I waited until I saw Wesley drive away.'

That sounded familiar.

'What were you doing in the barn?' Izzy asked.

'Same thing you were, I imagine. Looking for carbofuran.'

'We found it,' Izzy crowed.

Diana turned her head, beamed, then winced. 'Ouch!'

Izzy powered up her cell phone. While Diana looked on, she paged through the photographs she'd taken inside the bathroom.

'Damn,' Diana said. 'I've found carbofuran in chest freezers and hidden under loose floorboards, but inside a toilet tank is a new one. It's amazing the lengths people will go to hold on to that horrible stuff. I hope you've shared this information with DNR.'

'Done,' Izzy said.

'I've been lying here trying to piece it all together,' Diana said after a moment. 'I remember going into the barn and thinking I'd check out the loft. I was standing at the foot of the ladder when I heard voices outside. Wesley had come back, goddammit. Apparently, they'd forgotten to pack the kid's scooter board. He swore a blue streak at his wife for leaving the barn door open, then . . .' She shook her head gently, as if trying to shake the memory loose. 'That's absolutely the last thing I remember until you two showed up.'

'The doctor figured you'd been struck by something with a sharp blade,' I said, having overheard the conversation. I cast my mind back to the scene in the barn, but I'd been too busy worrying about Diana to notice anything else amiss.

'So, Wesley clobbered you with something, then just left you there to bleed to death?' Izzy said.

'Apparently,' Diana said.

'Worse than that,' I cut in. 'You didn't just fall into that heap of hay. Wesley took the time to cover you with it.'

'Maybe he planned to come back later and get rid of the body,' Diana said darkly.

'Well, imagine his surprise . . .' I said, as I pictured Wesley flailing around frantically in the hay when he returned from dropping his family off at the airport.

'You need to file a complaint with the police, Diana,' Izzy urged.

'No, no way,' she said. 'Wesley's word against mine, and no witnesses.'

'Cindy? The kids?' I asked.

'I'm pretty sure they stayed in the car,' Diana said. 'Besides, I was trespassing, so he had every right to protect his property.'

'But . . .' I began.

'It was an accident,' she said, her jaw set. 'If anyone asks, I was up in a juniper tree trying to rescue a barn owl with an injured wing. I fell. End of story.'

I gasped. 'Diana, you can't let Wesley get away with it! He could have killed you.'

'But he didn't.'

'Still . . .'

'You reap what you sow,' Diana said. 'Galatians six, verse seven. And if God takes his time about it, there's always Plan B.'

'What's Plan B?' Izzy asked.

Diana snorted. 'As soon as I figure it out, I'll let you know. One good thing, though . . .'

'What?' I asked.

She rocked her injured leg. 'At least it wasn't my driving foot.'

TWENTY

B y Wednesday, Izzy had heard nothing from Officer Fenelus other than a maddingly simple text back: *Thx 4 Pix.*

Diana had been released from the hospital and was recuperating at her home in Queenstown with her no-nonsense daughter, Jeannine, calling most of the shots.

'I'm out of your hair for a while,' Izzy announced briskly at breakfast over a cup of peach yogurt, black coffee and a honey-oat granola bar. There'd been some developments in another story she'd been working on – a proposed theme park expansion onto a state-owned nature preserve – and she was hot on the trail of one of the shifty – her term – developers who was in cahoots with a double-dealing – also her term – state legislator.

'I'll catch up with you at the Zoom session on Friday,' she promised as she collected her overnight bag from the front hall, slipped into her parka and out the front door. The Silent Sleuths – Jack, Izzy, Mark and I – hadn't held a meeting for a couple of weeks, so a Zoom call was long overdue.

Paul had gone down to the High Spot to commiserate over coffee and donuts with two long-faced, snowed-out golfing buddies, leaving me alone with the dirty laundry. I was stuffing a load of whites into the dryer when my cell phone began to chime with Noel's ringtone.

I picked up right away. 'Noel. Hi.'

'I . . . I . . . oh, golly . . . Mrs Ives, I . . .' She babbled on for a bit.

'Noel, slow down! I can't understand a word you're saying.'

'I was up all night, and, oh, I can't believe . . .' The girl sounded positively giddy.

'Breathe, Noel, breathe. Then you can tell me what this is all about.'

On the other end, Noel exhaled deeply, took a short, gasping breath and blurted, 'I think I found her, Mrs Ives. Unless I completely botched this GenTree business, I think I've found my mother.'

Now I had to take a moment to breathe. 'Hold on, Noel. I think

I'm going to have to sit down.' Carrying the phone, I drifted into the living room and plopped myself down in an armchair. 'OK, I'm sitting now. Tell me about it.'

'Well, I did what you said on GenTree and all, and followed up SharynG's tree to her great-grandparents, then . . .' She took a deep breath. 'Wait a minute. I was so excited I forgot to hold on to my notes.'

After a brief silence, she came back on the line. 'So, next I went to research my match with RPL. I still don't know exactly who he or she is, but the line goes up to our mutual great-grandparents, Howard and Letitia Smith, too, then down to his or her grandfather, Thomas Smith and his son, William who must be RPL's father. RPL has a slew of brothers and sisters, but on RPL's family tree they're just listed by their initials, so gee, thank a million, RPL. At that point, my eyes started to cross, so I decided to leave all those second cousins for later because, as you pointed out with SharynG, they were second cousins, not first, so that meant I probably descended from the third child, Felicity's line. Unfortunately, unless I missed it, there's no family tree for Felicity, and neither SharynG nor RPL expanded their trees out to relatives that distant.'

'That's the case more often than not,' I said. 'The best you can do is use Howard and Letitia Smith as a starting point and work down, building Felicity's tree from there.'

'Yay, me! That's exactly what I did!' I heard papers rustling, the clunk of a cell phone hitting the floor followed by a muffled, 'Drat!'

'Noel? You OK?'

'Yeah, trying to juggle too many things at once. Look, can I come over? This was all making sense at four o'clock this morning, but now that the sun's come up and I'm talking to you about it, I'm not so sure. I really need an expert opinion.'

'Absolutely delighted to help out, but do me a favor and have a nap first. One needs to think clearly in this biz.'

Noel snorted. 'I must be getting old. I haven't pulled an all-nighter since I was finishing my senior essay at St John's. Is three o'clock OK?'

'Perfect. I'll rev up the Keurig.'

'That'll be super, Mrs Ives. Right now I'm running on fumes.'

Noel arrived spot on time, bright-eyed, rosy-cheeked and bundled up against the cold in a hooded, lambswool duffel coat. While she unfastened the toggles on her coat, she handed me a clear plastic folder to hold, a folder so overstuffed that the snap wouldn't close.

I hefted the folder. 'You've done all this in a week?'

'Yeah. Working in split-screen mode was making me cross-eyed, so I've been giving the printer a workout.' Grinning, she draped her coat over a hook on the hall tree and stuffed her gloves in one of its pockets. 'Had to run out to Mighty Mart for a new set of ink cartridges, too. Honest to God, Canon could afford to give its printers away for free considering all the money they're extorting out of us for print cartridges.'

We made a brief detour to the kitchen where we brewed ourselves mugs of coffee, then adjourned to the dining room table where I'd set up my laptop and we'd have room to spread out. Before he left for the High Spot, Paul had lit the gas logs in the fireplace, so the room felt warm and cozy.

'First things first,' I said, as I powered up my laptop, waited for the screen to populate, then clicked on the GenTree icon. 'Let's see what you've been up to.'

Noel began leafing through the printouts in her folder, selecting those she wished to lay out on the table. 'Start with Howard and Letitia,' she suggested.

While Noel sat by silently, I took several minutes to review her work. She'd obviously identified the correct Felicity Smith who, on the 1950 US Census was five years old, living with her parents and two older brothers, Thomas eleven and Andrew seven, on East College Street in Granville, Ohio. 'Good work,' I said.

Noel beamed. 'I couldn't find a marriage record for Felicity online . . .' she began.

'Ohio marriage records are hit and miss,' I cut in. 'Some counties are online, some aren't.'

'Yeah, so I discovered. That's why I used the password you gave me to newspapers dotcom, and found an announcement in the *Granville Sentinel* for Felicity's wedding to a guy named Donald Miller in December of 1980.' Noel slid a printout across the table. 'She was thirty-five years old, practically an old maid.'

'I beg your pardon?' I said with a teasing frown.

'For back then, I mean,' Noel amended with a grin. 'Anyway, according to records in the Ohio Birth Index, Donald and Felicity had two kids. Ashley Lynn was born on November 12, 1982 and her brother, Jason Don in June, two years later. I'm twenty-seven, so it's not entirely outside the realm of possibility that Jason could father a child at age twelve, but it's much more likely that Ashley is my mother.'

Even though the room was toasty, I felt a chill. 'In that case, Ashley would have been fourteen when she became pregnant with you.'

'Yeah, creepy, isn't it? I wasn't able to find any birth records for a mother named Ashley Miller, so perhaps she had the baby in secret and gave it away?' Noel raised an eyebrow. 'It fits, doesn't it?'

'It fits, Noel, but that doesn't mean that's what happened.' I paused to collect my thoughts. 'Look, there's a good chance that Ashley and Jason are both still living. They'd be, what . . .' I did a quick calculation. 'Forty-two and forty, respectively.'

'I couldn't find any records at all for Ashley Miller, but that's not surprising. She probably goes by her married name now. But, according to the most recent US Public Records Index, a Jason D. Miller was living on McKinney Crossing Road in Newark, Ohio as recently as 2020. That's not even eight miles away from Granville. It's gotta be the same guy.' She slid another printout my way. Tapped it with a finger. 'He'd be my uncle. That's his address. If we can find him, we can hopefully find my mother.'

'Before we climb into the car and drive to Ohio, did you do a Facebook search?'

'No! It didn't even occur to me!'

I turned back to the laptop. 'Let's do it now, then.'

Jason Don Miller did have a Facebook entry, but it looked like he'd created the record ten years before when Facebook was all the rage, uploaded a profile picture of his dog, a ridiculously cute Yorkshire terrier, then completely neglected his account. He had ten friends, but none of them were named Ashley or even Miller.

Under the About tab, there was no contact information to show, although he did indicate he was from Newark, Ohio and had been born in 1984. 'Bingo,' Noel said when she read the birth date.

'This also says he works at OSU-Newark,' I pointed out.

'What's OSU?'

'Ohio State University. If we're lucky, he'll be a professor of something, listed under faculty and not working somewhere in administration or the athletic department.'

While Noel watched over my shoulder, I navigated to the OSU-Newark webpage, clicked Academics on the menu bar, then selected Faculty on the pull-down menu. For some reason known only to the OSU website developers, OSU-Newark faculty were alphabetized by first name, but they had provided a handy search box, so I typed in Jason Miller and hit return.

'Look at that!' I crowed.

Noel's uncle, if we were correct in our assumptions, was a professor of psychology at the university. We'd hit the jackpot. The faculty entry included his photograph, his email address at OSU. edu and a telephone number in the 740 area code. I tapped a few keys and sent the directory page to my printer.

Noel leaned in, so close that I had to scoot my chair over so we could scrutinize Jason's photo together.

Jason Don Miller was a young, genial-looking forty. He sported a stubbly, sand-colored beard and moustache, but his head was completely bald. Piercing blue eyes stared into the camera through the lenses of a pair of wire-rimmed eyeglasses. 'Hard to see a family resemblance,' Noel said, sounding disappointed. She cupped her forehead with both hands and scraped her hair away from her face. 'What do you think?'

Dutifully, my eyes flicked from Noel to her uncle and back, then I burst out laughing. 'Maybe, if you shave your head and grow a little beard.'

'There's another website we can check, too,' I said as I navigated away from Ohio State University. 'TruePeopleSearchdotcom is a free website where you can look up almost anyone by name, address or phone number.' I filled in the search boxes with what information we had on Jason and hit return. 'And there he is!' I whooped, as his record appeared. 'It's at the same address you already found on McKinney Crossing Road, but now you have his home phone number.' I sent that record to the printer, too.

'I can't believe this is happening.' Noel flopped back in her chair. 'What should I do now?'

I checked the time on my laptop screen. 'It's just a little after four o'clock on a Wednesday afternoon. Jason may be in his office.' I picked her cell phone up from where it lay on the table and handed it to her. 'You're going to call him, right?'

Noel pressed the phone, screen down, flat against her T-shirt. 'What if he doesn't answer?'

'You leave a message, silly.'

She blinked nervously. 'What will I say?'

'When in doubt, try the truth. Your name is Noel Sinclair, you're looking for Ashley Miller and you understand he may be Ashley's brother.'

'What if he hangs up on me?'

'Then you won't know any less than you know now.'

Noel held her phone at arm's length in front of her and stared at the screen. 'Oh, golly. I'm a bundle of nerves.'

I smiled in what I hoped was an encouraging way. 'Do you want me to dial the number for you?'

She shook her head so vigorously her gold hoop earrings bounced against her neck. 'No, no. I'll do it.' Noel took three deep, steadying breaths, counting each one aloud, then exhaled and began to punch in the numbers. In the seconds before the phone started ringing on the other end, she said, 'I'll put it on speaker.'

One ring, two, three . . . and then a brusque, professional voice answered, 'Good afternoon. This is Jason.'

TWENTY-ONE

Noel stared straight ahead, stunned, like a deer caught in the headlights. She opened her mouth, but no words came out. I poked her on the arm and mouthed, 'Say something!'

'Hello?' Jason said.

Noel took a deep breath. 'Hello, Mr Miller? My name is Noel Sinclair and I'm trying to locate a woman named Ashley Miller. I think you might be her brother?'

There was a long pause, then: 'Yes, Ashley was my sister.'

Noel inhaled sharply. 'Was? I'm sorry, sir, but has she passed away?'

Jason sniffed. 'Sorry, no. Unfortunate choice of words. What I should have said is that I haven't seen or heard from my sister in more than twenty-five years, so, frankly, I don't know whether she's alive or dead.' He paused. The silence lengthened uncomfortably. 'Can you tell me why you're looking for Ashley?'

'Well, I recently took a DNA test, two of them actually, and after consulting with a professional genealogist' – she dug her elbow into my ribs as if warning me not to contradict her promotion of me from 'amateur' to 'professional' – 'we think I may be your niece.'

'Oh. My. God.' Jason was quiet so long I thought perhaps he'd hung up.

'Sir?'

'Sorry, I just had to sit down. As you might imagine, this news comes as a surprise.'

Noel pressed on, sounding more confident. 'According to the DNA and the research we've done, I'm pretty sure Ashley is my mother. I'm guessing she never told you about me.'

'You guess correctly. After she left home we, uh, lost touch.'

'I'm sorry, sir. That must have been hard.'

'Please,' Jason said after a moment. 'Call me J.D. Everybody does.'

'I can understand that I might be coming as a shock to you after all these years, uh, J.D., but I'd be happy to pay for your DNA test if you'd like independent confirmation.'

'No, I'm quite comfortable with the two you've already paid for, Noel, was it?'

'Yes. Noel Sinclair.'

'But tell me this,' J.D. pressed. 'If you're looking for your mother, that must mean you don't know where she is either.'

'Sadly, I don't. In fact, I've never known where, or until now, even who she is. Twenty-seven years ago, I was abandoned on a doorstep when I was just a few days old. Fortunately, I was adopted by a wonderful couple who raised me as their own. I didn't find out until very recently that they weren't my biological parents.'

After a sharp intake of breath, J.D. said, 'Abandoned? Without a note or anything?'

'The only thing my mother left me was my name, Noel.'

'Twenty-seven years ago. *Shee-it*. That means . . .' J.D. paused and cleared his throat. 'Look, do you mind if we switch to a FaceTime call?'

Noel's eyes slid down to her lap, then over to me as if seeking confirmation that she was dressed appropriately for a face-to-face encounter. I nodded and gave her a thumbs-up.

'I'd like that,' she said. 'Call back on this number?'

'Five minutes,' J.D. promised. 'Give me five minutes.'

'This is the longest five minutes in my life,' Noel muttered as she stared at the screen of her iPhone and watched the minutes tick away. 'Do you think he'll actually call back?'

'Well, if he doesn't, you know where he is. You could write him a letter. Email him. Send pictures.' I reached out and squeezed her hand. 'He doesn't come across as the kind of person who'd simply write you off, though. Put yourself in his shoes. There he is, a college professor going about his usual day, grading papers, listening to some student's lame-brain excuse for why his term paper is late, and then, wham! Your phone call comes out of the blue. The poor man's probably reeling.'

We had reached the seven-minute mark and Noel was fidgeting in her chair, blinking rapidly as if fighting off tears.

When her cell phone finally rang she started, glanced at me as if to draw moral support, then accepted the call. 'Uncle J.D.?' Her voice was soft, tentative, as if experimenting with the sound of the unfamiliar name.

Once J.D.'s image appeared, she propped the phone up against the screen of my open laptop so she'd be hands-free and I could see him, too. I moved my chair carefully to one side so I'd stay out of the picture.

Noel's uncle was clearly returning the call from his office, surrounded by books arranged higgledy-piggledy on the bookshelves behind him. 'You've got hair,' Noel chirped.

J.D. laughed and casually brushed a wayward coppery-gold strand out of his eyes. 'You must be referring to my faculty mug shot. Don't know what I was thinking.'

'I . . . I . . .' Noel began.

'Please, Noel. Don't say anything for just a minute. Just let me look at you.'

From his side of the screen in Newark, Ohio, Jason Don Miller stared out at his new-found niece. Seconds ticked by. Finally, he swiped a cheek with his fingertips and said, 'I don't need any DNA test to confirm what you've told me, Noel. You look so much like my sister.'

J.D. swiveled in his desk chair and fumbled for something on the bookshelf behind him. When he turned around, we could see that he was holding a framed photograph. J.D. aimed it toward the camera and adjusted its position until the photo was centered and filled Noel's tiny iPhone screen.

A teenage girl smiled out at us slyly, rocking a profusion of coppery-blonde curls à la Carrie Bradshaw. In sharp contrast to the *Sex and the City* hairdo vibe, Ashley wore a high-necked ruffled blouse under a denim pinafore dress dotted with buttons.

I gasped. I couldn't help it. Noel was a clone of her mother.

'Ashley had just turned fourteen when this picture was taken.' J.D. managed a melancholy smile. 'Ashley hated that dress, but Bev insisted that she wear it when we went to Sears for a photo session. There's one of me somewhere, taken on the same day. Unless Bev cleaned house of that. Coat and tie, hair all slicked back, natch.'

'Who's Bev?' Noel wanted to know.

'Beverly. My dad's second wife. I refuse to call her my stepmother.'

Noel quickly moved past that, sensing correctly, as we later found out, that there was bad blood between J.D. and his stepmother. 'Can you send me a copy of my mother's picture?'

'I can, and I will. And I'll see what other photos I can turn up.'

Noel shared her email address with J.D., then said, 'I know you're probably very busy, but do you have time to tell me a little about my mother?'

J.D.'s eyes strayed to his right and back, as if checking a clock. 'All the time in the world, Noel. I'm just trying to think where to begin.' He scratched his beard thoughtfully. 'Ashley and I were very close, Noel, just two years apart. Our mom was already in her mid-thirties when she had us and was working full-time. She'd been married before to a guy named Danny, but he was killed in Vietnam in 1966 when she was only twenty-one. After that, she moved back in with her parents and took a job at the bookstore at Denison University. That's where she met my dad, at Denison, I mean. He was a track and field coach. By then, it was 1980, my grandparents had both passed away, and I think Mom heard her biological clock tick-tick-ticking. Anyway, she quit her job, married Donald, and had Ashley and me, bing-bing, and then, seven years later, she died.' J.D. paused to take a breath. 'Breast cancer.'

'I'm so sorry,' Noel said.

I had a flashback to the afternoon after my own breast cancer surgery when I woke up in a hospital bed to the anguished sobs of my daughter, Emily, out in the hallway. I could, quite literally, feel J.D.'s pain.

On the screen, J.D. shrugged. 'It was really, really hard, but what can you do? Dad remarried right away – he had two little kids who needed taking care of – and . . . well, let's just say that Ashley and Bev had their claws out from the git-go. Me? I pretty much stayed on the sidelines and silently rooted for my sister.

'Anyway, it was during spring break. Ashley and Bev had a big fight, it's always been a mystery to me what about, but Ashley made up her mind to run away. She came into my bedroom that night and told me she was going to hitchhike to Columbus. I was a pretty unhappy kid myself, so I decided I wouldn't let her go without me. Pretty gutsy for a twelve-year-old, huh?' He paused for a moment, tapping his chin absentmindedly with tented fingers. 'I figured it'd be a great adventure. I'd been to the Columbus Zoo and to the science museum, and they were super cool, but as it turns out, Ashley and I never got as far as Columbus. We were picked up almost right away at a truck stop on Interstate 70 by a guy heading east in a VW camper van.'

I squirmed in my chair, feeling antsy. The armchair detective in me silently screamed questions like: Who was the guy? What color was the van? Did you get a license plate number? But I didn't want to interrupt the flow of J.D.'s story.

'After a couple of overnight stops when we were eating Vienna sausages and beans out of a can, I started getting homesick, so they pulled off the Pennsylvania Turnpike at the New Stanton service area and I called Dad on a pay phone. Ashley waited in the van, watching out for me until Dad came to pick me up, but then she went on ahead with the guy in the van, and that's the last time I saw her.'

I couldn't keep my mouth shut one second more. I poked my head into camera range and asked, 'Didn't anyone report Ashley missing?'

If J.D. was surprised, his face didn't show it. 'Ah, you must be the professional genealogist Noel mentioned.'

'Hannah Ives,' I said, introducing myself. 'Don't listen to her. I'm just an old family friend.'

J.D. nodded. 'Noted. And to answer your question, Ashley wasn't really missing, was she? We knew she was with this guy, Bubs, and she sent postcards from time to time – addressed to me, by the way – saying she was OK, and I wasn't to worry. There were a couple of phone calls early on – one at Thanksgiving and the other just before Christmas, but . . .' His voice trailed off.

I was thinking what a scumbag Donald Miller must have been not to have called the cops on the pervert who had kidnapped his underage daughter. Our Emily had been twenty-one and already out of college when she ran off with Dante – now her husband – to follow the rock group Phish, but even still, Paul and I had been worried sick.

As if reading my mind, Jason said, 'Dad was pretty fed up with Ashley by then. She'd run away before, but she'd always come back within a day or two. And Bev? She said Ashley had made her bed and she'd have to lie in it.'

'At fourteen?' I was incredulous.

'You didn't know my dad. He died in a VA hospital a couple of years back, an embittered old SOB. After his death, I lost track of Bev. Don't know where she is. Don't care.

'The summer after my junior year at Duke,' he continued, 'I scraped enough money together from my summer job to hire a private detective to look for Ashley, but after working on it for four months, he came up empty-handed.'

'Did Bubs have a real name?' Noel wanted to know.

'If he did, I never heard it.'

'How old was he, do you think?' I asked.

J.D. leaned back in his chair and looked up, as if the answer were written on the ceiling, then he leaned forward, rested his elbows on his desktop and addressed me directly. 'I've thought about that a lot over the years, Hannah. To me, he seemed old, real old, but everyone looks ancient to a twelve-year-old, right? If I think about it logically, he had a drivers' license, so he had to have been at least sixteen. But he also owned the van, and you can't own a car unless you're at least eighteen.' He paused. 'Not long after he picked us up, Bubs got pulled over for speeding. The trooper checked his driver's license and registration, then let him go with a warning, so everything must have been on the up-and-up. Looking back on it now, I'd say he was probably in his early twenties. He was certainly older than the Denison students we were surrounded by all the time, but not by much.'

'Do you remember where Ashley sent the postcards from?' I asked.

'Bubs must have kept them on the move because they came from all over the east coast. New York, Pennsylvania, New Jersey, Delaware, Maryland, Virginia. Postmarks didn't mean much to me at the time, I'm afraid. I wish I'd paid more attention. I kept one postcard up on my dresser for a while, though, because she'd bought it at the National Aquarium and it had pictures of dolphins on it. She'd written, *I'll take you to see the dolphin show some day* and she'd signed it with hugs and kisses.'

'Do you still have the postcards?'

'That was more than twenty-five years ago, Hannah. When I went off to Duke, Bev converted my bedroom to a jewelry-making studio and pretty much sanitized the place. Not even my soccer trophies escaped the dumpster.'

While J.D. talked, I jotted down notes. Donald Miller and the Wicked Stepmother of the Midwest might have shown no interest in young Ashley's whereabouts, but even after all the water that had passed under the proverbial bridge, Noel and I certainly did.

Meanwhile, Noel gave her uncle the CliffsNotes version of her own life story and the direction her life had been headed before being upended by the results of an innocent recreational DNA test.

'Let's plan to meet, maybe sometime over the summer?' J.D. was saying to his niece when I tuned in again.

'I'd like that very much,' Noel replied. 'In the meantime, I promise to stay in touch. Let you know what's happening.'

'Same here,' he replied. After a beat, he added, 'Is Hannah still there?'

Noel nodded, then rotated her phone until J.D. was looking straight at me. 'Yes?'

'I just thought of something,' J.D. said. 'He'd be in his fifties now, of course, but back then, Bubs looked a bit like that guy in *Pirates of the Caribbean.*'

'Johnny Depp?' I suggested, my mind boggling as I tried to picture Ashley running off with a disheveled pirate with bad teeth.

'No, not him, the other one. He played in *Lord of the Rings*, too. The elf with the great hair.'

It'd been a long time since I'd binged on the movies in the *Lord of the Rings* franchise, but I knew exactly who J.D. was talking about. My granddaughter, Chloe, once had a poster of Orlando Bloom as Legolas taped to the wall of her room. 'In what way?' I asked. 'Certainly not the pointy ears.'

'It was the hair, I think. Platinum blond. Almost white. But now, who knows? He could be bald as an egg.'

'If we track him down, would you be able to identify him?' Noel cut in.

'Definitely. I spent two days and nights with the guy. You don't forget someone that easily.' He paused. 'He drank Labatt's Blue, by the way. Rooted for the Jets. And he snored.'

TWENTY-TWO

Zoom sessions with the Silent Sleuths were often on a Friday, usually at seven thirty and always managed to surprise, thanks to Izzy. Izzy had a green screen app and enjoyed playing around with her background image. Tonight she was calling in from the Great Pyramids of Giza.

'Thank you!' I said when I sat down with a glass of white wine and linked in to discover her sitting in front of a sun-drenched desert landscape. 'I dragged the trash out to the main road this morning and I still can't feel my toes.'

'Cheers!' Izzy raised her own glass of wine. 'It was either Egypt or the beach at Waikiki.'

'Oh, you really know how to hurt a guy, Iz,' Jack moaned a few seconds later after he Zoomed in from his home in Glen Burnie, dressed like a lumberjack in a red and black plaid shirt, his abundant silver hair looking as flyaway as his eyebrows. 'My furnace is on the fritz. I'm locked into the den with a space heater until the service guy shows up. If I suddenly disappear, you'll know why.'

Mark took a sip from a mug I knew was a favorite and most likely contained decaf coffee: *JESUS TAKE THE HELM*. 'Boo hoo, poor you, Jack. It got all the way up to twenty degrees in New Market today. Compared to us, Baltimore's having a heatwave.'

'You're dressed up tonight, Mark,' I observed, noting that he wore a dark green V-neck sweater over an open collar shirt instead of his more customary Navy fatigues.

'Reporting in from the Nativity Pageant from hell, ladies and gentlemen. Joseph got caught in the robing room nailing one of the shepherdesses, the donkey bit Melchior in the butt, and when I ran to fetch the first-aid kit, the goat ate my sermon. I was all for calling a halt to the whole damn thing, but seems it's a fifty-two-year-old tradition and the biggest money-maker of the year, so the deacons were unmoved.'

I tried to stifle a laugh, but failed. 'I'd pay extra to see that.'

Mark removed his wire-framed glasses and massaged the bridge of his nose between a thumb and index finger. 'You have no idea what it's like dealing with stage mothers convinced this pageant will be their toddler's big break into show business.'

'*Au contraire*, Mark. I've done my time, sitting for three hours on a folding metal chair in a school gym smelling of cold pizza and wet socks waiting to hear my grandson sing, "Rudolph the Red-Nosed Reindeer." There are even recordings.'

'One of the labors of Hercules,' Mark said. 'Exception noted.'

Izzy waved a finger. 'Play nice, you two.'

'Speaking of playing nice,' I said, 'since we last met, Izzy's dragged me out on a couple of expeditions, both related to the poisoned eagles that were rescued from the farm next door.'

'It's shaping up to be a podcast,' Izzy said, going on to describe our visit to the Hoots Raptor Rescue Center and her interview with Mee Semcken in some detail. 'But it's also a condemnation of the canned hunt business and an exposé of the lengths to which some people will go to protect their investments.'

'Like our neighbor,' I cut in. 'Wesley Butler poisoned those eagles, either on his own say-so, or because David Tuckerman asked him to. I'm convinced of it. Tell the guys what we found in the barn, Izzy.'

Jack had been leaning back in his chair nursing a longneck beer, but he suddenly snapped to attention. 'Barn? What barn?'

'We were searching David Tuckerman's barn for Hannah's cat,' Izzy lied smoothly.

'Bullshit,' Jack said. 'I was present the last time Hannah went looking for her imaginary cat, remember?'

Izzy bristled. 'Relax, Jack. Nobody caught us at it.'

'Legal issues aside for a moment,' Mark said, 'tell us what you found.'

'Two bottles of carbofuran hidden in a toilet tank and a carton of canned sardines.'

'So, what's the point?' Jack asked. 'It's not illegal to own carbofuran, and it certainly isn't illegal to keep a supply of tinned sardines around. Ask my wife. She piles sardines on crackers and dabs them with mustard.'

'I'm betting your wife doesn't store her sardines in the bathroom,' I said. 'Case closed as far as I'm concerned.'

Jack wagged his head. 'You took a huge risk going in like that. Trespassers have been known to get shot, and the last time I noticed, there's no shortage of guns in Tilghman County.'

'Nobody caught us, Jack,' Izzy repeated. 'All I took were pictures.'

'Izzy forwarded them to the officer from Fish and Wildlife,' I added helpfully. 'It's up to the authorities now.'

'Circumstantial,' Jack muttered, looking weary. 'Unless the lab results tie that particular formulation of carbofuran to the crime, that specific brand of sardines . . .'

'The Furadan was manufactured in Mexico,' I told him. 'And they were Titus brand sardines, packed in oil. Canned in Morocco.'

'Maybe . . .' Jack considered the beer bottle thoughtfully. 'But I sure as hell wouldn't count on it, ladies.'

'It can't be a coincidence,' I said. 'And if Fish and Wildlife doesn't come through, I have a Plan B.'

'And what might that be?' Jack asked.

'Talk to Wesley Butler about it directly, maybe con a confession out of him. For all he knows, Paul and I are totally in favor of what he did – many locals are.'

Izzy snorted. 'I wouldn't stoop so low.'

Clearly, until Izzy heard back from the Fish and Wildlife Service, with or without having to file a FOIA, this conversation was going nowhere. Besides, I had another issue I needed to discuss.

The night before, I'd slept fitfully, partly due to a cup of cappuccino I'd enjoyed too close to bedtime, but mostly because I was lying awake worrying about Noel's mother, young Ashley Miller. After Izzy's scoffing comment, she'd gone mum, so I jumped into the silence with both feet. 'Jack, I have a favor to ask, and Mark, you can help me out, too.'

'As long as it doesn't involve phantom cats,' Mark said, eyes focused directly on the camera, and at me, over the rim of his mug.

'No cats, I promise.'

'Run it by us,' Jack said.

'Not long ago, I ran into a young woman who used to babysit for my grandkids. Her name's Noel Sinclair. She and her sister thought it'd be a hoot to take one of those DNA tests and – you probably know where this is going – surprise! Not only are the girls not sisters, Noel isn't related to her parents at all. Long story short, it turns out Noel was abandoned on the doorstep of a church parsonage in Bentonville, Maryland, the minister and his wife decided to keep her, and the family doctor, a loyal parishioner, falsified Noel's birth certificate.'

'Falsified? That's a new one on me,' Mark said.

'Indeed. Noel and I have talked to the doctor, so I can fill you in later on how that bit of chicanery was accomplished. Fast forward to a couple of weeks ago. Noel came to me for help analyzing her DNA matches,' I continued. 'I'm still working on the paternal matches, which are thin on the ground. Fortunately, the matches on the maternal side were so good that it wasn't all that hard to identify the mother. Since then, Noel's talked to her mother's only brother out in Ohio, but he says the last time he saw his sister was in 1997, on the Pennsylvania Turnpike, riding off willingly with some dude named Bubs in a VW camper van.'

'How old was she at the time?' Mark wanted to know.

'Fourteen,' I said. 'The brother was twelve.'

'I hate stories like this,' Mark muttered.

'Yeah, me, too.' I heaved a sigh. 'Anyway, this is what I know. Twenty-seven years ago, shortly before December twenty-first, a pregnant girl who had turned fifteen only the month before, gave birth to a baby girl.'

Mark waved for attention. 'Not in a hospital, I gather, because of the falsified birth certificate.'

'Correct. The infant's umbilical cord was tied off with a shoe-string, according to the doctor.'

Mark groaned. 'Jesus, Mary and Joseph, as my good Catholic aunt used to say. Most fifteen-year-old girls I know are obsessing over their appearance, fearful of missing out, and worrying about being ghosted by some heartthrob on social media.'

'Yeah, sucks.' After a quiet moment to take a sip from the wine glass I'd been neglecting, I pressed on. 'So, this is why I'm worried, guys. Up until around the time the baby came, Ashley was sending postcards to her brother fairly regularly. After Christmas that year, nothing.' I paused to let that sink in. 'And although she always knew where her daughter was, she never tried to make contact, at least not as far as we know. There could be a reasonable explanation for that, of course, but . . .'

'You think something happened to her,' Mark said.

I nodded. 'I do.'

'Did anyone file a missing persons report?' Jack asked.

'According to the brother, no.' I ran an index finger thoughtfully round and around the rim of my wine glass. 'According to him, the stepmother was a piece of work. Washed her hands of the girl.'

'So nobody was out looking for her.'

'Sadly, no. You'd think a teacher at the high school she was attending would have made some inquiries, but if they did, the loathsome parents probably cooked up some plausible excuse to explain Ashley's absence.'

I revealed to the Sleuths that I had risen well before dawn that morning to comb local newspaper databases for any articles about bodies being discovered in the months immediately following the Christmas of 1997. 'I don't have much to show for it,' I confessed. 'I concentrated on the archives of the two local papers I could find online, the *Daily Times* out of Salisbury and Easton's *Star Democrat*. There were bodies, a few, but none that went unidentified. There's always the possibility that I missed something, though. Lots of news got buried under front-page hoo-hah over negotiations for the big Hyatt Regency resort and conference center that was being planned for Cambridge.' I polished off the wine and set the glass aside. 'About the time the sun came up, it occurred to me that I didn't need to go tripping down Memory Lane to the time when Bill Clinton and Monica Lewinsky dominated the headlines, because reading about the scandal over Lewinsky's blue dress reminded me that we already had Noel's DNA profile. We could definitely start working with that.'

'Have you uploaded Noel's profile to GEDmatch?' Jack wanted to know.

'Yes, I have. If I send you Noel's kit number, can you ask one of your police contacts to run it through CODIS and see if there's a match to any unidentified victims in the FBI databases?'

After Jack readily agreed, I turned to Mark for help with a more complicated assignment.

Mark Wallis was our team's expert on the Murder Accountability Project, or MAP, the nation's most complete compilation of case information for homicides, mostly unsolved, going back to 1976. You can search all kinds of data – geography, type of victim, method of killing, time frame – and even drill down to the age, race, sex and ethnicity of victims.

I was familiar with the database – culled from the FBI's Uniform Crime Reports, as well as police departments from all over the US – but while working on previous cases, Mark had perfected the art of navigating, manipulating and analyzing MAP data. He could make the software jump through hoops while the three of us looked on in awe.

'I'm forwarding a photograph of Ashley taken shortly before she disappeared,' I told Mark. 'We know she was alive on December twenty-first, 1997, when she left Noel with the Sinclairs, but after that . . .?' I shrugged. 'If she was still hanging out with this guy Bubs in the VW, they could have driven off anywhere, I suppose. But, if I had just given birth to a baby in the back of a camper, I don't think I'd feel like gallivanting all over the country, so maybe we should concentrate on the Delmarva Peninsula to begin with?'

'I'll get right on it,' Mark promised. 'Did Ashley have any identifying marks?'

I shuddered at the thought. 'You'll have to ask her brother about that.' As Mark jotted down J.D. Miller's contact information, I began to relax, feeling a wave of relief as that task was lifted from my shoulders and placed solidly on Mark's.

'What kind of name is Bubs, anyway?' Jack mused.

'The jury is still out on that,' I said with a shrug. 'According to Professor Google, it may be a shortened version of "bubba" which is a corruption of "brother." Or, it could also stand for "buddy," as in "Hey, bub, what do you think you're doing?"'

'Who'd want to go through life being saddled with a name like Bubs?' Jack muttered. 'Thank goodness my parents named me Jack. It's not short for John or Jackson or anything else. Just plain Jack.'

'Well, in the meantime, boys and girls, Just Plain Hannah is going to double down on Noel's biological father. So far, I've hit a brick wall. Noel has a strong eight hundred and sixty-six centimorgan match on the paternal side, but the guy doesn't have a public tree and isn't responding to messages. At that level, he could be Noel's first cousin, a half uncle, a great-grandparent or a great-grandchild. Applying common sense here, I can eliminate the great-grandchild, and any great-grandparent on that side is likely to be dead, so that narrows it down. Because folks often get test kits for Christmas, I'm hoping more people related to Noel will upload their data in the coming weeks. Ancestry adds about two million records per day, they claim, and GenTree almost as many, so I'll just keep going online to check. It'll give me something to do here over the holidays.'

'I thought you were going back to Annapolis,' Izzy said.

'We've decided to stick around for a while longer to see what an Eastern Shore Christmas is all about. We're planning to spend Christmas Day in Annapolis with Emily and crew, but otherwise . . .'

I shrugged. 'This time of year, it's hard to get their full attention. The spa's a zoo trying to squeeze in everyone who suddenly remembers they better schedule a full-body overhaul if they want to look buff for their holiday parties. There's also the annual run on gift certificates, not to mention when folks start calling on December twenty-sixth to make appointments to redeem them. Good for business, though, so can't complain. How about you?'

'Mother,' she said, casting her eyes upward in a dear-heaven-help-me gesture.

'I've got the kids for the holidays,' Jack added hastily, sounding almost apologetic. 'I'm taking them on a Disney cruise out of Fort Lauderdale.'

That answered the questions about Jack's wife, who I had never met and whose name I sat there trying to recall, and the status of their troubled marriage.

'I've paid in advance for the beer package,' Jack continued. 'And the kids qualify for the Teens Club, so I plan to spend some quality time lounging around the swimming pool working on my tan.'

'And if I survive this Christmas pageant,' Mark said, 'and that's a big if, I'm off to Stoweflake Mountain Resort for a hedonistic week of skiing and ice fishing with my brother, Abe. He's flying in from Philly.'

'You got any camels in your Christmas pageant, Mark?' I asked.

'No camels, but we've got the aforementioned donkey and goat, plus two sheep and a pig, all courtesy of the New Market 4-H Club. Why do you ask?'

'A cautionary tale. Back on December twenty-first, 1997, according to the *Star Democrat*, Ernie the camel slipped his tether and wandered away from the Nativity pageant at Kent Island United Methodist Church. The Wise Men, in full costume, chased him down Route 50, but alas, before they could catch up with him, Ernie collided with the front end of a Volvo station wagon and was killed.'

After several seconds of silence, Izzy and Jack burst out laughing.

'Absolutely true!' I chuckled. 'And the story went viral once PETA jumped all over the Methodists for precipitating this avoidable tragedy.'

'Gee, thanks, Hannah. You really know how to cheer a pastor up.'

I grinned straight at the camera. 'You're very welcome.'

TWENTY-THREE

E arly the following morning, as I was slicing a banana over a bowl of Cheerios, my cell phone began to vibrate where I'd parked it on the kitchen counter. Knife in one hand and banana in the other, I leaned over to check the caller ID.

Izzy.

I laid down my weapons, wiped my hands on a paper towel and swiped the screen on with a clean index finger. 'What's up, Iz?'

'Just called to report a miracle. Wesley Butler has finally stopped avoiding me. He just texted that he'd be home all day and that I should feel free to pop in.'

'That's good,' I said. 'But why are you telling me?'

'I'm thinking you'll want to come along.'

'*Moi?* Ha! Only if you let me give the SOB cookies laced with carbofuran.'

'Ah, when Hannah has her mind set, she is very hard to turn,' Izzy intoned.

'That's what Paul says.' I dropped the banana peel into the ceramic compost jar I keep next to the sink and replaced the lid. 'Besides, knowing what we know, what on earth are you going to talk to him about?'

'My article isn't a hit job, Hannah, not entirely anyway. For the full picture, I'll need the viewpoint of someone whose job it is to manage a reserve shooting area. I'm pitching it as a day-in-the-life-of sort of interview. You know, the challenges of dealing with an absentee landlord, for instance. Or the pernickety outfitters. Or clients from hell. Everyone opens up when they get the opportunity to talk about clients from hell.'

I snorted. 'OK, you talked me into it. What time?'

'I've got a blog to post, then I'll head out. Shall we say eleven?'

'See you then,' I said, and sat down to finish my breakfast.

People are creatures of habit. Sometimes they sign up with the same username across multiple social platforms. I was hoping to discover that Noel's first cousin, SimonSez, had been one of them, but had made little progress so far. I'd just finished scanning over one hundred SimonSezes in the Facebook search directory – ninety-eight to be exact – when Izzy rapped on the front door. I closed the lid on my laptop and went to answer it, opening the door with one hand and grabbing my parka off the hall tree with the other. 'Come in where it's warm,' I said. 'Ooops, I almost forgot.' I held up a finger. 'I'll be right back.'

'What's in the baggie?' Izzy asked when I returned from the kitchen.

'Chocolate chip cookies.'

Izzy squinted at the baggie suspiciously.

'No worries,' I said as I zipped out the door ahead of her. 'This time, I left out the carbofuran.'

Rather than walk, Izzy insisted we take her silver Hyundai for the short trip down to the Tuckerman place. Forty-eight degrees outside, according to my weather app, so I didn't argue. Five minutes later, she pulled into the driveway, parked behind a red, late model Kia Sorento, an SUV I deduced belonged to the Butlers from the stick figure decals affixed to the rear window – a dad, mom, two children and two dogs.

Izzy switched off the ignition, scooped up her keys and was halfway up the sidewalk by the time I climbed out of the passenger seat and caught up with her. I waited a step below while she marched up to the door and pressed the doorbell.

Nobody answered.

'Maybe it's broken,' I offered helpfully.

Izzy scowled, mashed her thumb down on the doorbell again, hard.

This time, the door was opened by a woman I judged to be much younger than her husband. Balanced on her left hip, a chubby infant about ten months old was giving a pacifier a good workout. In the living room behind her, a toddler sat on a braided rag rug amid a sea of oversized Lego blocks, building a wall around a Tonka dump truck. Even though it was winter, the children's mother was dressed in flip-flops, jeans and a short-sleeved T-shirt. Her chestnut hair was parted cleanly on the side and clipped back with a red plastic barrette. She squinted at us in the sunlight out of her right eye. The left eye was swollen shut, the skin surrounding it puffy and tinged with purple.

'Gosh! What happened to your eye?' fell out of my mouth before I could stop it.

She touched her eyelid lightly with the fingers of her free hand. 'Aren't I a mess?' She flashed a pained smile. 'Black flies,' she explained. 'Don't know where they come from this time of year. Wes says maybe they hatched out during that heatwave. I don't get out into the barn much,' she added, jiggling the baby by way of illustration. 'But lesson learned.'

'I'm Isabel Randall. Wes may have mentioned that I wanted to interview him for an article I'm writing on RSAs.'

'And I'm Hannah Ives,' I said, stepping up on the landing when Izzy made no move to introduce me. 'My husband and I own Our Song, the cottage next door.'

'Oh, right. And I'm Cindy. Wes mentioned he'd gone over to talk to you about the sick eagles.'

'Izzy and I visited the raptor rehab center the other day,' I informed Cindy. 'Sadly, one eagle died, but the other three they're treating have turned the corner. There's no reason they can't be released back into the wild once they recover fully.'

'I'm glad to hear that,' Cindy said in a voice so flat and listless it was hard to believe she actually cared about much of anything, let alone eagles.

'Is Wes here?' Izzy asked.

'Out back somewhere. I can't keep track of him, so I don't even try. Got enough on my hands,' she said wearily.

I produced the bag of cookies. 'Here. I made a double batch, thinking the kids might enjoy them.'

Cindy brightened, accepted the bag and held it close to her good eye. 'Chocolate chip? The kids will be lucky if there's any left after Wes gets ahold of them. But thanks. That was really thoughtful.'

The toddler, apparently bored with his construction project – or maybe because he'd overheard the magic word, *chocolate* – wandered over and aimed one curious blue eye at me from behind his mother's leg. I waggled my fingers in greeting, and he responded by wiping his runny nose clean on her jeans. The poor woman clearly had her hands full.

Izzy noticed, too. 'No worries. I'll just text Wes and tell him we're here, OK?'

'Sure,' she said, and even before we had time to turn around, closed the door firmly.

Izzy's mouth, which had been hanging open, snapped shut. 'Well, sooo nice to meet you and come back to see us again real soon, you hear?' Izzy drawled. As she stalked away, she dug her iPhone out of her pocket. Resting one hip against the hood of her car, she sent Wes a text, her thumbs flying over the screen. Not even five seconds later, her phone peeped. 'He's out back on the patio,' Izzy reported, dropping the phone back into her pocket.

Izzy trudged down the driveway with me hot on her heels. We found Wes, just as he had said, on the patio, a rectangular slab of plain concrete that extended out from a pair of sliding glass doors about twenty feet into the yard. A large, redbone coonhound lounged near his feet, its short, dense, coppery coat gleaming as sleekly as that of a prized racehorse in the low, noonday sun.

If the Butlers owned proper outdoor furniture, it had already been stored for the winter. The only things decorating the patio now, other than the dog, were Wesley Butler himself holding a can of WD-40 and a greasy rag, a rusty barbeque grill leaning crookedly to one side on three casters, a dog's stainless steel water bowl, three stackable polypropylene chairs – Walmart sidewalk specials – and what might be a motorbike, its parts disassembled and neatly laid out on the concrete as if straight out of a box from IKEA.

'Ah, just the person I was looking for,' Izzy chirped. 'We meet at last.' She extended her hand, then, noticing that Wes's hands were full, quickly withdrew it. 'Isabel Randall. I'm the reporter working on a story about carbofuran poisonings on the Eastern Shore.'

Wes's eyes slid from Izzy to me and back. 'As I told Hannah and Paul the other day, I haven't seen any of that stuff for years.'

I bent over the dog. 'OK if I pet him?'

'Sure. Beau's a sweetheart. Only kills when I give the order.' He raised a hand, grinned. 'Kidding!'

While I gave Beau a good scratch between the ears, Izzy pressed on, oozing innocence. 'Was carbofuran ever used on the Tuckerman farm?'

Wes shook his head and flat out lied. 'Not that I know of.'

From the depths of her handbag, Izzy produced a small notebook and a pen. 'I imagine it's a challenge to manage an RSA, Mr Butler, especially when the owner is in . . .' She paused, one eyebrow raised.

'New Mexico,' Wes supplied. 'Dave Tuckerman and I speak about every other day, so I like to think I know where he's coming from. Is this going to take long?'

'Just a few more questions, Mr Butler.' Izzy nodded in the

direction of the exploded motorbike. 'Then we'll let you get on with whatever you're doing.'

Wes's shoulders relaxed. He beamed at his project. 'It's an old Honda CR five hundred,' he explained. 'Four ninety-one cc two-stroke engine and sixty point eight horsepower. Well worth restoring. They don't make 'em like that any more.'

'I'll have to take your word for it.' Izzy smiled like an indulgent mother. 'Getting back to the challenges of running an RSA for a moment, what can you tell me about flock management?'

Wes heaved a sigh, as if waving his play time goodbye. 'I think we better sit down.' He reached for the stackable chairs. After he coaxed them apart and we were seated, he answered Izzy's question. 'We've got three ponds here and around five, six hundred ducks, give or take. It's an attractive habitat, so they pretty much take care of themselves. It's the predators we have to worry about. Foxes are a huge headache, but we've got coyotes, too, and skunks, raccoons, weasels, even the occasional stray dog. That's why some farmers put the poison out, Ms Randall, to kill the foxes. The eagles, osprey, hawks and owls are simply collateral damage.'

'But you don't.'

'Me? No. When it comes to foxes, I prefer to shoot 'em.'

I suppressed a moan. 'You can't shoot eagles, though.'

'No, Hannah, you sure aren't supposed to, but you know what? The US government is way behind the times. Bald eagles were removed from the list of threatened and endangered species way back in 2007. That's . . .' He paused to do the math. 'Um, sixteen, seventeen years ago, and yet every goddamn feather is still being protected.' He grimaced. 'Trust me, like rats, they're totally out of control.'

'I hear you.' Izzy's voice oozed with sympathy. 'You sound like a man who'd agree with Benjamin Franklin when he said the eagle was a bird of bad moral character who didn't earn his living honestly. Not sure what Franklin meant by that last bit, though.'

'Oh, the old dude's nailed it. Why bother to fish? As far as eagles are concerned, we're running a cut-rate cafeteria here. They come to eat, hanging out in the trees thick as Christmas ornaments. We offer a pretty good selection, too – mallards, pintails, canvasbacks. Tasty little morsels, those chubby, flightless ducklings. And it's brutal business, that.' He paused. 'Ever watch an eagle rip a live duck to pieces, tear it into bits to feed their chicks?' He raised a hand. 'You don't need to answer that.'

In the silence that followed, I found myself pondering the moral difference between feeding raptors infant ducklings or infant mice. As Mee Semcken commented when I acted squeamish about the pinkies, birds have to eat.

'Sometimes I'm reluctant to let Cindy bring Willie out to play on the patio, in case an eagle decides to swoop down and snatch him up,' Wes was commenting when I tuned back in.

I'd just met baby Willie. Twenty pounds and change would be a challenge for even the heftiest eagle.

Izzy snickered. 'Old wives' tale.'

'Says you!' Wes's crooked grin let us know he had been kidding about the baby.

'But you're fighting an uphill battle, Wes,' I cut in. 'Eagles are our national symbol.'

Wes snorted. 'Ha! Lions are the symbol of England, but you don't see any lions wandering around Piccadilly Circus, do you?'

Or kangaroos hopping around Sydney, I thought, or elephants galumphing around Bangkok, uh . . . wait a minute.

The sound of crunching gravel heralded the arrival of a white Chevy Silverado with a bold, gold stripe along the side. Black letters announced that this was a law enforcement vehicle belonging to the Maryland Fish and Wildlife service.

Wes sprang to his feet.

Izzy and I exchanged quick glances.

Whatever Fish and Wildlife's business, it must have been important enough to drive around both Izzy's Hyundai and the Butler's Kia and brake to a halt at the end of the drive, not far from the patio where we were sitting.

A door opened and an officer emerged from behind the wheel. He wore a long-sleeve khaki shirt under an olive drab jacket, each sleeve embellished with a distinctive Maryland Fish and Wildlife Police patch. A name badge over his right pocket read, *K. Fenelus*, and over his left was pinned an impressive gold badge. Officer Fenelus's belt was so loaded with law enforcement paraphernalia it was a wonder it could keep his pants up: a handgun, a fistful of keys and several little black pouches of goodness-knows-what all circled his waist. A cable snaked over his right shoulder, attached to a communicator that drooped within easy reach over his chest.

Fenelus was not alone. His partner, a female officer whose name badge read *E. Harmon* had frizzy red hair and fair Irish skin as pale as his was dark. Officer Harmon's petite, yet compact frame was so encumbered by the tools of her trade that she seemed to list to starboard.

Yin and yang, I thought. Good cop, bad cop? We'd soon find out.

Fortunately, Fenelus made no indication that he recognized Izzy.

'I'm glad Fenelus took me seriously the other day,' Izzy whispered to me, 'but, damn, the timing sucks.'

As the officers approached, Wes took a step backwards and half-turned as if making for the barn, then apparently thought better of it.

'Too late for a cleanup, if that's what you're thinking,' Izzy advised, pretty much blowing her own cover. 'Looks like that gal's carrying a search warrant.'

Wes stiffened. 'Shit.'

In a window of the house behind him, a curtain flicked aside, catching my attention. Cindy's face peered out, then disappeared almost immediately. Nobody else seemed to notice.

Officer Harmon's voice was unexpectedly husky for someone so small. 'Are you Wesley Butler?'

'Yeah,' he said.

'Sir, we have a warrant to search these premises for potential evidence related to the poisoning of certain bald eagles in violation of the Bald and Golden Eagle Protection Act, sixteen US Code six six eight (a) and the Migratory Bird Treaty Act, fifty CFR twenty-two. Do you understand?'

Wes nodded, but apparently a nod wasn't good enough.

'Do you understand?' she repeated, as she held out a piece of paper that I assumed must be the warrant.

'I understand.' Wes snatched the document from her fingers, glanced at it briefly, then folded it into thirds and tucked it into a side pocket of his thermal vest.

'Anything locked?' she asked.

Wes nodded mutely, unhooked a fistful of keys from his belt and handed them over. 'It's the one with the red key cap.'

Harmon marched straight into the barn, keys jangling as they dangled from her hand.

Fenelus remained outside, leaning against the makeshift barn door, arms folded across his chest, keeping an eye on Wes.

Izzy and I remained seated in the lawn chairs.

The search didn't take long, of course. Because of Izzy, Officer Harmon knew exactly where and what to look for. At the ten-minute mark, she yelled for Fenelus to fetch some boxes from the truck. When the two of them re-emerged about five minutes later, Fenelus was carrying a sturdy corrugated cardboard box preprinted on one side with evidence and chain of custody information, the top folded down and sealed with red and black tape. A smaller, white cardboard box was balanced on top, also sealed with tape.

While Fenelus loaded the boxes into the back of the truck, Harmon handed Wes another sheet of paper. 'Here's a receipt listing everything we've seized. But, you already know what that is, right?'

Wes didn't respond.

'Two containers of Furadan. One open,' she prompted.

Wes looked puzzled, but still said nothing.

'Do you know where we found them?'

Wes shrugged. 'I haven't a clue.'

'Let me refresh your memory, then. They were hidden inside an old toilet tank.'

Wes heaved a theatrical sigh. 'Really? Well, I don't know anything about that.'

'Anybody else managing this place, Mr Butler?'

'Nope. Just me. Besides, I know it's not illegal to have a bit of old Furadan lying around.'

'He better shut up while he's ahead. Jeesh!' Izzy whispered. She had her phone out, and had been busily thumbing away.

'We also found a stash of canned sardines we believe were laced with Furadan and used as bait,' Harmon added.

Wes's shoulders sagged. 'Look, this isn't my farm, I only work here.'

Harmon scowled. 'Yeah. That's what they all say. You'll be hearing from us again in due time, Mr Butler.'

After the officers drove away, Wes sat, slouched in his chair with his legs extended. 'That went well,' he deadpanned, his mouth set in a straight, hard line. 'A bit more of an interview than you bargained for, I bet.'

Izzy leaned forward, hands wrapped around her iPhone, forearms resting on her thighs. 'Until you're formally charged with something, Mr Butler, this will remain among the three of us.'

Wes gnawed on his lower lip, then said, 'Dealing on a day-to-day basis with Tuckerman is sometimes a challenge, but it's my job, it pays well, and I have a family to take care of. So, I do as I'm told.'

That got my attention. 'Are you saying Dave Tuckerman asked you to poison the eagles?'

'I was just following orders.'

I shot daggers at Wes with my eyes. 'That's what the Nazis said at the Nuremberg trials.'

Izzy piled on. 'And Lieutenant Calley after murdering Vietnamese civilians at My Lai.'

Red-faced, Wes fired back, 'It's not anything like that. There's no way I'm going to shoulder the blame for this when it's Tuckerman who calls all the shots around here.' He pointed at Izzy. 'You got a recording app on that phone?'

Izzy nodded.

'Good,' he said, his voice calmer. 'Turn it on when I say so.'

Wes dug his cell phone out of a vest pocket, swiped it on and tapped out a number. As the number began to ring, he activated the speaker. 'Go,' he mouthed silently to Izzy when someone on the other end answered.

'Hey, Wes. How's it hanging?'

'Look, we still got a problem,' Wes said without preamble. 'Damn foxes are out of control. Lost about a dozen ducks on the back forty overnight. Feathers all over the damn place.'

'Why waste your time calling me, then? You know what to do.'

'Yeah, but we got some collateral damage. Dead eagles on the property the other day, so Fish and Wildlife has been sniffing around.'

'But there's nothing for them to find, is there, Wes?'

Wes avoided the question. 'Just want to make sure you're aware of the risks.'

Tuckerman exploded. 'Risk! Don't talk to me about risk! The last goddam shipment of mallards set me back eight-seventy-five a head, up from seven dollars last year.'

Although Tuckerman couldn't see it, Wes raised a conciliatory hand. 'OK, OK. I hear you.'

'Good pay, house along with the job. There's a lot of family men who'd kill for a gig like that, Wesley,' Tuckerman said without a hint of irony.

'I don't need reminding,' Wes said.

'Good. Glad we understand one another.' And the line went dead.

Wes pocketed his phone, raised both hands in surrender. 'I'm done here, ladies. You need to hear any more?'

I got to my feet, feeling nothing but disgust for both men, but Wes was the only one I could dump on. 'Executing orders is no excuse, Wes. You knew the orders were unlawful. Where's your backbone?'

'I . . .' Wes began.

'You lied to me, Wes. That wasn't nice,' Izzy said as she pocketed her phone and retrieved her car keys. 'It's never a good idea to piss off a reporter.'

'I'm sorry I misled you, Ms Randall, but now that everything's out in the open . . .' He paused as if choosing his words carefully. 'It was never my intention to poison those eagles. I was going for the foxes. The eagles were simply collateral damage.'

'Collateral damage? Give me a break. That's just a euphemism for "innocent animals were murdered."'

For the first time that day, Wes actually looked worried. 'So, what are you going to do?'

'For now? Nothing.' She waved her cell phone dramatically. 'But after the police haul your ass away, all bets are off.'

TWENTY-FOUR

Around two weeks before Christmas, while I was puttering around the back yard giving long-overdue haircuts to the holly trees, my back pocket began to vibrate. I laid the clippers down and reached for my phone.

Jack texted: *CODIS hit. MAP confirms.*

While I had learned to appreciate Jack's 'just the facts ma'am' approach to crime investigation, reading those four simple words made my gut twist. Four words that almost certainly meant Noel's biological mother was dead. There'd be no happy mother–daughter reunion for Noel, not this, nor any Christmas.

Zoom in 10? Jack texted.

OK, I texted back.

Feeling lower than low, I gathered up the holly clippings I planned to use to decorate the mantel for the holidays, dropped them in the kitchen sink, then headed for the office where I planned to take the call. I didn't even bother to brush my hair or freshen up my face.

'Hey,' Jack said when he clicked me in. 'Really sorry, Hannah.' When I didn't say anything right away, he added, 'Mark's joining us, too.'

'A double header,' I muttered. 'Swell.'

As soon as chat windows for the three of us filled my laptop screen, I said, 'No small talk, please, guys. I need you to cut to the chase.'

Jack made a production of clearing his throat. 'My guy in Baltimore County ran Noel's GEDmatch kit against CODIS. He came up with a probable match to a female victim found not far from Tuckahoe State Park. The date is January six, 1998, which fits your timeframe to a T.'

Mark spoke up. 'I've just confirmed that information with MAP, Hannah. When I clicked through on possibles, there's only one case that fits. It's in the cold case files of Tilghman County, Maryland. January six, 1998, female, age fourteen to twenty-four, five foot two, blonde, green eyes.'

I was almost afraid to ask. 'What was the cause of death?'

'Massive head trauma, although there were indications of attempted strangulation.'

'Shit,' I said.

'Yeah,' Mark said, his face grave. 'But here's the kicker. According to the case file, the victim had recently given birth.'

We were offered a bird's-eye view of Mark's crew cut as he pawed through some papers on his desk. 'After a couple of days when nobody'd come forward to identify the victim, the police released an artist's sketch.' Mark held a copy of the sketch up to the camera lens.

The detailed, colored pencil image blurred as my eyes filled, then overflowed with tears. I could have been looking at a drawing of Noel. The guys had never met Noel, but my tears must have told them all they needed to know.

'It's a match, isn't it?' Jack said. 'I thought so when I compared it to the photo you got from the brother.'

'Yes,' I said simply. I snatched a tissue out of the box I keep on the desk, wiped my cheeks and blew my nose. 'I'm dreading having to break the news to Noel.'

'More bad news to come.' Jack spoke so softly that I might have missed it had I not been looking at his image on the screen.

'How could it possibly be worse than this?' I asked.

'In addition to DNA samples from unknown victims, CODIS also stores crime scene evidence like semen stains and blood splatters. The investigators collected fingernail clippings from this female victim. The debris they collected from under her fingernails contained DNA that matched Noel's profile, too.'

'That means . . .'

Jack nodded. 'Noel's biological father almost certainly murdered her mother.'

'Bubs.'

'Yes, Bubs. Whoever the effing hell he is. All we know is that he isn't a convicted offender.'

'Because . . .?'

'CODIS indexes sex offenders, primarily, but what gets submitted varies from state to state. Some states include DNA from persons convicted of murder, manslaughter, assault, robbery, carjacking, home invasion, stalking and endangering children. It's quite literally, all over the map.'

Thinking about the VW camper that J.D. told us Bubs had been driving, I said, 'They might have been camping in Tuckahoe Park, then. Do you think the park kept any records?'

'Nowadays you have to reserve a campsite in advance, but it was more loosey-goosey back then. Drive in, find a spot, stay for a night or two, drive out. Even if they had kept records, the retention period would have expired long ago.'

'Rats.' After a pause, I said, 'So, what do we do now?'

'Officially? Nothing. Baltimore County has turned our information over to the Tilghman County authorities who are in charge of cold cases. They'll take it from there. It's not a done deal until the medical examiner assesses the physical evidence, makes a positive ID and signs off on it. Once that happens, the officers handling the case will contact Ashley's next of kin. In this case, I'm guessing it'll be Ashley's brother.'

'Not Noel?'

'Noel's relationship to Ashley hasn't been legally proven, so no,' Jack said gently.

'This is going to be a hard secret to keep, Jack. No one wants to find out that their mother is deceased or in this case murdered, and by her biological father no less, but telling Noel the truth will allow her to move to the next chapter in her life rather than getting stuck searching for a mother who's no longer out there.'

'I know, but best to wait for a positive ID. You'll just have to trust me on this, Hannah.'

'Did the MAP records list any personal effects found with her body – a purse, wallet, anything?' I asked.

'Other than her clothing,' Mark said, 'only a silver pendant with a broken chain. The killer probably broke it in the struggle.'

Feeling embarrassed, I said, 'The *Star* or the *Times* must have covered the discovery of Ashley's body. I probably missed the story when I was browsing through the issues. Now that I have a firm date, I'll give it another go.'

'Let us know if you turn up anything new,' Jack said. 'Although I'm not optimistic.'

'You never know,' I said. 'If a reporter was actually on the scene when the body was recovered, there might be something in the article that the police didn't include in their official report.'

Jack's lip quirked. 'As a retired police officer, I'll try not to take that personally. To be fair, Hannah, the investigators did as thorough an investigation as they could given the limits of science at the time. And they get high marks for preserving the crime scene evidence.'

'No disrespect meant, Jack,' I said. 'Do you think you will be able to get your hands on the full case file?'

'Asked and rejected. They were super apologetic, but Tilghman County is holding on to everything while they reopen their investigation. Can't say I blame them.'

From prior experience, I knew exactly what a typical full case file looked like. Crime scene log. Death report. Evidence report. Lab report. Vehicle report. Victim information. Witness statements. Officer at scene notes. On and on and on until you get to Miscellaneous. Definitely more information than I had time to deal with anyway, and I admitted as much. 'That's OK, guys. What's on my plate right now is even more critical. Time to double down on locating SimonSez, and hope he can lead us to Bubs.' I puffed air out through my lips. 'The murdering sonofabitch.'

'Wrapping up for now,' Jack said, addressing Mark. 'How's the Christmas pageant going?'

'We have a new Joseph,' Mark reported. 'When the former guy withdrew citing a need to spend more time with his family' – Mark drew quote marks in the air – 'a local baker stepped into the role. Young guy, sells bagels so amazing that if you don't get to Flour Power before eight o'clock, you're out of luck. Anyway, he'd starred in *Joseph and the Amazing Technicolor Dreamcoat* in college and still has the dream coat to prove it. I'm not sure New Market is ready for Joseph dressed up like a drag queen, but his costume sure beats the hell out of a striped bathrobe.'

That made me laugh. 'Send pictures.'

'You got it, Hannah.'

After the Zoom session ended, I took a short break to download the document and Jpeg files that Jack and Mark had uploaded to our shared Google docs folder, then transferred some of them into a desktop folder I was saving for Noel. Then I signed on to Newspapers.com.

Once I located issues for the specific date in January 1998, I could see why I'd missed the reporting about the discovery of Ashley's body. In the *Salisbury Times*, the story had been relegated to a two-paragraph column below the fold, overshadowed by a long article – with three grainy photographs – reporting on the shenanigans of the newly-elected mayor of Snow Hill who was arrested on charges he used his office and full-time job as a former Worcester County sheriff's deputy to set up a series of covert pornographic photo shoots for an Internet sex site, including one with a naked woman atop his squad car. Johnson, forty-one and married, according to the paper, had offered an Ocean Pines couple his firearms, handcuffs, nightstick, and clout as the historic town's chief executive to help photograph the woman in explicit sexual poses at various area locales, including the Snow Hill firehouse and NASA's Wallops Flight Facility.

What a moron.

Snow Hill was a small town, population two thousand max. I knew it well as my father, a retired Navy engineer, had rented a cottage there for a few years while working as a contractor at nearby Wallops. It would be hard to pose naked on top of a cop car in Snow Hill without somebody noticing.

A much more comprehensive article appeared on the same day, January 8, 1998, in Easton's *Star Democrat.*

Body Found in Marsh at Tuckahoe State Park

The body of a young woman was found in the marsh at the edge of Tuckahoe State Park on Wednesday night. The investigation into what caused her death is just beginning, although foul play is suspected. The woman's body was discovered late in the afternoon, in a marshy grass area by a local resident walking her dog on a nearby nature trail, police said. Police had the area around the marshes cordoned off while they conducted their investigation. Her body was sent to the chief medical examiner's office in Baltimore, where a cause of death will be determined, police said. Police issued a statement describing the victim as between fifteen and twenty years old, 5ft 2in tall, weighing approximately 105 pounds with shoulder-length curly blonde hair and a light complexion. She was found wearing blue jeans, a Princess Diana memorial sweatshirt, black tennis shoes and pink-and-white striped socks. Police are asking for anyone with information on the identity of the victim to contact the Maryland State Police at 410-819-4747.

The article was accompanied by a black and white photo that had not fared well in the scanning process. That amorphous gray blob behind a stark white police cruiser and scrap of crime scene tape could have been anything – bushes, trees, a creature from the Black Lagoon. A quick check of the Talbot County Library online catalog told me that their newspaper holdings were all on microform, too, so as far as crime scene photos went, I'd remain, quite literally, in the dark.

A follow-up article appeared in the same paper a week later – *Police Probe Continues into Death of Young Woman* – in which the public learned that she had died of a blunt force head trauma and had been dead for only a few days when found. But following that, the newspaper returned to worrying about installing strobe lighting on school busses, recent outbreaks of pfiesteria, and whether to permit gambling at the proposed Hilton resort.

I spent some time wondering why none of the reports mentioned that the victim had recently given birth. I knew from watching crime shows on television that police often withhold details that only the killer would know as a way of confirming a suspect's guilt or eliminating a suspect who might be confessing to a crime he didn't commit. Perhaps that was their reasoning.

I paged through several more months of the paper and even checked the issues that came out on the first, fifth and tenth anniversaries of her death – nada. Hard to know how the police were following up, but as far as local newspapers were concerned, Ashley seemed to have been forgotten.

TWENTY-FIVE

I began to regret our decision to stay on at Our Song through the Christmas holidays when the Cast and Blasters started up again. *Boom-boom-boom! Boom!*

I decided not to let it bother me. It's Christmastime! The season of peace, love and goodwill to all men, even duck hunters!

I put everything on my To-Do List on the back burner – with the exception of an impassioned GenTree message to SimonSez asking him to contact me. Then I put my spreadsheets away, screwed in my earbuds and joyfully sang along to Simon and Garfunkel's greatest hits while busily rearranging the furniture in front of the French doors to make room for the Christmas tree we planned to cut at P&J Tree Farm later that week. Paul's chainsaw was propped up next to the front door, ready to go.

Boom! Boom-boom!

Oh, for the sound of silence, I thought, as I dragged an armchair to one side and began rolling up the area rug.

Earlier in the day, Paul had offered to help, but I'd waved him off on an expedition with our grandson, Timmy, who had begged to spend the first part of his school holiday with us. In Annapolis's New To You consignment shop across from the cemetery on Forest Drive, his sister, Chloe, had found the perfect Christmas gift for their mother – a set of blown glass apothecary jars – and Timmy, whose prior woodworking experience was limited to constructing a picture frame out of tongue depressors, was determined to build a wooden spice cabinet to house them. Paul had happily offered his workshop at Our Song and was serving as consulting engineer.

I was standing at the window taking a break from the dust I had kicked up, sipping a cold Coke direct from the can, when something caught my eye. An island, no, a flat, aluminum jon boat wearing a camouflaging hula skirt was gliding down Chiconnesick Creek toward our dock, a lone figure at the tiller.

My benevolence for duck hunters ends at our property line.

I ripped out my ear buds, cutting Paul Simon off in mid 'Coo, coo, ca-choo, Mrs Robinson,' wrenched open the door and ran out onto the deck. 'Hey! Hey!' I shouted at the helmsman, but the boat didn't alter course. Perhaps he couldn't hear me.

'Hey!' I yelled, louder this time, doing jumping jacks on the deck and flapping my arms like a lineman trying to flag down a speeding freight train. 'This is private property! It's posted. No hunting!'

But the little boat kept coming.

From my vantage point, I could see the helmsman, clothed head to toe in camouflage gear, was hunched over the tiller of the boat's stick-like, electric trolling motor. 'Wrong way!' I shouted, gesturing wildly toward the Tuckerman farm figuring the city slicker had simply drifted away from his shooting party.

The helmsman ignored me and aimed directly for our dock. As I watched, wondering if the guy was having engine trouble, the boat nosed up against one of our pilings, where it came to rest, bobbing gently in the wake of a passing powerboat. The helmsman made no move to tie up. In fact, as his little boat nudged rhythmically against our dock, he made no move at all. Something was amiss.

I hustled down the steps and across the frost-bitten lawn calling out, 'Hello? Do you need help?' By the time I reached the water's edge, I was close enough to see that the helmsman was doubled face down over the tiller, one arm dangling, the other slung over the transom. Had he had a heart attack? Or a stroke?

'Hello, can you hear me?'

The guy didn't move.

As long as the boat remained unsecured, it was in danger of drifting off when the tide changed. To prevent that, I'd have to get ahold of the painter, the braided nylon rope attached to the bow that I could see was coiled up uselessly in the cockpit. I briefly considered wading out and dragging the boat ashore, but it was mid-December, the water four feet deep, crispy at the edges, and a bracing forty degrees.

Sadly, the boat had chosen the most inconvenient spot to fetch up, midway between two dock ladders. I got down on my hands and knees and spread myself out on the wooden decking like a spatchcocked chicken, scooting as close as I dared to the edge. I reached down, straining to grab the painter, but it remained well below my grasp.

'Hold on,' I called out to the unconscious helmsman. 'I have another idea.'

I scrambled to my feet, crossed to the other side of the dock and

clambered aboard Paul's little Bayliner runabout. I lifted the boathook out of its stainless-steel holder and hurried back. Telescoped
out to its full twelve feet, the boathook easily snagged the painter
and I was able to draw it up to me. Once the painter was in hand,
I used it to pull the boat even with the nearest dock ladder where I
tied it securely with a figure-eight around a cleat.

Now what?

As I gazed down into the cockpit, I quickly realized that whatever
had happened, had interrupted the hunter's lunch. His shotgun, in
the broken position, lay open on the cockpit floor. Lying next to it
was a single-serve bag of potato chips, apparently unopened, an
empty bottle of Busch Light, and a half-eaten sandwich. A mandarin
orange rolled right, then left, then right again against the hunter's
shoe. Was he alive? I stared at his back, willing it to rise and fall,
but saw no sign that the guy was breathing. I'd need to check for
a pulse.

Holding onto the ladder with both hands, I backed down the
rungs and stepped into the boat, keeping a firm hold on the ladder
while the boat see-sawed under my feet. When it finally stabilized
and I was able to turn around, a sudden gust of wind sent a crumpled
wad of plastic wrap spiraling upward. Instinctively, I scooped it up
before it could be swept overboard into the bay where an unsus-
pecting turtle might mistake the plastic for a tasty jellyfish and
choke to death on it. I tucked the wrap into my pocket, then turned
back to see what I could do for the hunter at the helm.

My stomach lurched. The helmsman's pale ponytail lay across
his neck, dangling like a wet rope. Was he . . .? I brushed his hair
aside and felt his neck for a heartbeat, but nothing pulsed beneath
my fingers. His flesh was as cold as the air that surrounded us.

I sat back on my heels, tilted my head and leaned forward until
I could get a better look at the man's face. A pale dead eye stared
out of a face frozen in a grimace. Traces of vomit flecked the stubble
on his chin. I fell back in horror.

Wesley Butler had shot his last duck.

TWENTY-SIX

P aul jokes that my cellphone is surgically attached to my hip. That day, however, I'd set it aside while I was wrestling with the furniture, if only I could remember where.

I raced back to the house and wasted several minutes flailing around the disorganized living room until I finally found the phone, lying precisely where I had left it, its silver case essentially invisible against the gray stone hearth. Although I figured Wes was way past help, I snatched it up and called nine one one.

It took a bit of explaining to tell the dispatcher how to find our cottage, so I agreed to go out to the main road and flag the ambulance down, if necessary. Then I grabbed a jacket and hurried down the dirt track that led to the main road, where I leaned my back against a sun-bleached sign that read: 'Farm Fresh*Free Range Eggs*Honey*Vegetables*Just Ahead' and telephoned Paul.

'Where are you?' I asked when he picked up.

'At Exotic Woods on Whitehall. Timmy's still considering pieces for his project. I thought he'd settled on a curly cherry, but his head's just been turned by a slab of jatoba which looks pretty much like cherry to me, but since it comes from Brazil, that makes it special. Ka-ching.'

'Can Timmy hear me?'

'No, why?'

'Well, not to beat around the bush, Wesley Butler's dead.'

Paul snorted. 'Got into some of his own poison, huh? Serves him right.'

'Sick joke, Paul. But you know what? I think he may have.' I explained about the drifting boat, what I'd done to secure it, the rictus and the traces of vomit.

'Jeesh, Hannah. Are you all right?'

'Adrenaline pumping like crazy, but otherwise, I'm fine, honestly. I'm down at the mailboxes waiting for the ambulance now, but I'm hoping you can keep Timmy busy until after everyone leaves.'

'Not a problem. We're on the other side of the Bay Bridge, so it would take us an hour to get back anyway. After we settle on the

wood, I'll take him to Red, Hot and Blue for lunch. That'll kill
another hour. Sorry, poor choice of words.'

'I'm having a hard time working up sympathy for the guy, too,
but . . .' I took a deep breath. 'And, oh my God, who's going to
tell Cindy?'

'Are you sure it's Wesley?'

Wesley's dead face hovered like a fun house apparition behind
my eyes. I shivered, shook the vision off and said, 'Positive.'

'Look, sweetheart, I know your instinct is to dash down the road
like a marathoner and alert Cindy, but that's not your job. The police
will need to make a positive ID, then they'll do the job of notifying
Wesley's next of kin.'

'He's got two little kids, Paul! And I don't think Cindy works.'

'For all you know, she has a huge support network – big Italian
family, mega-church community – and if it turns out she doesn't,
then you can step in and start organizing day care and a meal train.'

'I wonder who they'll send, in the way of law enforcement, I
mean. Whose jurisdiction?'

'My guess? The sheriff of our fine county, Andy Hubbard.
Knowing how protective Andy is of his bailiwick, he won't call in
the Staties unless he has to.'

'Swell. Sheriff Hubbard already thinks the angel of death follows
me around like an acolyte.'

'Exactly. So, do yourself a favor, Hannah. Stay close to the
cottage, observe what's going on from the deck, offer coffee to the
first responders, whatever, but otherwise, stay well out of it.'

'You are a party pooper, Professor Ives. May I have your permission to use binoculars?'

'I'm serious, Hannah.'

'I know you are, and I'll behave. I promise.'

'Granddad, check this out!' Apparently, Timmy needed a second
opinion.

'Oh, oh. Looks like burl maple from here. Gotta go, sweetie.
Text me.'

'OK,' I assured the dead air between us.

Then I instructed Siri to call Izzy.

'Hannah!' Izzy said when she picked up. 'I was just about to
call you.'

'Must be telepathy,' I said. 'I need to—'

'I'm just out of a meeting with Roger,' she cut in before I could finish my sentence. 'Wesley Butler is a lying bastard. Collateral damage, my foot. Roger tells me the lab results on those eagles are in from the Fish and Wildlife lab. They died of carbofuran poisoning, all right, but that's not the surprising news. The big surprise is those foxes. They'd been shot, Roger says, and their carcasses laced with Furadan.' Her voice rose a few octaves, turning shrill. 'The *foxes* were used as bait, Hannah. Wesley Butler intentionally targeted those eagles.'

Izzy's news took my breath away, and for a moment, I couldn't speak.

'Hannah? Are you there?'

'Yes, yes, I'm here, just trying to take it all in.'

'What a silver-tongued devil. Admit to using just a teensy-weensy bit of Furadan, point an accusing finger at his employer, all the while . . .' She paused to take a calming breath. 'Roger says there'll be charges brought for sure.'

'Roger's charges have been overtaken by events,' I informed Izzy. 'That's why I was calling you. Wesley Butler's dead.'

'Get out of here!'

'Seriously. I'm out on the main road waiting for the ambulance right now.' I repeated to Izzy the information I had just given Paul.

'That's some seriously bad karma,' she said after I'd finished.

'I thought you might want to be on hand . . .' I began when I was interrupted by the *nee-naw-nee-naw-nee-naw* and flashing lights of an approaching ambulance. 'They're already here,' I said as a white vehicle with Tilghman County Emergency Services painted in blue on the sides screeched to a halt in front of me.

'I'm on my way,' Izzy said, and ended the call.

The window on the passenger side of the ambulance rolled down.

'It's down that way,' I told the EMT, pointing to the rank of mailboxes at the head of our rutted lane. He nodded to the EMT at the wheel, who peeled off to the right in a spray of loose gravel.

My work here is done, I thought, as I pocketed the phone and hustled along the lane back to the cottage. Sheriff Hubbard wouldn't need directions – he'd been to Our Song several times in the past – and if a crime scene unit was on the way, too, they could afford the time to get lost. Wesley wouldn't mind.

As I promised Paul, I stationed myself on our deck and observed the proceedings from there, bundled up against the cold. First to arrive after the paramedics – who had driven straight across the

lawn and parked their ambulance at the head of the dock – was
Sheriff Hubbard at the wheel of a white police cruiser. If you didn't
recognize the blue and gold seal of office plastered to his cruiser's
door, the word *SHERIFF* printed in black on a pale blue stripe left
no doubt: Sheriff Andrew J. Hubbard was on the case.

The EMTs were finishing up just then, two of them kneeling on
the dock packing up their gear while a third hovered over them
looking important. Sheriff Hubbard parked on the narrow gravel
strip that ended at our garden shed, then trotted down the lawn and
onto the dock, piloting his compact, stocky frame between the EMTs
like Moses parting the Red Sea.

I scooted my deck chair closer to the edge of the deck, steadied
the binoculars on the railing and watched while he pulled on a pair
of rubber gloves and climbed backwards, like I had done, down the
dock ladder and into the boat. When I twiddled with the focus, I
could tell he was taking photographs with his cell phone.

Four or five minutes later, Hubbard climbed back up the ladder,
stripped off his gloves and handed them to the nearest EMT. I
couldn't hear what they were saying, of course, and my lip-reading
skills were piss-poor, but by the way Hubbard paced and kept
checking his watch, I guessed he was wondering what was keeping
the crime scene investigators.

They didn't keep him waiting much longer. A white Ford
Econoline van with *Forensic Services Crime Scene Unit* lettered on
the front, back and sides came bumping down the lawn towards the
dock. I held my breath and crossed my fingers, praying to whomever
was the patron saint of well-tended lawns. All spring and summer,
Paul and Rusty Heberling, our man of all work, had lavished tender
loving care on that lawn. Now we'd need divine intervention to
keep those heavy-duty tires from leaving unsightly ruts, even on
the frozen ground.

'You-hoo!'

Not Paul, but Izzy, announcing her arrival as she rounded the
cottage from the side yard and hustled up the short flight of steps
that led up to where I sat shivering on the deck. 'I knocked and
knocked, so I figured you must be out back where the action is.'
She turned away from me and faced the scene, leaning forward,
both hands resting on the railing.

We watched in silence as one of the crime scene investigators
exchanged a few words with Sheriff Hubbard then returned to the

van. Seconds later, two other CSIs emerged from the side of the open van and began to suit up like moon men in jumpsuits, hoods, booties, face masks and goggles. As a final step before lugging their kits down to the crime scene, they helped shove each other's hands into latex gloves.

'Goggles?' Izzy mused.

'If it's Furadan that killed him, I would, too, wouldn't you?' Izzy turned to face me, eyes wide. 'But, Hannah, you boarded that boat!'

'Only for a couple of minutes, honest, and I didn't touch anything. Uh . . . well, except Wesley's neck.' I shuddered. 'But I haven't dropped dead yet, so I'm probably in the clear.'

Izzy pulled up a chair and sat down in it. Like me, she was in it for the long haul. She brought me up to date on her meeting with Roger. 'The lab totally debunked Wesley's claim that he'd baited the foxes with poisoned sardines. There was no trace of sardines in any of their stomach contents. He'd shot them all.'

'With what? A shotgun?'

'Nope. Apparently he used a rifle, a Remington two twenty-three.'

I leaned back in my chair, wrapping my arms around myself more for warmth than anything else. 'Ah, the mighty hunter,' I mused, and then, because it floated into my consciousness from some filing cabinet deep within my brain, I began to recite from 'A Mighty Hunter Before the Lord.'

Izzy eyed me sideways through her lashes. 'Horses and hounds? What the hell brought that on?'

'Dunno. It's a poem I had to memorize in high school. It seemed apropos somehow.'

'I agree. But, who wrote it?'

'A British poet named Cecily Fox Smith. Maybe it was the "fox" in her name and the subject of hunting that brought the poem to mind.'

'You never cease to amaze me, Hannah Ives.'

I turned and aimed a grin at my friend. 'I can recite the whole of "The Rime of the Ancient Mariner," too, if you like. All one hundred and forty-two stanzas.'

She raised a hand. 'Please. I'm easily traumatized. Never recovered from being forced to read *David Copperfield*.'

Down at our dock, the CSIs still crawled all over the jon boat,

but it looked like Sheriff Hubbard was ready to move on. After the
EMTs pulled out, tires spinning in the muddy grass near the water-
line, making me cringe, Hubbard glanced our way.

I sprang to my feet and gave him a friendly wave, hoping he'd
wander up and join us. He acknowledged the invitation by touching
the brim of his ranger's hat, then, as I had hoped, trudged straight
up the sloping lawn.

'You must be freezing, Sheriff Hubbard,' I said when he stepped
onto the deck. 'I know I am. Would you like some coffee?'

Hubbard rubbed his hands together briskly. 'Yes, please. Thanks.'
He bobbed his head toward Izzy. 'Who's your friend?'

'Oh, sorry. May I introduce Isabel Randall.'

Izzy popped up from her chair and extended a hand. 'Izzy.'

'Sheriff Hubbard,' he said, removing his broad-brimmed hat as
he stepped forward to greet her. 'But everyone calls me Andy.'

Hubbard's prominent nose descended in a straight line from his
backward-sloping forehead. Except for a tidy fringe of salt-and-
pepper hair around his ears, he was completely bald. In weather
like this, he needed that hat.

'Let's go inside where it's warm,' I suggested as I slid the patio
door open.

A minute later, the sheriff's hat was hanging on a hook in the
hallway and Izzy and Andy had seated themselves across from one
another at the kitchen table while I organized coffee mugs and began
punching buttons on the Keurig.

'Full disclosure,' Izzy volunteered. 'I'm an investigative reporter
working on a story about the eagle poisonings on the Tuckerman
farm. Hannah and I are friends going way back,' she told him,
shading the truth just a tad. We'd met not even a year ago, but while
working together as members of the Silent Sleuths, we'd grown
close. 'After Hannah discovered the sick birds, she gave me a call.'

'Cream and sugar?' I asked, handing Andy a steaming mug.

He wrapped his hands gratefully around it. 'Just black, thanks.'

'You're a cheap date,' I said with a grin.

'Less fuss,' he said, taking a careful sip.

'Hannah tells me the dead guy is her neighbor, Wesley Butler.
Is that right?'

Andy nodded. 'Never met the guy myself, but that's the name
on the driver's license we found on the body. Photo on it matches.'

He rested the mug on the tablecloth, but kept his fingers curled around it. 'Tell me what happened, Hannah.'

I laid it out simply. 'I noticed the boat drifting this way. When it bumped up against our dock, I secured it before it could float off. I did climb aboard and check for a pulse, but Wesley must have been dead for a while. He was stone cold.'

He raised an eyebrow. 'That's it?'

'Scout's honor,' I said, as I carried the coffee I'd brewed for myself over to join them at the table. 'Any idea what killed him?' I asked once I sat down.

His upper lip quirked. 'You know we'll have to wait for the M.E. on that.'

I decided not to share my theory about carbofuran poisoning. I knew there could be other explanations for the symptoms I noticed, because I'd Googled them on my cell phone. Epilepsy. High blood sugar. Drug overdose. I didn't wish death on anyone, but if it was Wesley's time to go, there could be no more fitting way than by carbofuran poisoning.

'I interviewed Butler at the Tuckerman farm the other day,' Izzy commented as she spooned sugar into her mug. 'He confessed to using Furadan on the eagles. Accidentally.' She sniffed. 'Today my contact at Natural Resources tells me the poisoning was intentional and that federal charges would most likely be brought against Butler and the landowner, David Tuckerman.'

Andy nodded in confirmation. 'They gave me a courtesy call before they went for the warrant. Now, they'll just have to worry about Tuckerman, working with the feds in Arizona.'

'New Mexico,' I corrected.

'Whatever. Not my problem, thank goodness. I've got enough on my plate as it is.' He drained his mug, set it down on the tablecloth and stood. 'Look, I'd better be going. I'm meeting one of the female deputies over at the Tuckerman place. We'll need to inform his widow.'

I escorted Andy into the hallway, lifted his hat off the peg and handed it over.

Holding his hat in both hands by the brim, he turned it round and round as he spoke. 'We're sending a private ambulance to pick up the body and drive it up to the M.E.'s in Baltimore. Shouldn't be long now.'

I opened the front door, he took a step toward it, then turned back. 'And before you ask, we'll be towing the boat away shortly, too. Thanks for the coffee.'

'Andy?'

'Yes?'

'After you notify Cindy Butler, will you let me know if there's anything I can do? She's got two little kids, and . . .'

Andy settled the hat on his head, adjusting the fit. 'I know. Damn it. And just before Christmas, too. Sometimes I hate this job.'

TWENTY-SEVEN

Two days later, Paul and Timmy were busy in the workshop, so I was taking advantage of their absence to wrap Christmas presents. From somewhere among the rolls of wrapping paper my iPhone pinged. My fingers were – literally – tied up with tape and ribbon, so I ignored it at first. But when the phone pinged and pinged again, I untangled myself, dropped the scissors and leaned over to check out the display.

Big scoop! Izzy texted. *COD carbofuran.*

Followed by: *My source says tuna salad.*

And then: *Call me.*

So, I did.

Izzy picked up right away. 'Crazy around here today,' she said.

I knew better than to inquire about Izzy's source of information. As a long-time reporter, she had cultivated dozens of reliable ones. 'Suicide or murder?' I asked right away.

'Could be either. They're treating the death as suspicious.'

'I noticed half a sandwich in the boat,' I told her. 'Could have been tuna.'

'Bingo,' Izzy said. 'It acted so fast, Wesley still had part of the sandwich lodged in his esophagus.'

I shivered. 'TMI, Izzy, TMI.' After a moment's thought, I added, 'Though it does seem odd that a guy would pack himself a picnic lunch if he intended to off himself.' I reminded her of the chips, orange, and Busch Light I'd also spotted in Wesley's boat. 'And why mix poison into a tuna sandwich when it might go down a lot easier with beer?'

'People do strange things. I once covered a story where a woman climbed into her fireplace before dousing herself with kerosene and setting herself on fire, presumably because she didn't want to burn the house down around her.'

'Still, why not use his shotgun? Guns are much more of a guy thing than poison.'

'Good question. I'm sure it's occurred to the sheriff, too.'

Thinking about the uneasy feeling I'd had about Cindy's relationship with Wes when meeting her for the first time, I asked, 'Where was Cindy when Wes died, do you know?'

'Williamsburg Premium Outlets. Drove down the night before. Left the boys with her parents in Lightfoot for the day so she could go Christmas shopping.'

'Doesn't sound like someone who's plotting to murder her husband.'

'Doesn't sound like someone who isn't, either.'

'I'll make a point of checking in on Cindy later today. I picked up a couple of stocking stuffers for the boys that I'd like to deliver.'

'Good. Put on your deerstalker cap and see what you can find out.'

I changed the subject. 'Any word from Jack on Ashley?'

'Not yet. But, as you know, anything involving DNA usually takes time.'

'Frustrating, but just as well, I suppose. Confirmation would certainly cast a pall over Noel's Christmas.'

'Indeed,' Izzy said. 'Well, I'd better . . . oh, gosh, wait a minute! I almost forgot. I got a call from Mee Semcken at Hoots late yesterday. The eagles are ready to be released. She wants to do it as close to where they were found as possible, but even though Wesley's, uh, you know, she's still wary about the Tuckerman farm, so that means your place. Around two tomorrow, she thinks. If that's OK, I'll call back and give her the go-ahead.'

'Tomorrow around two is great,' I said. 'My grandson, Timmy, is with us and he'll be thrilled.'

'Back to you on that, then, Hannah. Have a good day.' And the line went silent.

Only later did I pause in the middle of fashioning a bow out of curling ribbon to wonder about Wesley's coonhound. Where was Beau? Steve Heberling had implied that Wesley and Beau were joined at the hip; he never went hunting without him. Beau should have been in the boat, too.

Could I imagine a scenario where a man – facing a hefty fine and the possibility of prison time for violating federal wildlife protection laws – would hope to escape his problems by ending his life?

No. The chances of Wes doing time for a first offense, especially while operating under orders from the landowner, were slim. He had to know that.

What I could imagine was a frazzled young mother of two

toddlers, stuck in what could be an abusive relationship, hoping to escape her marriage by poisoning her husband's lunch.

In driving to Virginia, had Cindy been clearing the decks? Getting herself, the children and the dog out of town in preparation for the Main Event?

Leaving the wrapping paper, ribbons, tape and scissors spread across the dining table, I gathered the gifts I'd wrapped for the Butler family – a pinwheel bath toy, a sticker book and a twenty-five-dollar McDonald's gift card – and popped them into a small shopping bag. I made a pit stop at the refrigerator to grab a spaghetti casserole out of the freezer – Timmy would pout if he discovered it missing, but he'd get over it – slipped it and a small container of oatmeal-raisin cookies into a Trader Joe's cool bag and headed for the car.

Earlier in the day, on his way back from Home Depot, Paul had driven past the Butler house and reported seeing their vehicle in the drive, so I figured she'd be home, and he was right. But this time, Cindy had backed the SUV into the driveway. The rear hatch yawned open and she'd half-filled the cargo hold with plastic tubs and cardboard boxes. Going or coming? It was hard to tell.

Cindy answered the doorbell promptly, and a welcoming wave of overheated air whooshed over me. She dredged a smile up from somewhere and pasted it on her face. 'Oh, hi, Hannah.' Still holding the door, she stepped aside. 'Come in. Excuse the mess.'

Going, I concluded.

Three shiny, hard-sided suitcases – one with a Toy Story design – lay open on the sofa and piles of children's clothing teetered precariously on the coffee table. Cindy tossed the stuffed giraffe she'd been holding into a plastic laundry basket full of toys. 'Dave Tuckerman's just given us until December thirty-first to move out.'

'Generous of him,' I deadpanned.

'Yeah, well . . .' She shrugged off whatever would have come next.

'Cindy, I'm so sorry about Wesley.'

'Thanks,' she said simply.

Feeling no further words would be adequate at this point, I set the bag of gifts down next to the front door and held out the cooler bag. 'I've brought you a spaghetti casserole. Three-hundred-and-fifty-degree oven for an hour. My grandkids love it, and I hope your boys will, too.'

Cindy produced a genuine smile and accepted the bag. 'That's really thoughtful, Hannah. Let's take it into the kitchen, OK? I haven't managed to mess that up yet.'

I followed as she forged a trail through the clutter to an L-shaped kitchen area at the back of the house, then stood leaning against the refrigerator while she unpacked the bag. She set the aluminum-foil-covered casserole dish out on the counter with a flourish and announced, 'That takes care of dinner tonight!' Turning to face me, she said, 'I've just made coffee. Would you like some to go along with the cookies?'

'That would be lovely.'

Cindy indicated I should sit in one of the high stools at the kitchen island where she joined me a minute later carrying two mugs. 'Cream and sugar?'

'Yes, please.'

'No cream, I'm afraid. Will milk do?'

I smiled. 'Of course.'

I was grateful for the milk. It made the bitter, watery instant brew almost drinkable. As I took a second sip and tried not to make a face, I was distracted by the *click-click-click* of toenails on the bare floorboards. Beau, the redbone coonhound, trotted into the kitchen. He sniffed my shoes where they rested on the rungs of the stool, then settled down at the foot of Cindy's stool. She reached out and gave his ears an absent-minded scratch. 'Beau likes to nap with the boys. They'll be up soon, I suspect, and then . . . well, welcome to the madhouse.'

'You'll be needing help with the move,' I observed. 'There's a lot to pack up.'

'Not really,' she said, nibbling on a bit of cookie. 'This house came fully furnished. None of it's ours, really, except for some photographs and a few knickknacks. Oh, and the swing set and wading pool out back. Dad's driving up with a U-Haul in a few days, so no worries about any of that.'

'Where are you and the boys going, Cindy?'

'A place you've probably never heard of. Lightfoot, Virginia, just outside of Williamsburg. Dad's a dermatologist at Sentana Regional Medical Center. We'll stay in the condo with my parents for a while. Just until I get back on my feet,' she hastened to add. She finished off the cookie and wiped her fingers clean on her jeans. 'Believe it or not, I'm a certified massage therapist. I was working for a sports medicine practice in Virginia Beach when I met Wes.'

'How did you and Wes end up here, then?' I asked.

She managed a smile. 'Wes liked to tell his pals he was heading for Virginia when his car broke down. Couldn't afford to fix it, so he got a job with Perdue, driving the chicken trucks.'

'Ugh,' I said.

'Could have been worse,' Cindy said. 'We know someone who's in charge of night shift evisceration.'

I moaned.

'Anyway,' she continued while reaching for another cookie, 'driving the truck he got to meet a lot of the farmers, and eventually one of them down near Fruitland offered him a job managing his sharecroppers.' She shrugged. 'That was long before I came along, though.'

'How old are you, Cindy? Do you mind if I ask?'

She wagged her head. 'Twenty-three.'

From the look on her face, she knew I must be counting years off on my fingers. 'Wesley likes, uh, liked 'em young.' She shrugged. 'I wasn't a great brain, so the minute I got out of high school, I enrolled in the massage therapy program at Centura College. I really enjoy the work, Hannah. You feel like you're helping people in a meaningful way.'

'Not everyone can say that about their jobs,' I commented, thinking about the countless hours I wasted commuting from Annapolis to Washington, DC. When I was offered a buy-out from Whitworth and Sullivan, the accounting firm where I had worked for decades as a records manager, I snatched it up and have never looked back.

While we were talking, Beau got to his feet, wandered over to his water dish where he lapped briefly, then sat down next to what could be a pantry door, half-open, his eyes bright, tongue lolling.

Cindy smiled indulgently, hopped off her stool and reached into the pantry. 'We keep his treats in here,' she said, coming out holding a package of Pup-Peroni.

Beau's tail beat a quick *ratta-tatta-tat-tat* on the kitchen floor.

'Who's a good boy?' Cindy gave Beau's head an affectionate pat before sending him off to concentrate on his chew.

'What about the dogs?' I asked as Beau disappeared around the corner, carrying the chew in his mouth like a stick. 'When you move, I mean.'

Cindy cocked an eyebrow. 'Dogs?'

I gestured vaguely in the direction of the family's SUV. 'The stick figures on your rear window. There are two dogs.'

'Oh, you noticed. Yeah. One's Beau, of course, and the other was a sweet little Jack Russell named Bandit.'

'Was?'

'Wesley killed him.'

I nearly fell off the stool. '*What?*'

'I don't suppose there's any reason to be all hush-hush about it now. A few months back after a long talk with Tuckerman, Wesley began messing about with the sardines . . .'

I held up a hand. 'Good, Lord! Stop! Don't tell me.'

Cindy's face clouded. 'Wes claimed it was an accident. "I just turned my back for a minute, Cyn, honestly,"' she quoted, pitching her voice low. Cindy reached for a roll of paper towels mounted on the side of a cabinet over the sink, ripped one off and used it to dab at her eyes. 'I was livid,' she continued after taking a moment to collect herself. '"What were you thinking, asshole? You have two babies!" I screamed like a maniac. I was standing right here, too, holding a saucepan, so I clobbered him over the head with it.

'That went about as well as it usually did,' she continued. 'He hauled back and gave me a solid punch in the gut.' She began rubbing her side, as if the spot were still tender.

Our conversation had taken a disturbing turn, but I sensed an opening, so I plunged in. 'What are the police telling you about Wesley?' I asked.

'It's ironic, isn't it?' Cindy said, almost dreamily. 'Somebody poisoned Wesley's tuna salad sandwich with carbofuran. Imagine that!'

As she talked, Cindy had been unconsciously shredding the paper towel with her fingers. She looked down at what remained of it now, almost in surprise, then laughed, balled it up and disposed of it in the trash can under the sink. When she turned back around, she considered me with a wan smile and said brightly, 'You know what they say. Start playing with fire and you're likely to get burned.'

TWENTY-EIGHT

B ack home, thoroughly creeped out and decompressing with a cup of high-octane coffee loaded with cream and sugar, I waited for a moment to be alone with Paul to dissect what had happened at the Butlers.

Had Cindy just confessed to murdering her husband?

Certainly not in so many words.

But one thing was perfectly clear: Cindy Butler was not the grieving widow. Before I left, she'd practically been dancing a jig on her husband's grave.

I had finally extricated myself from her hair-raising stories of physical and emotional abuse – Wesley had once locked her in the basement to 'teach her manners' – and retreated to the front door, where I snatched up the bag of stocking stuffers I'd purchased for the boys and handed it over. Cindy thanked me profusely and, in return, insisted on showing me the spot in the flower bed where Bandit had been buried. The older boy, Wally, had marked it with a rock, finger-painted with Bandit's pawprint.

I knew Paul would insist I report what I'd just learned to Sheriff Hubbard, and I was totally on board with that. The sheriff could take the information, especially the tip about poor Bandit, and run with it. I'd made no promises of confidentiality to Cindy.

I was so engrossed in composing the email I planned to send Sheriff Hubbard, phrasing and rephrasing it for clarity, that I must have conjured the man up.

My cell phone rang, startling me.

'What the blazes is going on, Mrs Ives?' Noel was speaking in a whisper. 'Sheriff Hubbard showed up at the parsonage a while ago and asked to speak with my father about Wesley Butler. They were locked up in my father's office for over thirty minutes.'

'Wesley? How odd. I wonder how your father knows Wesley.'

'Exactly what I thought. When I ran into Mr Butler that time at your house, he said he wasn't much of a churchgoer, and I've never seen him at services here, that's for sure.'

Something didn't sound right. I didn't know Sheriff Hubbard

well, but I couldn't imagine him, or any law enforcement officer, volunteering information like that. More likely, he'd show up at the door, simply ask to speak to Reverend Sinclair, then take the man someplace private to talk.

'Noel, how did you know the sheriff wanted to speak to your dad specifically about Wesley Butler?'

After a long silence, Noel cleared her throat and fessed up. 'It's an old house, Mrs Ives, with forced air heating. Ginny's bedroom is right over Dad's office. My sister discovered a long time ago that if you put your ear to the heat vent on the floor in her bedroom, you can hear a lot of what's being discussed down below.'

'Naughty girls!' I teased, smiling as I pictured the scene.

'Yeah, I feel bad about that now.' She sniggered. 'No, that's a lie. I don't. How else could Ginny and I find out that the director of our Vacation Bible School was having an affair with the pharmacist at the Rexall?' She paused. 'The woman was a battle-axe. We weren't sorry when she got the old heave-ho.

'But I digress. I haven't done it in years, believe me, but after Dad took the sheriff into his office and shut the door, I couldn't help myself. I high-tailed it up to Ginny's room and put my ear to the floor.'

'So, what's your father's connection with Wesley?'

'That's what Sheriff Hubbard wanted to know. They obtained Mr Butler's cell phone records, and you aren't going to believe this, at least I didn't, still don't, but Mr Butler made nine calls to my dad's number over the past several weeks.'

Thinking about all the trouble the late Wesley Butler was in over the carbofuran, I asked, 'Could Wesley have been coming to your father for counseling?'

'That's what Dad told the sheriff, but I don't believe it. Wesley wasn't a parishioner, and Dad doesn't make a habit of taking walk-ins. He's super conservative. Won't even marry people unless at least one of them is a member of the church. The mayor once offered him a thousand dollars to make an exception for his daughter, but Dad turned it down. They were Lutherans, he said.

'But I haven't even gotten to the crazy part yet,' she continued. 'If I hadn't already been lying on the floor, I would have fallen over when the sheriff asked about a five-hundred-dollar withdrawal Dad made from the ATM down at the corner – which isn't even his bank! Seems that same day, Mr Butler deposited five hundred dollars in his own account. That *can't* be a coincidence.'

'Maybe I watch too much true crime television, but blackmail could be one explanation,' I suggested. And blackmail far too often leads to murder, I thought to myself. At least it does in crime fiction.

Noel sighed. 'I hate to say it, but that's what sprang to my mind, too, especially when Dad started tap-dancing like crazy. He told the sheriff the money was a one-time personal loan to help a guy through a temporary situation. Possible, I suppose, since money can be tight for some folks around the holidays, but not very likely.'

After a thoughtful silence, Noel said, 'And now that Mr Butler is dead, I'm worrying the police think Dad had something to do with it, which would be *totally* crazy.'

Maybe, maybe not, I thought. Aloud, I said, 'Don't worry, Noel. Sheriff Hubbard's probably just dotting all the i's and crossing all the t's. I learned this morning that Wesley died from carbofuran poisoning. Somebody spiked his tuna salad sandwich with the stuff. I can't imagine your father rustling up a tuna salad sandwich for Wesley's picnic lunch.'

'Dad? Make tuna salad? That's a laugh. He can barely manage peanut butter and jelly. Mom does all the food prep in our family. If anything ever happens to her, he'll be having Pop Tarts for breakfast and eating dinner across the street at Denny's every night. But why the heck would he give somebody he barely knew five hundred dollars?'

'You could ask *him* why the sheriff stopped by, I suppose. All casual like,' I suggested.

'I did, Mrs Ives! But Dad made up a totally lame story about being invited to speak at the March meeting of the Rotary Club.' She snorted. 'Practice what you preach, they say. You'd think Dad had never heard of "Thou shalt not bear false witness."' She sighed. 'But, then there's "Honor thy father and thy mother," to worry about, so color me conflicted.'

'Speaking of fathers, have you done any more work on GenTree?' I asked.

'Last time I looked at my parental matches, it made my eyes cross, so no. I'll have to leave that up to you, Mrs Ives. You're the expert. Besides, it's totally nuts here around the holidays.'

'I hear you, we still don't have a tree. But, if you can spare a couple of hours tomorrow afternoon, Mee Semcken from Hoots is coming over to our place bringing the eagles. They're well enough to be released.'

'Oh, wow!' she said. 'I wouldn't miss that for anything. I've been praying for those poor birds every Sunday since that terrible day we found them. Thank you, Jesus! What a miracle!'

I had to agree. God had been guiding the hands of the experts. 'Two o'clock, then. OK?'

'Don't even think about trying to keep me away, Mrs Ives.'

'As if,' I said.

TWENTY-NINE

B y the time Mee Semcken arrived with the caravan from Hoots, her audience had already assembled. Timmy had helped Paul drag several of the kitchen chairs out onto the deck and they'd arranged them, along with the two Adirondack chairs, theater-style along the railing. We had acquired additional pairs of binoculars, too, and although the temperature had climbed into the high fifties, I'd dug Navy football lap blankets out of the closet in case anyone needed one for extra warmth.

Noel came early, bringing a carrot cake to share. 'I hope you don't mind that I've invited Roger,' she said as she set the cake down on the dining room table where I'd laid out an assortment of snacks – all the usual suspects, including chips and dip, cheese and crackers and a platter of fresh fruit.

'Of course not,' I told her. 'Roger's an integral part of this story.'

'He's bringing smoked bluefish,' Noel said. 'I hope that's OK.'

I grimaced. 'Just as long as it's not tuna.'

Izzy bopped through the sliding glass doors just then and I realized, with some surprise, that she and Noel had never met. I made the introduction, then left them fussing over the arrangement of silverware and cocktail napkins to make room for Izzy's crudités while I answered the doorbell and invited Roger and his appetizer in.

'Sorry I'm late,' Roger apologized as he handed me a paper plate covered with tin foil. 'I got called away to fish a two-foot alligator out of somebody's koi pond.'

That made me laugh.

'All in the line of duty.' He grinned and dashed off to join everyone out on the deck.

Last to arrive was Diana Kingsley, clomping down the driveway in a sturdy walking cast. Paul intercepted her and escorted her to one of the Adirondack chairs. 'Take a load off,' he said as he popped out its footrest.

Not even a broken ankle kept Diana down for long. Before coming to us, she'd picked up a red-tailed hawk who'd been struck by a car outside of Chestertown. Turning the injured bird over to the rehabilitators at our place would save her a twenty-minute drive, but she also came to watch the release.

Paul met the Hoots van at the head of our drive and directed Mee to a parking spot near the shed, roughly the same spot where Sheriff Hubbard had parked his police cruiser only days earlier. While everyone kept a respectful distance, Mee and her assistant, Charlene, unloaded the first of three large cardboard boxes from the back of the van. They set the box down at the edge of the yard, just at the point where the lawn began its long, gentle slope toward Chiconnesick Creek.

Gently, they tipped the box, easing it over on one side. Charlene stripped off the tape that had been holding the flaps shut. Mee, standing at what had once been the bottom of the box, reached over from behind and eased the flaps open.

Then, through binoculars, I saw the eagle. From the size, I guessed it was one of the two females. Her enormous yellow talons were nestled in a fluffy, terrycloth towel and a sheet of newspaper waved loosely behind her. She shook one talon free from the towel and, blinking in the sudden light, stuck her snowy feathered head out into the cool December air. Head swiveling, she did another slow blink, then glanced around as if wondering, *Where the heck am I now?* before stepping cautiously onto the lawn. A few feet away from the box, she spread her wings, flapped them experimentally, folded them again against her sides before hopping a bit further down the slope. At one point, she turned and gazed back at Mee and Charlene who stood straight and silent beside the box, like proud parents. Was she requesting their permission to leave? Then, she spread her wings wide, flapped powerfully and took off, skimming low over the creek then rising, higher and higher, soaring over the Chesapeake Bay until, even with binoculars, I lost sight of her.

I didn't realize I'd been holding my breath until Timmy said, speaking for all of us, 'That was awesome!'

The procedure was repeated and each of the eagles – first the male, and then the second female – stepped out of their boxes, tested their wings and returned joyously to the wild.

'Is that our eagle?' Timmy asked as the last eagle skimmed over the golden-tipped cattails in the marshes that adjoined our property, rose, circled the woods to the north and disappeared. 'Is that Hobbes?'

'There's no way to tell for sure, Timmy,' I said. 'We'll just have to wait and see.'

But I was wrong. We didn't have to wait long. Unexpectedly, the third eagle reappeared and circled twice, three times over the creek. She lit briefly on a piling at the end of the dock, shifted from foot to foot, surveying the area as if to confirm she was well and truly free. Nobody approached. Nobody tried to coax her back into the cardboard box that had so recently been her cage.

She spread her wings wide, flapped and flapped – as if shouting, *Huzzah! Huzzah!* – and lifted off.

Again, she lazily circled the woods.

There was a collective gasp as suddenly, propelled by her powerful wings, she shot straight up-up-up where she floated for a moment riding the thermals, silhouetted against a powder blue winter sky. Abruptly, she went into a steep dive, plunging toward earth. Only inches from the ground – or so it seemed – she pulled up short and shot straight up again. As we watched, she dipped and soared, performing loop-de-loops like a roller coaster.

'She's like a Spitfire on a strafing run,' Timmy observed as she flew directly toward us.

No, not toward us, exactly. Toward the bare, stark-white branches of the dead tree at the head of the creek.

Hobbes had come home.

THIRTY

A week had passed, and still no official confirmation from the M.E. that the body found in Tuckahoe State Park twenty-seven years ago belonged to Ashley Miller. But, based on Noel's close DNA match to Ashley's brother, Jason, the Silent Sleuths and I knew the truth.

That Ashley had been murdered by a transient named Bubs seemed clear.

That Bubs was Noel's biological father seemed equally clear.

CODIS contained no record of Bubs' DNA, so he wasn't a known criminal.

The information we needed was locked inside a recreational database called GenTree, hanging on a family tree managed by a first cousin named SimonSez, and only his permission would allow us to unlock it. SimonSez had not responded to either Noel's or my requests through the GenTree messaging service. His silence was frustrating.

For the doggedly persistent, all was not lost, however. On her paternal side Noel had fourth- and fifth-cousin matches in the hundreds, individuals more distant than SimonSez with whom she shared third and fourth great-grandparents. Tracking down Bubs' identity could require climbing through branches of public family trees dating as far back as the 1700s, looking for commonalities. But with enough time, it could be done.

I parked myself in a chair in front of my laptop, logged onto Noel's GenTree account – she'd named it *XmasCarol* – and prepared for the long haul.

Sometimes, miracles happen.

There was a message in Noel's GenTree inbox from SimonSez. I held my breath and clicked it open.

> Hello, XmasCarol. Sorry I missed your texts. Writing my PhD dissertation. Nose to the grindstone and all that. Super cool to have a close relative – maybe? – I've never heard of. Happy to share my family tree with you, but can we talk first?

SimonSez signed off with his real name, Simon Everhart, and gave Noel his phone number.

I wasted no time in dialing it, pacing back and forth across the carpet in the front hall as Simon's number rang and rang.

When the call went to voicemail, I swore silently, left a detailed message and hung up. Then I opened my mouth, took a deep breath and screamed.

Footsteps came thundering down from upstairs. My grandson, Timmy, to the rescue, his floppy hair – the same straw color as his mother's – still wet from the shower.

He screeched to a halt at the foot of the stairs, hand clutching the newel post. 'Grandma! Are you OK?'

'Sorry, Timmy. I'm fine. What you just heard was a primal scream.'

'Jesus, I thought you were being dismembered or something.' He tucked a disobedient strand of hair behind his right ear, where I knew it wouldn't stay for long.

I briefly explained what the scream had been all about.

'He'll call you back,' Timmy said, reasonably. 'You waited this long. Another hour or two won't matter.'

'You're right,' I said, stepping forward and surprising him with a hug. He smelled fresh and clean, like Bazooka bubblegum. 'I appreciate your willingness to save my life.'

'Yeah, well . . .' he said as he shrugged out of my embrace. 'Guess I better get back to my project. Grandpa's waiting for me out in the workshop.'

'Off with you, then,' I said, giving him an affectionate shove.

Back at my desk, I used TruePeopleSearch.com to do a reverse lookup on Simon Everhart's phone number. According to their records, he was thirty-one years old, lived in West Windsor, New Jersey, a township just outside of Princeton. Simon was married to a woman named Megan, also thirty-one. As far as I could tell, neither one of them was on Facebook or Twitter, but if I were writing a PhD dissertation, I wouldn't waste my time Facebooking or Tweeting, either. I decided to wait until after Simon returned my call – or not – before paying extra for an in-depth report on the guy.

The big hand on the kitchen clock crawled around to noon. I put a saucepan of water on the stove, and when it came to a boil, dropped in half a dozen hot dogs and turned the gas down to a simmer. I'd set a bag of hot dog buns out on the kitchen table along with squeezy bottles of mustard, ketchup and relish, and had just started to mince a sweet onion when Simon returned my call.

'Hannah Ives? This is Simon Everhart.' His voice was deep, silky as a late-night radio DJ.

'Thank you so much for calling,' I said, as I wiped my hands dry on a paper towel. 'May I call you Simon?'

'Of course.'

I repeated some of what I'd told him in my voice message, that I was an experienced genetic genealogist and that Noel, a close family friend, had asked for my help when a DNA test revealed she'd been adopted. 'You match with Noel at eight hundred and sixty-six centimorgans which, based on your relative ages – Noel is twenty-five – means there's a high probability you're first cousins.'

Simon chuckled. 'Well, I'll be damned.' He paused, as if organizing his thoughts. 'As soon as we hang up, I'll send you an invite to access our tree. Noel's going to have more relatives than she knows what to do with, I'm afraid.'

'Since she has none at all right now,' I said, conveniently leaving Noel's maternal side out of the equation, 'that will be a pleasant change.'

'Full disclosure,' Simon said. 'My mother, Linda, did most of the work on our tree. She turned it over to me about a year ago. She'd been trying to locate her brother but got discouraged over the lack of close DNA matches. She finally convinced herself that he'd been murdered, his body buried somewhere in a shallow grave. How else to explain that he dropped completely off the radar?'

My antenna began to vibrate. 'Her brother?'

'Yup. I was still a toddler when Uncle Bubs disappeared – around 1997, I think it was – but Mom never really gave up hope of finding him.'

'Yes, yes, that sounds like our guy,' I said, struggling to hold my voice steady. 'If we're right, he'd be Noel's biological father. But surely his mother didn't name him Bubs.'

Simon chuckled again. 'No. They nicknamed him Bubs because Aunt Susan, my mother's sister, had a lisp and couldn't say her brother's name properly. Bubs was a junior, named after their father, Wesley Butler, Senior.'

I swayed, grabbed onto the back of a chair to steady myself. I sat down, my knees weak and wobbly. I must not have said anything for a while because I heard Simon say, 'Hello?'

'I'm here,' I reassured him. 'Just trying to find a pencil so I can write all this information down.'

In truth, a ballpoint pen and a pad of paper sat on the kitchen table smack-dab in front of me. I'd taken time out from writing a grocery list to fix lunch for the guys.

I scrabbled for the pen. 'What can you tell me about Wesley Junior?'

'Only what I've heard from my mother, I'm afraid. He was the youngest of three kids – my aunt Susan is the oldest, then came my mother, and then Bubs. We're all Pineys from the region around Medford, New Jersey where Granddad owned a garage. Granddad's dead now. Heart attack back in 2007. Anyway, Bubs went to Rutgers, I know that for sure, where he got some Mickey Mouse bachelor's degree in Exercise Science and Kinesiology. After graduation, he started working somewhere as a high school coach, but after two years he left to quote "pursue other interests" unquote.' Simon puffed air into the phone. 'In other words, he got shitcanned. Never heard why.'

Thinking about young Wesley's preference for teenage girls, I could guess why, but decided to keep that suspicion to myself.

I filled Simon Everhart in on his newfound cousin's background as a Sinclair, skipping the part where she'd been abandoned on their doorstep one cold, December night. I explained how we'd come to know one another and described Noel's work for Warner Protective Services and her prospects with the firm.

As we wound up our conversation with an exchange of direct email addresses, telephone numbers and promises to keep lines of communication open, I agonized over keeping mum about Wesley's gruesome death. I decided to pass Simon's contact information on to Sheriff Hubbard promptly and give him the thankless job of contacting Wesley's next of kin.

I felt sympathy for Wesley's sister, Linda, whose fears about her brother's fate had been realized, just decades later than she thought. And she'd been half right, too. If my theory was correct, Wesley had been murdered, but he wasn't lying in a shallow grave. He was lying on a slab in the office of the Chief Medical Examiner in Baltimore, dead of carbofuran poisoning.

I'd figure out later how to explain to Simon that when I found out my dead neighbor was his uncle, I'd neglected to mention it.

In the meantime, I had a more urgent problem on my hands: how to break the devastating news to Noel that the phantom father she knew as Bubs had been living less than fifty miles from her home in Bentonville, and one day, not so long ago, she'd crossed paths with him in the entrance hall of our cottage.

THIRTY-ONE

S ome days you wait ages for a bus, and then three of them show up at once. Today was one of those days.

Immediately after ending my conversation with Simon, I texted the Silent Sleuths:

Bubs = Wesley Butler! Deets to follow.

I opened my laptop and was halfway through writing an email detailing my conversation with Noel's first cousin, Simon Everhart, when Jack responded with a text to the group.

Heads up! Ashley Miller positively ID'd. Live press conference at 2. WBNF-TV.

Izzy chimed in almost immediately.

Advance copy of statement leaked. Butler ID'd as killer.

I sat back, stunned, but impressed. Apparently, Sheriff Hubbard and his cold case team were one step ahead of us. We may have taken different routes, but both the Silent Sleuths and the Tilghman County Sheriff's department had reached the same conclusion: twenty-seven years ago, Ashley Miller had been brutally murdered by Wesley Butler.

I knew one thing for certain. There could be no delay in keeping secrets from Noel, not now. In less than two hours, the whole state of Maryland would find out exactly what we knew.

I texted Noel, but she had notifications silenced. Since time was critical, I decided to drive to Bentonville and catch up with her there. Stu Warner had given Noel a short-term assignment reviewing security camera footage for an attorney in a stalking case, but I knew she didn't report to the law firm in Salisbury until four o'clock, so I might still catch her at the parsonage.

Thirty minutes later, as I stood on the parsonage steps, finger poised to ring the doorbell, I could hear angry voices raised just on the other side of the solid oak door.

'Lies, lies, lies!' Noel screamed, her voice shrill. 'My whole life, lies! You, the doctor, Mrs Short and you, too, Father! How *could* you! You're supposed to be a man of God! How can you look yourself in the mirror?'

Her father replied, his voice low, muffled, indistinct.

'Bullshit! You didn't call the police! You made precisely *zero* effort to locate her. If you had done either of those things, my mother might still be alive!'

I stood on the doorstep shivering in my lightweight jacket, shamelessly eavesdropping. Obviously, I was too late. Noel had already heard the news. Ashley Miller, her biological mother, was dead. The weight of bringing Noel the bad news had been lifted from my shoulders. I felt embarrassed by the wave of relief that washed over me.

'I can't stay in this house one more minute!' Noel yelled.

Seconds later, when the front door flew open, I staggered back.

Seeing me, Noel pulled up short. Her face was flushed, her cheeks damp, her eyes red and swollen.

'What's wrong?' I asked, reaching out with both hands, hoping she'd assume I'd only just arrived.

'Everything!' she sobbed.

I took in Noel's outfit – blue jeans and a long-sleeved cotton T-shirt – and said, 'You can't go out without a coat. You'll freeze to death.'

'I don't care!' she sobbed.

'Let's go back inside where it's warm,' I said reasonably.

She shook her head. 'I can't. I can't stand to look at them, I'm so furious.'

Using my thumb, I gestured at the restaurant across the street. 'Want to go to Denny's and talk about it?'

Noel took a deep, shuddering breath, squared her shoulders and nodded.

I linked my arm through hers and led her across the street and into the restaurant, crowded with local workers making the most of their lunch hours. Noel remained silent while the hostess showed us to a booth tucked away in a back corner. 'Coffee?' I asked Noel before the hostess could get away.

Noel caught her lower lip between her teeth and nodded.

'I'll tell your server,' the hostess said, and left us alone.

Noel eased onto the brown vinyl banquette across from me where she sat hunched over, hands folded in her lap. I moved the standup menu and condiment holder aside so I could look directly into her eyes when I softly urged her to tell me what was wrong.

'Ashley Miller's dead,' she said.

I decided not to pretend I hadn't heard. 'I know,' I said. 'Izzy texted she had it from a confidential source that Sheriff Hubbard would be announcing it at a news conference today. I called you right away, but when you didn't pick up, I decided to come find you.'

Noel looked puzzled for a moment. 'Oh, my phone. God only knows where I left it. After Uncle J.D. called . . .' She shrugged, lips trembling. 'I'm afraid I came unglued.'

'Ah, Ashley's brother. I should have guessed. As next of kin, he would be the first to be told.'

Noel sniffed, unwrapped the napkin from around her silverware, unfolded it and used it to blow her nose. 'He was super kind, but the bad news hit me like a ton of bricks. After we hung up, I simply snapped. I confronted my parents. This stupid charade has been going on for twenty-seven years. Enough is enough.'

Our server – a young twenty-something wearing a black Denny's uniform shirt and sporting a high, Fifties-style straight-as-a-stick ponytail – arrived just then carrying two steaming mugs of coffee.

'Want some lunch?' I asked, as she set the mugs in front of us. 'My treat.'

Noel shook her head, curls trembling. 'Not hungry.'

'Soup?'

'No, but thank you.'

I smiled up at the server whose nametag read *Olivia*. 'Give us a few minutes, OK?'

Behind a pair of crimson eyeglasses, Olivia's dark eyes darted from me to Noel and back again. She nodded in silent understanding. 'I'll check in with you a bit later, then, OK?'

I found it troubling that Noel had not mentioned the biggest bombshell of the day – to my way of thinking, at least – the true identity of Bubs. 'Did your uncle tell you anything else about the upcoming press conference?' I asked as I tore open a packet and dumped sugar into my coffee.

'Just that they had a DNA match to her killer, too,' she said. 'But that was no surprise to me. Who else could it be but Bubs?'

So, she didn't know. I decided to break it to her gently. 'Noel, this morning when I logged onto GenTree, there was a message from SimonSez.'

She'd been absentmindedly stirring her coffee, but she looked up at that, one eyebrow cocked. 'That guy who might be a grand, a half or a cousin?'

I nodded. 'Exactly. He's authorized us to look at his family tree, but I haven't had a chance to do that yet because, well . . .'

She snorted. 'Because you're busy babysitting me.'

I managed a wan smile. 'That, too,' I said. 'But, listen to me. He sent me his contact information, and we were able to talk. Simon's full name is Simon Everhart. He's married to a woman named Megan and they live in New Jersey. I figure he's about your age. Simon's mother is Bubs' older sister, so he's definitely your first cousin. There's another sister, too.'

Noel was no dummy. She knew I was taking my time, dawdling on the way to whatever point I was trying to make.

'Don't tell me Bubs isn't my biological father because I won't believe you. Ashley wasn't pregnant when he met up with her on that turnpike in Ohio, not if I was born ten months later in Maryland. Who else could it be?'

I spit it out, blunt and cold. 'Simon's Uncle Bubs was Wesley Butler.'

For the longest time, Noel simply stared. Not at me, not at the funky light fixtures, not at the posters mounted on the wall. She had gone away somewhere and when she snapped out of her trance-like state it was with words I'd never heard her use before. 'Jesus H. Fucking Christ!'

I don't generally use such words either, but I had to agree.

Noel folded her arms on the tabletop and rested her forehead on them. We sat together in silence as patrons, waitstaff and bussers hustled around the busy restaurant, politely avoiding eye contact.

I waited patiently, sipping my coffee.

My mug was empty, and I'd flagged Olivia down for a refill by the time Noel raised her head. 'That kind of explains everything,' she said, dry-eyed. 'Wesley must have been blackmailing Dad. About me. I wonder how he found out?'

'I'm just guessing, but do you remember that time at our house, where you met him for the first time? He compared you to that actress on *Game of Thrones*. That was total bullshit. He recognized you, Noel, because you look like your mother.'

Her hand flew up to her mouth. 'And I told him where I lived!'

'You did.'

'And that's how he found my parents. How he figured it might be worth a few bucks to them if he promised to keep their secret about my phony adoption.' She smiled ruefully. 'For my dad, being holier-than-thou is part of the job description, Mrs Ives. He'd be an easy mark.'

I checked the time on my cell phone, surprised at how late it was. 'We're missing the press conference, Noel.'

She puffed air out through her lips. 'So what? They aren't going to tell us anything that we don't already know, are they?' She pressed both hands flat against the tabletop, leaned back against the cushions, took a deep breath and let it out slowly. 'Wesley's dead, so case closed,' she said. '*Doink-doink.*'

'Except for finding whoever killed Wesley,' I pointed out, thinking how tragic it would be for Noel if, on top of everything else, either of her parents turned out to be Wesley's killer. Or the old family physician, Dr Stone. He'd be an easy mark, too.

Noel leaned forward until her chest pressed against the edge of the tabletop. 'Do you see the least spark of concern in my eyes, Mrs Ives? Whoever killed that horrible man did the world a big, fat favor. I'm still a bit of a noob when it comes to computers, but I do know GIGO. Garbage in, garbage out.' She snatched the laminated menu out of its holder, her eyes on scan. 'I think I'll have some of that soup now, please.'

THIRTY-TWO

P aul and I were engaged in a cut-throat game of Scrabble – I'd just played ZITHER on a triple word square – when Timmy, who was out on the deck, opened the sliding glass door, stuck his head inside and shouted, 'Grandma, Grandpa, quick, quick!'

I leapt to my feet, jostling the Scrabble board, scattering the letter tiles over the tabletop. 'What's the matter?' I yelled in panic.

'Sorry,' Timmy said when Paul and I joined him on the deck. 'No emergency, but you just gotta see this.' He waved a pair of binoculars in the direction of the creek. 'Hobbes has a boyfriend!'

After my heart rate returned to normal, I reached inside the door to retrieve my own pair of binoculars, put them to my eyes and focused on Hobbes's tree.

Timmy was right. The Widow Hobbes was no longer alone.

As I trained the binoculars on her nest, a male eagle flapped to a landing in the nest beside her, bearing a small branch in his beak, perhaps as a housewarming gift. He dropped it at the rim of the nest, pecked at it for a while, stepped back and stared as if considering how best to weave his modest offering into her already substantial home.

Hobbes had her own ideas. After studying him critically, she picked up the branch, waddled with it to the opposite side of the nest where she fussed with the arrangement, turning the branch this way and that before tucking it in. She stepped back, seemingly satisfied. If HGTV had a makeover program called *Nestorations*, Hobbes would be its star.

Next to me, Paul, who had acquired a pair of binoculars of his own, muttered, 'So, Hobbes has a suitor!'

'Apparently so,' I said, 'and the way they're standing next to each other rubbing wings, it doesn't look like she's going to kick him out of the nest any time soon.'

'No,' Paul agreed. 'I noticed she'd been tidying the nest recently. Now that there's a boyfriend involved . . .' He paused and waggled his eyebrows. 'Come January, we might even see some eggs.'

'Maybe we should install an eagle cam,' Timmy suggested, his voice eager, ready to hop into the car and drive out to Best Buy and purchase the wherewithal for the installation.

'I don't think so, Timmy. We don't need a twenty-four-seven live feed,' I said. 'We can monitor their nest just fine from here.' I lowered the binoculars and caught Paul's eye, then turned back to Timmy. 'How would you feel having a camera watching you twenty-four-seven? It's spooky, I can tell you from experience,' I said, recalling the three surreal months I spent with twelve other cast members living in Annapolis's historic William Paca House being filmed for a reality show called *Patriot House 1774*.

When I looked again, Hobbes and her boyfriend were taking a break from nestoration to roost in neighboring branches at the top of their tree. Suddenly, Hobbes lifted her wings and flapped away. The male eagle gave chase. The pair circled their tree, then peeled off in the direction of the Chesapeake Bay, rising higher and higher as they flew.

'It's just like the other day,' Timmy exclaimed, as Hobbes and her suitor floated, wings spread, at the apex of the arc they were tracing, then plunged toward the ground and back into the sky again.

'After we observed her behavior the other day, I did some research. It's called sky-dancing, Timmy.' Before I could continue, Hobbes made an abrupt U-turn and chased after her suitor. Faster than he, she swooped in and grabbed him, hard, by the talons. Together the pair cartwheeled, talons locked, tumbling rapidly toward the ground.

Timmy leaned dangerously forward, bracing himself against the railing. 'What the heck is going on? Holy crap! Are they fighting?'

'Sure looks like it, but no,' Paul said. 'Sky-dancing is an eagle aerial courtship ritual. Your grandmother and I watched a couple of videos about it on the YouTube Nature Channel.'

Timmy lowered his binoculars. 'So, are they "doing it," Grandpa?'

Paul chuckled. 'No, that happens later, usually in the nest. They're just revving up for doing it.'

In a dizzying display, Hobbes and her suitor continued their daredevil plunge, like skydivers sharing a single parachute, hurtling toward earth. Timmy jumped up and down. 'No! No! They're going to smack right into the ground! Pull the ripcord already!'

As if the birds heard, and seemingly inches from disaster, they released talons and soared back into the sky, spiraling off in opposite directions.

Until that moment, I didn't realize I'd been holding my breath.

'Good Lord,' I gasped. 'That certainly gives new meaning to the term falling in love.' I looped my arm through Paul's. 'Don't know about you, sweetheart, but if I were one of those two love birds getting that close to the ground, I would seriously consider faking it.'

Paul laughed out loud.

I nudged him in the ribs. 'Now that they seem to be married, I should tell you that her husband's name is Sonny.'

'Sonny and Hobbes?'

'No, sorry. Hobbes informs me she's petitioning the court for a name change. From now on, she wants to be called Cher.'

'You win, Grandma. There was only one Calvin.' Timmy turned to look at me, this wise, caring, fifteen-year-old boy who in six short months had shot up like a weed, outgrown two pairs of chinos and now stood almost as tall as his grandfather. 'I wonder what happened to Calvin?'

I explained about the National Eagle Repository in Colorado. 'Eagle feathers carry powerful medicine for Native Americans. They symbolize courage, strength and hope. Calvin's feathers will live on for years in the headdresses and ceremonial costumes of our Native American relations. Your cousin, Julie, was even awarded an eagle feather by the Red Cloud Indian River School where she's been teaching. It's a huge honor.'

'Oooh, better have a look,' Paul said, nudging me, gesturing toward the nest with his binoculars.

The three of us stood at the railing shoulder-to-shoulder, binoculars raised, like spectators at the Kentucky Derby.

Cher – the eagle formerly known as Hobbes – had returned to the nest, and so had Sonny. As I fiddled with the focus, Cher turned her back, shifted her tail feathers to one side and . . . I lowered the binoculars and, channeling Marlon Perkins, pitched my voice low and said, 'Viewers, this is where we draw the curtain, if all goes well . . .'

'They're doing it, aren't they?' Timmy cut in, binoculars practically screwed into his eye sockets.

Paul chuckled. 'They're doing it.'

Paul's hand slid off my shoulder, caressed my upper arm and drew me close, so close I could feel his heart beating against my side. 'Eagles mate for life, don't they?'

'According to the Nature Channel, they usually do,' I said.

'Wise birds.'

'You're confusing eagles with owls.'

'I was a wise old bird when I married you, Hannah Ives.' Paul learned over, tipped my chin up and pressed his lips, soft and full and tasting sweetly of rum against mine.

When I came up for air, I said, 'Guess I'm not going to kick you out of the nest anytime soon, Professor.'

'Uh, mmm,' Timmy said, shaking his head.

After the patio door slid closed behind him, Paul and I couldn't stop laughing.

THIRTY-THREE

J ust before six thirty on the Thursday evening before Christmas, I bundled up against the cold, coaxed the engine of a reluctant Volvo into life and headed for Bentonville, where I'd arranged to meet Noel at First Christian Church before choir practice began. On the outskirts of town, a fine mist began to fall. The *swoosh-swoosh-swoosh* of the windshield wipers kept time as I sang along with Andy Williams to 'O Holy Night' on the twenty-four-hour Christmas station. According to the weatherman who had just broken into the broadcast with a travel advisory, the temperature was expected to fall below freezing, so I drove with extra caution. By the time Brenda Lee began rockin' around the Christmas tree, I was approaching the stoplight at the intersection of Market and Church Streets and began hunting for a parking space.

I hadn't accounted for Midnight Madness.

The shops along both sides of Market Street glowed warmly from within with holiday spirit. Outside, for several blocks in each direction, the streets were illuminated by colonial-style lampposts decked out in holiday finery – candy canes, snowflakes and holly berry wreaths. Here an inflatable Santa Claus, there a Frosty the Snowman waved crazily in the breeze.

A red and green banner sagged across Main Street – *Happy Holidays * Buy Local* – and it looked as if everyone in the county had showed up to do just that. The sidewalks thronged with holiday shoppers, arms laden with shopping bags, laughing, clutching one another for support as they wandered from shop to shop, their feet slipping and sliding on the icy sidewalks. At the restaurant on the corner, a server wearing a white apron tied snugly over his ski suit, stood under a red-and-maroon-striped awning distributing paper cups of steaming liquid to passersby. *Hot spiced cider!* read a sandwich board propped up near the crosswalk. *Happy Holidays from Denny's!*

When the light turned green, I drove on cautiously, past Denny's, the Daily Grind, Lillie Belle's Boutique and Kendall Barfield's old real estate office, up to the intersection with First Street, where I turned left and circled the block, heading for the church parking lot on Pine. Several years prior, the lot had been donated to the church and repurposed from an old Sunoco station, the only clue to its former life being faint rectangular outlines on the concrete pavement where the gas pumps used to stand and the skeleton of a coin-operated air and vacuum machine.

I sandwiched my car into the narrow space between two SUVs, opened the door as far as it would go without dinging the adjoining vehicle and wriggled out. As I emerged from the gap between the parked cars, a sudden gust of wind snatched my breath away. I drew my scarf up over my mouth and tucked it more securely under my collar, patted my pocket to make sure the little package I'd brought with me was secure and trudged off.

The shortest route from the parking lot to the church led parishioners directly past the parsonage. In spite of the biting cold, I paused on the sidewalk in front of the Sinclair's long-time home and tried to put myself in Ashley's shoes. What thoughts had been running through the teenager's mind as she stood near the place where I stood now, cradling her newborn daughter on that cold, rainy night?

Had she admired the buttery Victorian house as much as I did now, with its fairy-tale tower and twisty brick chimney stack? Had there been a tree in the window then, too, decorated with blue and silver balls and wreathed in twinkling lights? Was the entrance hall illuminated by the same crystal chandelier, shining cheerfully through the stained-glass fanlight over the front door? I swallowed hard. To a fifteen-year-old on the run from an impossible situation, it must have looked like sanctuary from the storm. An oasis. I swiped a tear from my cheek with the back of my glove before it had a chance to freeze, and turned away.

Next door on the church lawn, the life-size Nativity scene had already attracted a small crowd of holidaymakers, iPhones flashing away. Everyone from Bethlehem seemed to be awaiting the arrival of the Christ Child. Mary, Joseph, the Three Kings, assorted shepherds and lowly beasts all braved the worsening weather as a herald angel, arms raised, rained blessings – and raindrops – down on the creche. The manger, bathed in a spotlight, was filled with straw but far from empty. When He eventually came, the Virgin Mary would need to evict the orange tabby curled up there now. As the crowd dispersed and I slogged by, the cat opened one eye, considered me dispassionately, then went back to sleep.

I'd driven by the church sign – a lightbox with changeable letters – many times before. This coming Sunday, the sign announced, services would be at nine thirty a.m. and eleven a.m., when the good Reverend Robert Sinclair would be preaching on 'Hollow Day, Holiday, or Holy Day: Luke 2:10–11.' There'd be a coffee hour afterwards in the parsonage. Would there? Would he? After all that had happened in the past few weeks, I wasn't so sure.

Leaving the sign to my left, I carried on up the sidewalk to the welcome crunch of rock salt beneath my boots. A maintenance man, who had obviously anticipated the turn in the weather, stood in front of the church doors. 'Door's open,' he said, as he dipped a gloved hand into a plastic bucket and continued sowing the steps with salt.

'Thanks,' I said, as I grabbed the carved wooden handle and pulled the door open to a welcome wave of hot air. 'Stay warm, you hear?'

He paused to smile up at me, his fist full of salt. 'Choir's in the basement.'

'I know,' I said. 'I'm meeting Noel in the sanctuary.'

He nodded sagely, then scattered the salt. 'Have a blessed Christmas, ma'am.'

'I'm working on it,' I said with a smile, then pulled the door firmly shut behind me.

Electric candles twinkled in the windows that flanked the sanctuary, six windows on each side. Up front, additional candles flickered in two six-arm, floor candelabras that stood tall on either end of the altar rail.

The children's choir was still in rehearsal. Strains of the traditional Polish carol, 'Infant Holy, Infant Lowly' drifted up the winding staircase that led from the narthex down to the fellowship center below.

I'd arrived a bit early, so I thought I was alone in the sanctuary, until a sudden movement caught my eye. A lone figure, her hair a nimbus of gold backlit by the candles, knelt at the altar rail. It had to be Noel. Not wanting to interrupt her at prayer, I tiptoed up the aisle and sat down in the first pew to wait.

Thus rejoicing, free from sorrow,
Praises voicing greet the morrow
Christ the babe was born for you!

Children's singing voices filled the church. Then, over the angelic choir, I heard sobbing. Someone wasn't free from sorrow.